WIRED STRONG

PARADISE CRIME THRILLERS BOOK 12

TOBY NEAL

"Yesterday I was clever, so I wanted to change the world. Today I am wise, so I am changing myself." — Rumi

CHAPTER ONE

Pim Wat
Same time frame as the end of Wired Ghost

P<small>IM</small> W<small>AT</small> <small>STARED</small> at her reflection in the mirror.

She was supposed to be meditating. The Master wanted her to learn to manage her emotions, her mind, her body.

And technically, she *was* meditating—on the ruin of her once beautiful face.

One eye was higher than the other, because a broken cheekbone hadn't been set. The other eye wouldn't open all the way—the lid had been torn and had healed crookedly, giving her the look of a drunkard. Scar tissue twisted across her face like a snake, and her jaw had been broken and reset poorly, causing a droop to her mouth.

The dandelion fluff covering her skull, gone white from suffering, she could grow out and dye.

But her face?

Pim Wat was a gargoyle now, a travesty. She had no intention of reining in her emotions about that. She picked up the heavy, expensive bottle of perfume resting on her vanity, and hurled it at the mirror.

The flask broke with a satisfying crash that flung shards of crystal and glass all over the luxurious chamber, filling her hair and peppering her skin with "shrapnel" that reeked of jasmine and roses. She smiled through the pain, letting the shards impale her where they would.

Pim Wat welcomed the searing of a thousand tiny cuts.

Pain was a friend. That sensation woke her up; it was a spur in her side, driving her to greatness. She was done being a malleable doll that the Master could mold into someone loving, forgiving, passive. She'd never been those things. This outward ugliness didn't suit her, either.

The Master called her "my beautiful one," and "my deadly viper."

Pim Wat wasn't those things now, but she would be again.

She'd rise from these ashes like a phoenix to strike terror into her enemies; she'd rain death on those who'd stolen years of her life—beginning with that disloyal whore who'd handed her over to the torturers.

She'd enjoyed the masquerade of asking Sophie's forgiveness. Now her daughter wouldn't see vengeance coming.

A knock at the door. "Mistress? Are you all right?" The quavering voice of Pim Wat's attendant was muffled by the heavy wooden portal. The woman was a peasant, the wife of Number One's houseman, Nam. The couple had recently been brought to the Yām Khûmkạn compound as refugees, hiding from the raid that the U.S. Department of Justice had made on their home. Kupa should be grateful to be allowed to serve Pim Wat, but the woman continually needed discipline.

"Bring a feather duster, broom, and pan, Kupa," Pim Wat said. "There's been an accident."

"Right away, Mistress." The maid's footsteps hurried away.

Pim Wat finally shut her eyes.

She could meditate now, sitting in outward stillness, and plan what came next.

2

CHAPTER TWO

Marcella
Day 1, four weeks after Wired Ghost

SPECIAL AGENT MARCELLA SCOTT shut the door of the office at the Fight Club gym in downtown Honolulu, and turned to face her friend. "Did you wand the room for surveillance?"

Sophie Smithson rose from the chair behind the battered metal desk. "I did." The chair was a relic from a time when the prosperous gym had been small and struggling; they'd both been working out here since then. Sophie held a device in her hand and approached Marcella. "I need to check you, too."

Marcella rolled her eyes. "Really? There's no room in this outfit for anything but my tits." But she extended her arms and allowed Sophie to sweep the palm-sized device over the exercise bra and tight workout shorts she wore. "I can't believe we've come to this."

"I don't think you'd intentionally try to entrap me." Sophie switched off the handheld detector and set it on the desk. She, too, wore workout clothing: yoga pants, and a spandex racerback top that displayed well-defined lats, deltoids, and abs. "But there are agents in your office who'd do anything to be able to take me down."

"Special Agent Pillman of Internal Affairs, you mean." Marcella made a rude Italian hand gesture. "The man's a menace, and that's on a good day."

Sophie gestured to the leather couch against the wall. "Let's get comfortable. It's been too long since we caught up, and we have a lot to cover."

"I know. I'm the one who asked you to meet me, remember? I'm sorry that I haven't seen you since Jake's memorial." Marcella ran an eyeball over her friend. Sophie wasn't looking half bad, considering she'd lost her fiancé in a volcano-related tragedy only three months before. Prone to depression, Sophie had been known to take to her bed without eating for days at a time. Marcella had feared that Jake's death, coupled with the departure of Sophie's daughter and nanny to Kaua'i for their custody month with the child's father, might have brought on such an episode.

Instead, Sophie's tawny skin glowed, and though there were bags under her eyes, an unfamiliar roundness filled out her cheeks, breasts, and hips. Her hair, usually short, was nearly touching her shoulders in a riot of thick brown ringlets. "Are you ready for some sparring? You look like you're getting a little soft."

"Not today." Sophie sat on the couch and patted the open area beside her. "Now that we've made sure the area is secure, you need to tell me what is going on with this multi-agency FBI investigation into the Ghost—my friend, Connor."

"Okay. I'll tell you what I can, but it isn't much." Marcella flopped onto the old leather couch, smoothing back her sleek ponytail. "They won't let me anywhere near the case. But I've heard whispers around the office indicating that there's a faction that wants to take you into custody in order to capture Connor."

"How?" Sophie raised her elegant brows.

"By using you as a combination of hostage and bait. I had to listen at Waxman's door to get this—and thankfully, he wasn't in favor. I don't think I could forgive him if he were."

They'd shared Waxman as a Special Agent in Charge during Sophie's five years at the Bureau; in that time Marcella had found him to be a hard boss, but someone with basic integrity.

"Who was in the meeting you listened in on?" Sophie's honey-brown eyes were intent.

"Pillman and Gundersohn." Pillman was with Internal Affairs and had a cruel streak; Gundersohn, a slow-moving Swede with a procedural mindset, had been known to get stubborn once he had an idea. "With Interpol, the Secret Service, and the CIA on that task force too, Pillman argued that they could let those guys do the dirty work of picking you up and storing you at Guantánamo or something, and pretend not to be involved." Marcella laid a hand on Sophie's arm, squeezing it to impress Sophie of her worry. "I'm not sure even the ambassador's influence is going to be enough to keep you safe from them right now. You have to go somewhere. Hide."

Sophie frowned. "No. I've 'lawyered up' instead. And so far, Bennie Fernandez is worth every penny I'm paying him."

"That awful little man!" Marcella tossed her head and laughed, picturing the defense lawyer's cherubic, Santa Claus appearance and wicked legal aptitude. "Never thought we'd be on the same side. He's kicked our asses in court half a dozen times. I'm a little less worried about you now."

"Ever since Connor came out of hiding in Thailand to rescue Jake and me from the volcano, that task force has been relentless. We've been through two full searches of the Security Solutions building. Subpoenas of our records and computers. They're trying to squeeze Connor by seizing his property and any assets they can find; but he saw that coming a long time ago, and transferred ownership to me. Now I'm the one dealing with all the pressure." Sophie shook her head. "I wish they'd give it up. He's untouchable at the Yām Khûmkạn compound in Thailand, and he doesn't care about any of this anymore."

"I'll be honest, Sophie." Marcella leaned forward and made eye contact. "I don't trust that man, whatever name he's currently going by, as far as I can throw him. The more time that passes, and the longer he's involved with that weird-ass Thai organization, the less I think he has your best interests at heart."

"You've believed that for a while, and I understand why." Sophie rubbed the back of her arm. "I know you mean well, Marcella, but Connor and I have a bond. I owe him my life. He'd never betray me or let them take me."

Marcella bit her lip to keep from responding. *She didn't believe that for a minute.*

The man who called himself Connor had many names, and various other loyalties. He always had—or he'd have protected Sophie better than just dumping everything, including his dog, on her and leaving her to deal with it. "I felt duty-bound, because of our friendship, to warn you about what I heard. What if the CIA just grabs you, lawyers be damned, and whisks you off somewhere? Threatens to torture you, and forces you to communicate with him so he comes to get you?"

Sophie was still rubbing the back of her arm, an odd habit. "I've thought of that. I do need to do something to deal with that possibility. But hiding isn't the answer—these organizations work in the shadows. No, I need to stay in the light to be safe, even though it goes against my natural inclinations—especially now."

Marcella stood up in agitation. She stalked over to the water cooler and filled a plastic cup with filtered water for each of them. She handed one to Sophie, eyeing the lovely antique diamond engagement ring her friend wore in memory of her fiancé. "What do you mean, 'especially now'?"

"Instead of hiding, I need to be even more visible. Involved with the workings of Security Solutions as its CEO. Surrounded by a security team at home and at the office, twenty-four hours a day. Going to society and government events on my father's arm as his plus-one; playing the role of United States Ambassador's daughter. I need to be seen—even in my current condition." Sophie smoothed her left hand, decorated with that sparkler of a diamond, over her waist. "You're right that I'm going soft, Marcella. I'm twelve weeks pregnant with Jake's baby."

Marcella's eyes flew open. "What? No—seriously? Again?" She immediately clapped a hand over her mouth, wishing she could take back the words. "I didn't mean that the way it came out. I only meant —how hard it is for you already, as a single mom to Momi. Jake's baby, too—oh my gosh, you—you must be . . ."

Sophie's full lips tightened into a flat line and her brows drew down. "I expect that kind of response from a lot of people, Marcella, but I didn't expect it from you."

"Gah. I'm sorry, darling. If you're happy, I'm happy." Marcella lifted her hands in a "surrender" gesture. "Jake's baby. Wow! His family must be ecstatic."

"They don't know. No one knows but Dr. Wilson. And now you." Sophie's hand still rested protectively over her abdomen. "This baby is all I have of Jake. All I'll ever have." Her eyes filled. "And I can't help but believe that it's meant to be, because of that. No matter how challenging the situation is."

"I can't imagine." Even more, Marcella didn't *want* to imagine Sophie's situation. She was happily married to the love of her life, Honolulu Police Department Detective Marcus Kamuela. Someday they hoped to be parents, but she'd never want to have to deal with pregnancy and a child—alone. *Jake Dunn's death seemed even more tragic now.* "I'm so sorry." Marcella reached out to hug her friend.

Sophie pushed Marcella away and stood up. "I think you'd better go. I told Alika I'd check out the bookkeeping here at his office." Sophie's gaze went to the computer resting on the desk. "I've got at least an hour's worth of work here." Sophie's ex-boyfriend, Alika, owned the gym. Sophie and Alika seemed to be solid friends as they co-parented their two-and-a-half-year-old with the help of Armita, Momi's dedicated nanny. "Let me know if you hear anything new at the FBI."

"Hey. I'm sorry I didn't respond the way you wanted about your news, Soph, but I'm here for you. I'll help however I can." Marcella made a tossing gesture. "Maybe you've got spaghetti cravings? I make a mean pasta primavera."

"That won't be necessary. Everything's handled." Sophie walked around behind the desk and sat down, turning on the computer. "Have a good workout."

Marcella stood still for a long moment, but Sophie didn't look up. She busied herself behind the monitor as if Marcella had already gone.

Marcella's shoulders sagged in defeat. She walked to the office's door, and shut it gently behind her as she went out into the main area of the gym.

She wanted to leave—to run away from this echoing, smelly gym with all its memories, and meet her husband at home. She'd get a hug from Marcus—maybe even make love—and reassure herself that they were *alive* and *together*.

Her whole being lit up at the thought of being in Marcus's arms. Safe. Treasured. Passionately desired.

Sophie's tragedy wasn't hers.

But what kind of friend did that make her?

Marcella'd given Sophie an uncensored, negative response when she was the first person other than Sophie's therapist entrusted with the news of her pregnancy. Sheer selfishness to run to her husband for comfort when Sophie had no one.

Marcella wasn't perfect, but she was a better friend than that.

She'd stay at the gym, do her workout, and see if Sophie wanted to talk after she was done in the office.

Marcella went over to one of the exercise bikes, got on, and set it for a rigorous mountain climb, keeping one eye on the door. Then weights, still watching for Sophie.

Ninety minutes passed. Eventually, Marcella's Catholic guilt was assuaged by the sweaty workout—but when she finally went to the office and tried the door, it was locked.

The blinds were closed. No light showed in the crack under the portal.

Sophie had found a way to leave, alone.

CHAPTER THREE

Connor
Day 1, four weeks after Wired Ghost

CONNOR WAS VERY aware of the men encircling them as he and the Master sparred at the Yām Khûmkạn compound in Thailand. Around the circle that defined the practice area, ninja trainees stood five deep in the courtyard. Gray stone walls encrusted with lichen and moss surrounded; the humid jungle air smelled of flowers and sweat.

Connor spun and lashed out with his foot in an attempt to catch the Master under the chin. But, as usual, the man seemed to float just out of reach. The Master was so light on his feet that it was as if he barely touched the ground, while Connor's breath labored in his lungs, and his body felt as heavy as if wearing a suit of armor.

The Master hit him in the chest with a blow from a closed fist, shooting Connor back three paces and stealing his breath.

Connor longed to pause, to center himself, to have room to go inside where time and space became elastic, and he could anticipate the Master's moves.

But the man gave him no time. No space. And not even room to breathe.

Instead, the Master was a tornado, a storm moving in to batter at Connor from every direction. Connor rolled, ducked, and fled before his power.

The Master's "Number One" was about to be humiliated in front of the entire courtyard filled with trainees. The more self-consciousness tightened Connor's chest and shortened his breath, the more the Master's blows and kicks registered as pain.

He was a human punching bag and unable to stop it.

The Master paused suddenly, settling into stillness, his immaculate white _gi_ falling into place. His long black hair, unbraided today, flowed down his back in a silver-streaked river; his tawny skin gleamed like polished wood. Compelling dark purple eyes met Connor's sea-blue ones. "Let's take a break."

"Yes, Master." _Thank God! He was getting freakin' killed by the bastard!_

Connor folded his hands and inclined his head, mirroring the Master's respectful stance. His body throbbed and screamed and twitched; he worked to control his ragged breathing.

He couldn't worry about the humiliation of being defeated in front of the men.

He couldn't worry about how he appeared to others.

If Connor could manage his body, if he could tap into that internal energy source that allowed him to transcend time, he could make a comeback.

"Shut your eyes," the Master said. "Don't open them. Come at me when you're ready, with your eyes closed."

The men murmured among themselves at this direction. Connor felt the crackle of their anticipation to see his humiliation, their lust to see his defeat. They were young and easily excited by such things; they still loved the smell of blood. That's what had drawn them to the Yām Khûmkạn, to train to be spies, operatives, ninja assassins. The Master knew that, but he had much more for them—mysteries that Connor was coming to know.

Connor shut his eyes.

Self-consciousness fell away.

That quiet place, that deep stillness inside him, rose up and enveloped him.

He was pure energy, a column of bright aqua blue with a white-hot core.

Connor could see the Master behind his closed eyes—a lustrous, deep violet energy form. He perceived the color signatures of the men watching and witnessing around them; the light of their presences created a pulsing container in which he and the Master would pit themselves against each other—not in a fight, but a *dance*.

Connor moved forward, coming in from the side, slowing time so that his movement cut through space like a scythe severing silk. The Master matched him, blow for blow and kick for kick.

They wound around each other in an intricate choreography, never quite connecting, their patterns bouncing and reflecting, variations on a theme. Around and around they went, atoms in a molecule, ever spinning and perfectly balanced: a lightning storm of energy discharges that hurt no one.

Connor opened his eyes—he wanted to *see this!*

The two of them were about twelve inches off of the ground, whirling like dervishes.

The second his brain processed the realization that he was aloft, floating in the air, Connor crashed to the ground—*and it hurt like a mofo.*

The Master drifted down to land on the stones beside Connor. The gasps and murmurs of the men were silenced as he turned to face them.

"Now you see the ultimate of what we train for. Once the martial arts forms of your training are memorized, and once you have mastered your bodies, you can transcend physical limitations. All is ease and flow; matter is just energy moving through space. If you are willing to make the sacrifices necessary, if you are willing to surrender your beliefs about what defines us—you too, can dance on the air." The Master caught Connor's hand, hefting him to his feet.

He held Connor's fist up into the air. "Behold, my Number One! Give him your respect."

Hundreds of trainees fell to their knees and bowed, touching their foreheads to the ground. They rose and cried in one voice, *"Number One! Number One!"*

Connor shut his eyes, overwhelmed, and let their energy swirl around him, lifting him off the ground once more.

LATER IN THE EVENING, Connor sat on top of the six-foot-high, one-foot-wide tiger's eye column in the Master's garden, his legs folded beneath him in lotus position.

The Master sat at the tea table under his favorite flowering orchid tree. He was eating, but Connor would not. That was discipline for Connor's breach of faith in the sparring ring.

The Master finished his meal and sat back. "You have questions."

Even though fifty feet or so separated them, Connor could hear the Master perfectly. "They are more like concerns, Master," Connor said.

"Tell me."

"I want a leadership partner to help run the compound when you're away. I would like to focus on the administrative side of the Yām, and continue my vigilante justice activities via computer." Connor saw no point in prevarication. "I had hoped Pi would be my partner, but that was the wrong choice, as you know. In his stead, I would like to nominate my man Nine. I trust him. He is completely loyal to both me and the Yām Khûmkạn."

The Master poured himself more tea from an elegant china pot. He'd braided his hair, and his sternly handsome profile was turned toward the lotus pond, as he watched the darting of a dragonfly over the blue-purple flowers blooming on the water. "Nine is not a leader. He is loyal, yes, but he does not inspire. We don't have anyone right now with that potential, but we will, eventually. I will resume the day-to-day leadership of the men and their training for now as we search for such a candidate, and you can develop our online presence and further our agenda from the top room."

"Thank you, Master. I am grateful. This will be a better situation for the Yām Khûmkạn long term."

The "top room" was the computer lab, located in the highest tower in the compound, where they could get the strongest satellite wireless signal. In the time the Master had been away with his consort, Pim Wat, Connor had re-done that room to his own specifications.

"I have another concern, Master." Connor tried to ignore the tightness of apprehension in his chest about bringing this up, but it had to be dealt with. "It is about my servants from Phi Ni, Nam and Kupa. Nam has been helping in the garden, but does not feel like that is enough for him to do. And his wife, Kupa, is a gentle soul. She has been very unhappy in her role as Pim Wat's personal servant."

The Master sighed, and set down his teacup. Per usual, he answered only what he chose to. "Nine does have certain potential. Credibility, if you will. He is technically good with the martial arts forms; therefore, I will have him work with the men on their morning routine. That will free my time as well." The Master crumbled a bit of bread in his fingers. "Pim Wat will be back soon from her surgeries, and I will spend more time with her. She torments those near her when she's bored." The Master gestured to the beautifully flowering beds that lined the stone walls of his inner sanctum. "I will reassign Nam to be your personal assistant since Nine will be busy with the men. But Nam clearly knows plants. He can spend any remaining time he has assisting the gardening staff. As to Kupa, she came here as a refugee; it is unfair to use her in such a way. But she will have to endure until we can find a replacement."

Relief loosened Connor's spine. He inclined his head. "Thank you, Master."

"I would assign one of the men to attend to Pim Wat, but I would not trust them to resist her allure," the Master said darkly.

Connor suppressed an internal shiver. Pim Wat did indeed weave a spell, and it was a seductively malignant one. The woman was an amoral psychopath. He'd hoped that she was "healed" by her time with the Master on his secret island; but Kupa's reports had informed him that, if anything, she was more lethal than ever. He would have to find a way to coach Kupa to guard her mind and emotions from Sophie's sadistic mother. *But how?*

The Master spoke as if Connor had said the words aloud. "Tell Kupa that, in her way, Pim Wat cares for her. She hurts the ones she loves."

"I hesitate to ask this, Master, but—I had hoped, for Sophie's sake, that Pim Wat would be different after you rescued her and she healed with you on your island. But the things Kupa tells me indicate that her basic nature is—intact."

The Master gazed at him, unwavering. Connor felt the power and weight of that gaze. "Pim Wat is who she is. I love her for her extremity, for her dangerousness, for how, as the years have gone by, she remains true to herself and becomes more and more of her essence. I would never try to change her, nor anyone. Have you not learned that yet?"

Connor blinked.

That statement was true. The Master nurtured and shaped what already existed in a person's character. He had done that with Connor himself. "But I don't understand how you can love someone who is —so cruel."

"Acceptance is a form of power," the Master said. "Maybe someday you will understand that Pim Wat is a part of the duality of all things. Without darkness, where would the light be? How would it exist?" He took a sip of his tea. "Stay where you are on that column for three more hours, and think on these things."

"Yes, Master," Connor said, and shut his eyes.

CHAPTER FOUR

Sophie

THAT EVENING, after working through Alika's computer issue at the gym and slipping past Marcella to go home and change, Sophie slid into the padded leather booth at her father's club. She settled herself across from the ambassador and accepted a large wooden menu with the specials of the day clipped onto it. "You always want to eat here, Dad."

Frank Smithson smiled, removing reading glasses from a pocket on his tailored summer-weight jacket to examine his menu. "There's always a table waiting for me, you can't beat the food, and we don't have to worry about privacy."

"Good reasons. We're a bit overdue for a catch-up, and there's always something classified to discuss." Sophie took a moment to appraise her father. He was looking dapper as always, though a bit tired around the eyes from being in Washington until this week. "I'm glad you're back in the Islands."

"Only for a month or so, alas. So much for retirement."

Frank always complained, but continued to answer the call of duty when it came. He'd never really retire if he could help it—he loved his work as much as she loved hers.

The waiter approached. "Good evening, Ambassador. And who is this lovely lady?"

"My daughter, Sophie. Sophie, this is Jack."

Jack. The name was way too close to her fiancé's. Sophie suppressed the twinge of grief any such reminder brought. "Good to meet you, Jack. Can I get a virgin Blue Hawaii?"

"Sure. And for you, sir?"

Her father ordered a dry martini with a twist.

Frank raised his brows as the waiter walked away. "Since when do you order one of those awful drinks without even the benefit of booze?"

"The Blue Hawaii is my favorite. I don't care how silly it is." Sophie took a deep breath, let it out, and met her father's gaze squarely. "And I'm not drinking alcohol because I'm pregnant."

Her father's eyes widened. "Oh, my dear."

Sophie's hand shook as she reached for her glass of water. "At least you didn't say 'Oh no, not again!' I've already had that once, today." She took a steadying sip. "I'm twelve weeks along. Jake is the father."

"What a blessing to come from tragedy." Frank reached over to cover Sophie's hand where it rested on the table. The deliberateness with which her father spoke told Sophie that his words were thoughtfully considered—but she loved him the more for his kind diplomacy.

"Thanks, Dad. That is what I have been telling myself." Sophie liked the rich chocolate of his skin against the tawny gold of hers, as she always had. *What color would her child add to this mix of shades?* She turned her hand over to clasp his. "Of course, it wasn't planned, but I've come to be happy about it."

Frank leaned forward. "How could I be anything but happy for another grandchild? Momi was a surprise, and she's been the best thing to happen in this family since you brought home Ginger."

"You just compared my daughter to a dog, but I appreciate the sentiment." Sophie was able to smile, and so was he.

Jack delivered their drinks and took their dinner orders. When he left, Frank lifted his martini toward Sophie's large, bright blue, umbrella-decorated glass. "To delightful surprises." They chimed the rims of their drinks and sipped.

"That wasn't the other only bit of private news I needed to discuss with you, Dad." Sophie set her glass down.

Her father cupped his cheeks with his hands in a mock *Scream* face. "Not sure my heart can take any more."

As far as Sophie knew, the ambassador was aware that the CIA had tried to recruit her a few years ago to spy on her mother, when they'd both discovered that Pim Wat was an operative for the clandestine Thai espionage organization, the Yām Khûmkạn. He didn't know anything more, and she'd tried hard to keep it that way. Until now.

"It's not a joking matter, unfortunately. The task force that's digging into Security Solutions, looking for evidence that we're involved with this computer vigilante called the Ghost, has crossed the line into harassment. I've been warned that they might take me into custody in order to leverage the fugitive they're after. Just— keep me prisoner somewhere to try to force him to come for me."

Her father's frown was fierce. "Who's bothering you? I want their names and badge numbers."

"That's not important. What is important, is that I need to be sure I'm protected, especially now." She touched her belly. "I was wondering if I could move back in with you during the months that Momi and Armita are on Kaua`i. I can keep a security detail in the Pendragon Arches apartment next to us when they're in town, but I want to be extra careful right now, and I feel secure in your apartment."

Sophie caught an unguarded expression on her father's face—it looked a lot like guilt, or relief. "Of course, darling. *Mi casa es su casa.*"

Sophie smoothed her own expression into a neutral mask. Why would her father feel guilty or relieved? She was about to invade his quiet apartment by re-occupying her old room, and bringing two large, rambunctious dogs along with her. "I really appreciate it, Dad. I'm happy to pay rent."

The ambassador flapped a hand. "Ridiculous. I won't hear of it. How soon can you come?"

The rest of the dinner passed with conversation about when and how she'd return to his penthouse apartment and her room there; Frank's semi-retirement was not proceeding rapidly, but he swore he'd try to be in Honolulu when she was at his place. "I want to be a part of this new baby's life, from the very beginning."

She'd take his words at face value. She really couldn't afford to probe for the mixed emotions her father no doubt had about her situation; feelings she continued to deal with herself. "Thanks so much, Dad. You're always there for me."

A flash of that expression again, quickly hidden. "Of course."

Sophie went on. "Furthermore, I'd like to volunteer to be your plus-one at any diplomatic dinners or events you have coming up. I want to be seen on your arm—that's the safest place I can be, right now."

Her father's smile was genuine this time. "Excellent. I happen to have a fundraiser dinner at Iolani Palace coming up, and I'd love to show you off."

Sophie's presence in his apartment was no doubt going to interfere with the ladies he spent time with, but Frank didn't seem to mind—and Sophie couldn't afford to worry about that. "I'll come to your place tomorrow, Dad, and we can figure out where everything goes."

CHAPTER FIVE

Raveaux
Day 2

Private investigator Pierre Raveaux followed Kendall Bix into the Security Solutions' CEO's office. The president of operations seated himself at the small round conference table. The CEO, Sophie Smithson, sat behind her executive desk in the corner. When she looked up at them, Raveaux saw puffy dark circles under her beautiful brown eyes. Three months after her fiancé's death, it still looked like she was crying herself to sleep every night.

"I'm not interested in any new cases," she told Bix sharply. "I've got my hands full dealing with this FBI multi-agency probe."

"We need to carry on with business as usual." Bix was calm, assertive, and well-groomed, as always. He opened a slim laptop. "Trying to anticipate the task force's moves is driving us all nuts. Staying busy with a new case will keep our minds off of whatever shenanigans they're dreaming up to capture the Ghost. We need to keep working."

"I disagree." Sophie clicked her mouse a final time. Raveaux noted her crisp white button-down shirt, worn over a pair of stretchy black dress pants with pearls at her ears—she looked fresh and professional, even though her eyes were tired and sad. She joined them at the table. "What do you think, Pierre?"

"I get to have an opinion?" Raveaux felt that unfamiliar tug to his mouth that meant he'd almost smiled. "I'm growing a bit stale on the Jack Reacher novels. Another case to take my mind off the tourists cavorting in my backyard would not be amiss."

"Cavorting. I like that." Sophie's dimple made an appearance. "All right then, since Pierre is in favor of us taking another job, let's hear what you've got for us, Bix."

Bix harrumphed. "This is strictly a white-collar job; nobody's going to be getting their hands dirty or fleeing a volcanic eruption on this one—but it's sensitive. Needs a diplomatic touch and tech skills. This is why I want my two senior investigators to work it, since there will likely be a need for forensic computer investigation. The client is actually waiting down in my office, hoping to meet with the two of you." Bix turned the monitor of his laptop, so that they could see the logo of one of the premier privately funded schools in Hawaii. "Are you familiar with Kama`aina Schools?"

"Somewhat. They specialize in delivering college preparatory education to primarily Hawaiian children," Sophie said. "They've got deep pockets that aren't filled by parents—the schools are funded by a land trust created by the Hawaiian monarchy at the turn of the century. Those funds come from the lease fees of major properties owned by the trust in downtown Honolulu."

"Correct so far," Bix affirmed. "This new client is an independent auditor who has been hired by the Board of Directors for Kama`aina Schools. The board suspects there has been some kind of embezzling of the trust."

"Why are we working with the auditor and not the board?" Raveaux straightened the pleat in his slacks and cocked an ankle over one knee, settling in.

"The endowment funding the schools is in the millions of dollars every month. The bookkeeping is overseen by a very well-respected accounting firm. Until recently, if there were any concerns, they were kept tightly under wraps and dealt with between the board and the firm. Recently, though, one of the board members with a background in accounting has made enough fuss to get an independent audit approved. That auditor has come to us on her own initiative to ask for help."

"That is unusual." Sophie reached back to pick up her electronic tablet off the corner of her desk. Her fingers flew over it as she made notes. "Why would the auditor want to work with a firm like us? We don't specialize in forensic accounting."

"I think we should let her present that herself, but the two of you have the unique skills we'll need to assist her in this audit. One of you should work directly with the auditor and interface with the players in the case—Raveaux can play that part nicely. Sophie, you can run computer analysis on everything our intrepid investigators get access to and bring in. Between the two of you, you should be able to provide our client the support she's looking for."

"Call the client to join us," Sophie said. "My curiosity is piqued."

"Your wish is my command, boss lady." Bix gave an ironic lift of his brow.

Raveaux had noticed the byplay between Sophie, as CEO, and Bix as Operations Head, on numerous occasions—they seemed to enjoy it, and they worked well together.

The three Security Solutions representatives stood respectfully as Bix performed the introductions a short time later. "Hermione Leede has come to us with a matter in need of skill and diplomacy."

The client was a petite woman with a crown of intricately braided white hair encircling her head. She wore a bright scarlet suit, Mary Jane heels, and she carried a well-worn, top quality brown leather satchel that much reminded Raveaux of the messenger bag he used himself.

"Very pleased to meet you." Leede enunciated her words with the crisp, tony accent of the British upper class. "I look forward to your assistance in this delicate matter."

"We are delighted to help." Sophie gave the warm smile Raveaux remembered, but hadn't seen lately. She extended a long-fingered hand that engulfed the client's petite, beringed one. "Would you like a cup of tea?"

A delighted smile wreathed Leede's face. "Perfect. It's so seldom that I am offered a cup of tea here in Hawaii, or hear the accent of a countrywoman."

"I'm not British, but I'd be lost without my tea." Sophie went over to the sideboard and pressed the button on her instant hot water pot. "I was educated in Europe, though."

Raveaux sat back and waited as Sophie prepared the tea things and the two women chatted. Bix pushed a contract over in front of Leede eventually, when the client sat at the table. "Here's our standard agreement for your review. Would you like to pay our hourly rate, or a percentage?"

"How interesting that you would offer those options." Leede cocked her head. Raveaux was reminded of a sparrow eyeing a nice bit of seed. "I've hired on for this audit for a recovery fee that's a percentage of the funds regained through my investigation—plus an hourly rate. If I fail to find any inappropriate losses, I'm paid the hourly rate only."

"That kind of payment structure is often indicated in insurance recovery investigations," Bix said. "We can work with that."

They negotiated for a few minutes, agreeing on a princely hourly rate with a fractional percentage, if the money was recovered.

Sophie returned with the loaded tea tray. Leede's pale brows lifted and she clapped her hands in glee. "I can't believe you have real chocolate biscuits! And what kind of tea can I look forward to? Loose leaf, no doubt?"

"Of course. This tea is very special—a blend of new leaf tips dried and produced in my home country of Thailand," Sophie said. "I have it delivered monthly, directly from the family that grows it."

"I shall look forward to tasting this exotic treasure." Leede accepted a teacup, saucer, and spoon.

"Let's let it steep for a moment." Sophie turned over the tiny hourglass that accompanied the set. She picked up her tablet and stylus from the table. "Now that we've observed the niceties, I have just one burning question. Why did you enlist our firm's assistance? The Kama`aina Schools' Board has entrusted you to do the audit on your own, and you would be entitled to the entire payment if you completed it. Why do you want us to get involved?"

"Because it's too big a job for one person," Leede said. "And I don't feel safe."

CHAPTER SIX

Raveaux

RAVEAUX LEANED FORWARD, making eye contact with the tidy, petite auditor. "Tell us more about that. In what way don't you feel safe?"

Hermione Leede adjusted the bright gemstone rings on her fingers in a habitual gesture. "Tempers are very high on the Kama`aina Schools' Board, and they don't want anyone to know that the audit is going on. A large bureaucracy supports the schools, and whoever is siphoning off this money will not want it to be discovered. I worry about the lengths someone might go to stop the audit. Not only that, I worry that I might need an additional witness to what I uncover, as well as more manpower for the various tasks I foresee." Leede paused to take a sip of tea, and when she replaced her cup on the saucer, it rattled against the china. "In addition, I'm a traditional accountant. There will be forensic computer records analysis, and that's not my specialty. Give me anything to do with a calculator and a spreadsheet, and I'm your girl—but searching a dozen computers for deleted files is not something I've ever wanted to learn."

"Fair enough," Sophie said. "Sounds like we're a match, because

I'm excellent with computers, and Raveaux here can provide all the protection you might need."

The sideways compliment from Sophie warmed him, and Leede's eyes twinkled at Raveaux from behind rhinestone-studded, cat eye glasses. "It definitely won't hurt my reputation to show up with *you* by my side, Monsieur Raveaux."

They wrapped up the meeting, and Raveaux made an appointment to meet Leede at her office the next day to begin the audit.

As Leede and Bix headed out, Sophie stopped Raveaux with a hand on his arm. "Can we speak for a minute?"

Her touch sent a zing of awareness through his body. "Of course." Raveaux sat back down.

Sophie went to her desk and took out a surveillance wand. She ran it over him quickly and expertly; he bit the inside of his cheek and held very still. He didn't blame her a bit for wanding him; he'd been bugged the last time they spoke privately. "Should we turn on the fan?"

"Not necessary. This room is swept daily." Sophie put the device away, and sat down across from him. She poured more of the fragrant tea through a strainer into their cups. "I've been meaning to catch up with you since you warned me about the raid on Phi Ni, but with all the security concerns we've been going through, I didn't want to draw attention."

"I understand." Raveaux had been leveraged to get Sophie to return to the United States from her private island sanctuary in Thailand with a fabricated story. The multi-agency team that was after the Ghost had planned to raid the island and capture him; Raveaux's warning had given Sophie time to warn Connor. "I know everything worked out, because you came back and it's been business as usual —but what happened over there?"

"After I dodged the agents sent to detain me in the conference room—again, thank you Pierre, for that warning—I took our corporate jet to Phi Ni to check on what had happened. The Department of Justice had marked all of the buildings and the entire island for seizure. No one was there." Sophie's honey-brown eyes darkened with remembered stress. "It was terrifying."

Raveaux's brows drew together. "What had happened to everyone?"

"Connor took his houseman Nam and Nam's wife Kupa back to the compound in Thailand. That place is so heavily armed that there's no way anything less than an act of war could remove him from there. Just before they fled, he put Armita, Momi, and my dogs on a private plane back to Hawaii. And they were waiting for me when I got back." Sophie's cheeks flushed and she dropped her eyes. "I died a little bit that day, and came back to life when I found my loved ones at home. They'd have been taken to use against me if you hadn't warned me, Pierre."

Raveaux cleared his throat. "Don't mention it again. What now?"

"I've decided to guard against the task force. I've arranged a meeting for us with my defense lawyer, Bennie Fernandez. He needs to interview both of us to determine if there are any conflicts of interest that might preclude him from being able to defend you."

"Thank you." He had heard the defense lawyer was one of the best in Hawaii. "But I am here on a work visa. I have few rights. I believe that I'm only still here in the United States because the team is still assessing if they can use me. Against you, and the man called Connor."

Sophie met his eyes for a brief moment. "That's why I want you protected."

"You have my word that your interests will always come first with me." Raveaux said it like a vow, each word precise and definite.

Sophie's expression remained carefully blank. She consulted her tablet, fingers flying, and his phone pinged. "I just forwarded you the date and time of the Fernandez consultation. We'll meet in this office since it's easiest to control security. Now, have you had any further communications or threats?" She met his eyes. "I don't want to come into work one day and find out that one of my most trusted colleagues has been deported, or worse."

Raveaux shook his head. "Nothing, thankfully. I sent a communiqué to some of my old friends on the French police force and in Interpol, asking them to be on alert on my behalf." He shrugged. "I felt better having warned some good people that I might be in need of assistance."

"Absolutely." Sophie fiddled with her stylus. "I'm taking my own security measures. In addition to hiring Fernandez, I'm moving in with my father every month that Momi and Armita aren't here. I'm going to be seen with him as much as possible and take advantage of my position as his daughter."

Raveaux's conscience pricked—the ambassador was secretly working with the multi-agency team, and had been the one to try to recruit Raveaux to use Sophie to trap her friend Connor. Raveaux hadn't told her of that a month ago because her grief over Jake was so fresh. *Should he tell her now?*

"In any case, that's all I wanted to say." Sophie stood up. "They must be watching you, so be very careful." She walked over and sat down behind her desk, still carrying the teacup. "I'll see you at the meeting with Fernandez."

Raveaux stood up—clearly, their meeting was over. "*Bonne chance*, Sophie, *merci*."

CHAPTER SEVEN

Sophie
Day 2, Evening

SOPHIE SPOTTED a tail following her SUV as she drove home to the Pendragon Arches apartment after work. The surveillance vehicle didn't break off until she turned into her building's underground garage.

Her heart rate escalated—maybe she should pack tonight and go to her father's apartment now, instead of the next morning as they'd discussed. She had no doubt she was being watched, every moment —even now as she let herself in and was greeted by Ginger and Anubis.

The dogs whined and jostled about anxiously as she packed her bags with just enough clothing and bathroom supplies to last the month. She'd return to this unit when Armita and Momi came back from her custody month on Kaua`i. Keeping Momi, a strong-willed toddler, on her schedule was challenging enough, without adding a new environment to the mix.

That thought reminded Sophie of the beautiful month she'd spent on Phi Ni right after Jake's death. If only the three of them could return to that pristine white beach and beautiful house on the cliff overlooking the Gulf of Thailand with its picturesque atolls—but the island, though deeded over to her, had been seized by the Department of Justice, and its ownership was tied up in the courts.

Sophie turned to the dogs and made a hand signal. "Sit."

Anubis, his sharp Doberman ears pricked, sat immediately. Ginger, Sophie's yellow rescue Lab, had eventually learned the basics through two rounds of obedience school. Whining reluctantly, she lowered her plump hindquarters to the floor. Sophie tossed them each a small dog biscuit. "Ginger, stay. Anubis, patrol."

Anubis leaped up and trotted off, following an established route of checking for intruders that Connor had trained him to do. Ginger remained sitting, whining low in her chest, intelligent eyes fixed on Sophie's backpack duffel bag.

Anubis gave a short, sharp bark—*his warning bark.*

The front doorbell dinged.

Sophie frowned. She didn't expect anyone at this time in the evening. She hit an app on her phone that activated a tiny security camera set over the door.

Two men in suits that bulged at the hip with sidearms stood in front of the aperture. *Agents!* They must have overheard her conversation with her father, and decided to pre-empt her move to his place. Because they'd followed her, they likely knew she was inside. The door was locked, but they might try to break in if she didn't answer it.

Time to disappear.

Sophie snapped her fingers for the dogs, picked up her tightly packed duffel, and slid her arms into its handy backpack straps. She put her phone into her pocket and headed for the closet, leashing the dogs as she went.

Sophie opened the interior security portal in the back of the closet and walked both dogs through the opening. Early in her relationship with Connor, she'd discovered this secret entrance to an office he owned in the apartment next door. The steel-reinforced door closed soundlessly and was automatically concealed behind a rotating shoe rack filled with footwear she seldom wore.

Sophie stifled a sneeze as she exited Connor's closet into his former bedroom, the dogs at her side. This secondary apartment was where the Ghost had really lived and spent time, but Sophie rarely used it. The lights were off and the air smelled musty.

Sophie entered what had been Connor's computer lab, the only room she did use, and then only when she needed privacy and security for some online task.

This room was completely soundproofed and had no windows— it could even be sealed as a "safe room," but she didn't want to do that in this instance unless she had to.

Sophie sat down on one of two office chairs in front of the computer work area, and re-activated the phone app.

The two agents had escalated to pounding on the door of her apartment. The camera didn't have audio, and she couldn't hear it in this sound-dampened room—but she could feel their blows as a vibration in the walls. Ginger whined anxiously, pressing against her leg, while Anubis's chest rumbled with a silent growl.

"Settle, my lovelies," Sophie crooned, and stroked their heads reassuringly as she watched the app.

One of the agents waited against the wall beside the entryway while the other headed for the elevator. They were likely going to get the building's supervisor to open the door for them.

Sophie settled into stillness. The dogs lay down at her feet.

She watched the entire drama as the reluctant building supervisor, prodded by the agents, unlocked the door—she'd had to give him the code and keys as part of the building's safety protocol. The agents drew their weapons and moved into her apartment.

Now was the time to move. She couldn't take the risk that they'd somehow uncover her secret exit.

Sophie stood up, tweaked the dogs' leashes, and headed for the front door of the secondary apartment, using a workaround she'd already programmed into her phone to deactivate the building's security cameras in the hall. Once the cameras were off, she slipped out and trotted lightly down the well-padded length of the hall to the elevator, bypassing that and hitting the stairs.

They might have left another agent to watch for her in the lobby, so she'd exit another way.

Sophie got off on the fourth floor, where the building's gym and indoor pool were located. She slid her keycard into the gym's door and hurried through the deserted workout area with the dogs close to her side, taking the service elevator that was accessible only on this level. The elevator dead-ended in the basement, bypassing the lobby altogether.

Unless the agents had studied the building's schematics, they wouldn't know that she could take an emergency side door out of the basement, go up a flight of metal stairs, and come out in an alley behind the building through a one-way, exterior-locked metal exit door.

The night smelled of the trash bins in the alley. Sophie's delicate stomach lurched. She breathed through her mouth, pushing through the queasiness, and broke into a jog, taking the dogs through the alley to the next street.

Once Sophie was out of the narrow throughway, she breathed easier, scanning all around as she cinched down the duffle pack. *No one in sight.*

She ran easily through the warm night, Ginger on one side and Anubis on the other.

Cars whizzed by. The businesses of downtown Honolulu were closed, but brightly lit from inside. A few tourists strolled, arm in arm. Sophie kept her weapon available and her eyes moving—the agents could still try to drive alongside her and throw her into a vehicle.

She couldn't take the risk of getting her car out of the garage at the Pendragon Arches. She'd send a Security Solutions operative tomorrow to fetch it and bring it to her father's apartment garage.

She called Security Solutions, requesting a team from Bix. "Agents are searching my apartment. They came to grab me."

"Damn, Sophie, I'm sorry you're dealing with that," Bix said. "I didn't think they'd be this aggressive. Do you need a pickup?"

"No. I'm almost at my father's address on foot. Was able to evade them." Sophie slowed to a rapid walk. "Put together a security detail to cover me starting tonight. I'm going to want an operative at my father's building keeping an eye out for me there, too, and to escort me to and from work."

"You got it," Bix said, and ended the call.

Sophie resumed running, the dogs bounding happily at her side, until she reached her father's building.

Her heart rate was back to normal by the time she stood in front of the red lacquered door of the penthouse apartment at the top of the high rise. Ginger was already whining with excitement to see Frank, one of her favorite people, as Sophie pressed the doorbell and checked the overeager Lab. "Quiet, girl."

Her father opened the door. Frank wore his favorite black satin pajamas and a pair of velvet slippers, a glass of cognac in his hand. "Sophie! I thought you were coming in tomorrow."

"I almost got taken by some agents." Sophie held his gaze and both of the dogs in check on their leashes. "Are you sure you want to deal with what I might be bringing through this door?"

Frank Smithson's well-groomed black brows drew together in a frown. "I can't believe you think you need to ask that question. Get inside, and we'll sort this out."

Sophie stepped into the open living area that had been her home for her first five years in Hawaii. She unclipped the dogs so that they could ecstatically greet her father—Ginger pushed her head into his crotch, while Anubis rubbed his sleek body against the ambassador's legs. Frank greeted them with just as much enthusiasm.

Sophie turned and locked the door, then unbuckled the waist strap of the duffle pack and slid it off. Her tee was damp at the waist and middle of her back; she was glad she'd changed into her yoga clothes after work. "I ran here on foot. That's why I don't have the dogs' beds, or any of their accoutrements."

"I'll get them some water." Frank headed for the kitchen area, Ginger and Anubis trailing him. "What happened?"

Sophie took a moment to enjoy the vista that was her favorite thing about her father's place: floor-to-ceiling windows showcasing an iconic view of Diamond Head and the Waikiki hotels, sparkling with colored lights. The ocean filled most of the window, moonlight streaking the water with its silver gleam. "I almost forgot how gorgeous this view is, Dad."

He'd filled bowls of water for the dogs in the sleek kitchen, separated from the living area by a granite island. Ginger and Anubis lapped noisily as Frank came over and pulled Sophie into a hug. "I'm so glad you're here," he said into her ear. "You'll be safe now."

Sophie shut her eyes and relaxed into her father's embrace, accepting his comfort. "Thanks, Dad. I really appreciate it." She pulled back and eyed her father. "But I'm an independent woman. I don't like to have to run home to my papa because bad guys are after me—and I'm not even sure how bad they really are." She cocked her head. "Furthermore, I'm not sure this whole thing is much of a surprise to you."

She spotted that flash again, quickly hidden by her father's diplomatic poker face. "I won't know what you mean until you tell me what happened. Let me fix you a drink." He turned away, heading toward the wet bar cabinet near the kitchen.

"No alcohol," Sophie said automatically. Frank stiffened, and then nodded.

Yes, there were unspoken currents between them. Maybe this time at home would be a chance to clear them up.

CHAPTER EIGHT

Sophie

SOPHIE CARRIED her duffle pack into her old room. The triptych of her computer monitors was gone from the black lacquered desk, but the bed was still inviting and topped with the jade-green silk coverlet. The blackout blinds still rolled shut and provided a feeling of security as she pushed the button.

Her body sagged suddenly with one of the waves of exhaustion that seemed to be part of the first trimester. Sophie flopped face down on the queen-sized bed, giving in for just a moment. To rest her eyes . . .

Her father's gentle shake on her shoulder brought Sophie awake with a start. "Honey. If you hadn't told me you were pregnant, I'd have known right away from seeing you like this. I hate to wake you, but I'm pretty sure you didn't plan to go to bed in your sweaty running clothes."

Sophie pushed a handful of damp curls off her forehead and squinted at the clock. "Dad! You let me sleep for an hour!"

"You must have needed it." Frank headed for the doorway. "Why don't you take a shower, get into your jammies, and I'll meet you in the living room for that drink I made you."

"Okay. Thanks." Sophie did want to speak with her father, but she felt like she'd been sandbagged at the back of the head. She blinked the sleep out of her eyes and made her way between the dogs, who were curled up on beds Frank had made for them from beach towels.

Under the fall of water, using familiar coconut-smelling soap left in her bathroom from when she'd lived there before, Sophie reflected.

Her dad was alone, here in this beautiful apartment. He dated a lot; but he'd never seemed to let himself get attached enough to remarry after his disastrous first union with Pim Wat. Frank didn't seem to dislike women, just not to trust them—and Sophie understood that particular response all too well. "Mother would be enough to put anyone off of women," Sophie muttered.

Frank hadn't changed a thing in her room. He must be telling the truth when he said he'd welcome the company of her and her dogs. And even if she brought Armita and Momi, too, he'd likely be happy —though there definitely wasn't room for them all to be comfortable in the two-bedroom place, spacious though it was.

She wrapped up in one of the fluffy white cotton towels hanging on the warming rod, and then put on a sleep tee. Donning her favorite dragon-covered silk robe and blotting her hair with the towel, she rejoined her father in the living room. "This will be a mess tomorrow if I sleep on it damp. I miss the days of just keeping it buzzed."

"You look beautiful with it short, but I love your curls now." Frank was seated on the semi-formal loveseat with the Wall Street Journal on his lap. He set the paper aside, got up, and went to the little refrigerator inside the wet bar unit. "I made you something special." He took out a frosty-looking blue drink in a tall glass, complete with an umbrella. "After you told me you were coming over, I had Augie stock the bar with the ingredients for your favorite drink, and some of the food you like is in the fridge."

Augie was Frank's housekeeper, driver, and general helper. Sophie wished she had someone like that to help her every day. "You're sweet, Dad. Tell Augie, thanks."

She accepted the frothy concoction, which had begun to separate a little during her nap. She stirred the drink with its straw, and took a sip. The cool sweetness felt nice on her throat, and it was definitely alcohol-free. "This is delicious."

Frank sat on the corner of the loveseat, closer to her, and extended his goblet of cognac. "Cheers." They clinked glasses. "Now. Tell me what happened, exactly."

Sophie told him about the surprise visit from the agents, that she'd spotted them using the app on her phone, but not how she'd been able to get out of the apartment undetected. "I've already asked Bix to set up an ongoing security detail for me." She waggled her phone. "He texted me that they'd meet me tomorrow morning outside your place. I'll call the building's security and let them know." She took a moment to do that, then lifted her eyes to meet her father's. "Should I have them stay outside the door all night too? After all, these are legitimate law enforcement people, supposedly, though their tactics so far have not been aboveboard."

Frank shook his head. "I've alerted my Secret Service detail. They told me they'd be monitoring anything here at my apartment."

"If they want to take me in, they legally can. The security detail is just to make sure I go to a legitimate interview site and that Bennie, my lawyer, is called and on his way should they try to detain me." Sophie took a sip of her drink. "Bennie's terrific, by the way. Thank you for reminding me about him. He had been the Security Solutions' legal counsel, but I had forgotten how good he is."

Should she tell the ambassador about the meeting she'd set up with him and Raveaux? No. Her father wouldn't be interested in what was going on with Raveaux, a mere contractor in her company.

"I knew Fernandez was good." Frank sat back with a satisfied smile. "Glad he's working out."

Sophie eyed her father over the rim of her drink. "Speaking of Secret Service. I've had confirmation that they are a part of this multi-agency investigation that's harassing me. Have you heard anything about that from Katie?"

Kate Smith was her father's Secret Service agent when needed, and security liaison and consultant other times. Sophie had found the agent to be smart, kind, and competent.

Her father gazed into the amber-brown depths of his drink and swirled it. "No. Katie doesn't tell me about her other cases."

"Well, I'm surprised that she hasn't mentioned it, since I'm involved in this one, in however peripheral a way." Sophie kept a sharp eye on her father.

"I'll ask her about it, if you'd like." Frank's dark brown eyes met hers, blandly expressionless.

"Please do." Sophie finished her drink and stood up slowly, stretched and yawned. "Need any other information gaps filled in before I go to bed?"

"I don't think so." Frank set his drink aside and stood too. "Anything I should know about what's coming up?"

"I have no idea from one day to the next." Sophie shook her head. "Let's take it as it comes, Dad."

"That sounds best." Frank kissed her cheek. "See you in the morning."

Sophie headed to her room and shut the door gently. Brushing her teeth, she frowned.

Her father absolutely knew something about this team, this case, and whatever the hell they were trying to do—but he hadn't taken her hint to share. She'd have to be more direct the next time they talked.

CHAPTER NINE

Marcella:
Day 3

MARCELLA DRAGGED a brush through her hair and wound its smooth length expertly around her fingers, pressing the thick roll of choco-late-brown locks against the back of her head and anchoring it with bobby pins; a style she called "The FBI twist." Her features were so bold—her eyes long-lashed, her brows strongly-marked, her lips full —that anything more than a touch of lipstick, for daytime, looked overdone.

She stepped back from the mirror, tugged down her neatly buttoned blazer, and brushed a bit of lint off her sleeve. Ben Waxman, her Special Agent in Charge, was a stickler for dress code and protocol, and she was about to barge into a large, multi-agency team meeting and ask to sit at a table where she wasn't sure she'd be welcome. "All they can say is no," Marcella told herself out loud. "And I won't let them say no."

She had to get on the task force to help Sophie. Offering intel would open that door. Marcella wanted Connor caught. Only when that man was behind bars would her friend be safe. Be great if Sophie's sicko mother Pim Wat went down too, while they were at it.

Giving her jacket another tug, Marcella headed for the door of the women's room, enjoying a glimpse of her gleaming gold-toned pumps beneath regulation navy trousers. A girl needed a good pair of shoes to boost her confidence, and Marcella had those in a rainbow of colors and styles.

Marcella pulled the door open and headed for the FBI's conference room, walking fast, her head up and arms swinging. The meeting room door was closed; she had expected that. She knocked, two loud raps, and then opened it and stepped inside.

As she had anticipated, Waxman was seated at the head of the table, with agents ranged around him beneath the FBI logo prominently displayed on the wall. She recognized three: Agents Pillman and Gundersohn. Neither of them had ever been a friend. The only other female in the room, Secret Service Agent Kate Smith, assigned to Sophie's father, was at least a familiar face.

"Good afternoon. I'm sorry to interrupt, but I have some important information to share with the team," Marcella said.

Waxman's brows went up, but his gaze looked relieved—apparently the meeting had not been going well. "Pull up a chair, Marcella. Everyone, this is Special Agent Marcella Scott, one of our finest."

Waxman was sparing with his praise. He was probably trying to pave the way for her intel, but regardless, Marcella's neck warmed at the compliment. "I'm sure I can catch all of your names later. I'd like to volunteer to be a part of the investigation."

Waxman's eyebrows snapped together; he didn't like that. She should have gone through the chain of command, but the chain of command would have dead-ended with a pat on the head. "Some new information about how Sophie Smithson was rescued on the Big Island, along with her deceased partner, Jake Dunn, has come my way." That was a mouthful. Marcella forged on. "Sophie is a personal friend of mine. She told me that using a chip with satellite tracking capabilities embedded under her skin, the Ghost found them."

The conference room door opened again. Marcella turned to face whomever had entered—and shock widened her eyes. "The group is already aware of this, Marcella," Ambassador Smithson said, as he advanced into the room. "I gave them that intel."

Waxman speared her with his icy blue gaze. "Why didn't you come to me directly with this, Agent Scott?"

"I got it only yesterday evening, when I met with Sophie." Marcella pulled out a chair and seated herself in an open space. She looked around the table, making eye contact with five different people. Only the blue-eyed brunette Secret Service Agent smiled at her. "I have more confidential information to share, but I would like to be formally added to the team first."

Pillman scowled. "That sounds a lot like you're trying to leverage us, Agent Scott."

The man sitting closest to Marcella turned toward her, and extended a hand. "This FBI infighting is to our benefit! I am all in favor of you joining the team. I'm Stefan Voise of Interpol. We tried to grab Sophie last night to interview her, but she evaded us at her apartment. We still can't figure out how."

Marcella bit her bottom lip on her startled exclamation—*Sophie grabbed at her apartment?*

"As to that." Ambassador Smithson had seated himself closest to Waxman. His resonant voice rumbled with angry authority. "My daughter is grieving. She's also expecting a child. She is not to be harassed any further. I've cooperated with this investigation because I want her separated from the negative influences of Connor, her mother Pim Wat, and whoever the hell the Master is. But my agreement with this task force was that no one would interfere with my daughter or try to bring her in. An attempted grab at her apartment violates that agreement."

Marcella had guessed that Frank was here to protect Sophie the minute she saw the ambassador—*why else would he get involved with something like this?* But now he'd stolen her thunder. Marcella had been planning to share the news of Sophie's pregnancy as intel; what else did she have to offer?

The room broke out into raised voices and arguing.

Marcella knew about the secret office and exit Sophie had used to ditch the team; but that wasn't likely to be valuable unless they could use it to trap Connor or something. "Dammit," she muttered under her breath. She was about to get kicked to the curb if she didn't do something to prove her value.

The ambassador stood up and buttoned his jacket, apparently not satisfied with the justifications being offered around the table. "I won't be assisting this group any longer unless I can be assured, in writing, that my daughter, her nanny, and my granddaughter, will not be used as bargaining chips to access those Thailand connections. I've lost confidence in the team's ability to bring these criminals to justice. Any further communications with our family can go through my attorney." He slapped a business card down in front of Waxman, and swept out.

Kate Smith hurried after him. "Frank! Let's talk about this!" *She'd probably been the one to bring him onto the team.*

The door shut behind them. The room was in chaos. Marcella held her seat and her breath. They needed her now; she was the only one who could get close to Sophie, who had her trust. She would sit tight, and wait until they realized it.

That didn't take long.

Waxman pinned her with his cold blue stare. "We'll expect your full cooperation with this investigation, Agent Scott. You'll answer directly to me."

"Absolutely, sir," Marcella said. "What can I do to help?"

CHAPTER TEN

Sophie

Bennie Fernandez looked much the same as he had the first time Sophie had met him during one of her FBI cases years ago. The short, round defense lawyer's apple cheeks, snowy beard, and bright eyes never seemed to age.

Sophie had already drawn the blackout drapes and wanded her office for surveillance devices that morning. As an additional precaution, she had set up two fans on tall stands that created white noise across the corner seating area where Raveaux had joined them for the meeting to talk about his representation.

Sophie snuck a glance at Raveaux out of the corner of her eye. He looked haggard; dark circles surrounded his intelligent brown eyes, and the silver streak at his temples seemed a little wider today. This must be one of those times when he wasn't eating or sleeping well. She could certainly empathize with that, since her shoulders still ached from running through Honolulu at night carrying a heavy backpack.

Sophie prepped the tea things as Fernandez engaged Raveaux. "Sophie is already my client, and she asked for this meeting to see if it's appropriate for me to take your case as well. We have to make sure that there are no conflicts of interest that would interfere with supporting you."

"I am fine with other representation, if you need to make a referral," Raveaux said. He straightened his trousers, and cocked one ankle over his knee.

"I want Raveaux to have the best, Bennie. And you're the best." Sophie brought the tray with the tea things and set it on the coffee table. She seated herself in the armchair that faced the loveseat and couch in the corner of her office. "I owe Pierre all the help I can give him for his current situation, since it is, at least in part, due to me."

Fernandez's tufty white brows arched comically. "What exactly is the situation? If I could get a recap for the record." His appearance was one of his greatest weapons; that cherubic face hid one of the keenest legal minds Sophie had ever encountered. "Be candid with me, please. Attorney-client privilege covers all matters disclosed in this meeting."

Sophie met Raveaux's eyes for the first time. "Should you tell him, or should I?"

Raveaux looked away and fiddled with his cuff. "Why don't you explain the situation, Sophie."

Sophie turned to face Fernandez. "As you already know, a multi-agency law enforcement task force is trying to leverage me to cooperate with capturing the international fugitive known as the Ghost. Remember when I first engaged your services a few months ago? I was responding to a warning that Raveaux gave me. He had been approached and threatened with deportation and worse, by agents from the CIA and FBI." Sophie gestured to the drapes and the fans. "We had to take all of the security steps that you currently see here, in order for him to advise me of an incipient raid on my private island to capture my friend Connor. Monsieur Raveaux had also been tagged with a personal surveillance device, without his consent. And unless I'm wrong, he's been under continual scrutiny ever since, threatened with deportation and even being taken overseas for interrogation."

Fernandez made a note on a tablet. "Hmm. What is your status here in the United States?"

"I am a French citizen here on a work visa." Raveaux rubbed at a scuff on the immaculate leather loafer resting upon his knee. "Since the original incident, I have also cooperated with two additional interrogations at the FBI headquarters, where I was not-so-subtly threatened with torture and deportation. As far as I can tell, though, my warning to Sophie was not detected. If it had been, I have no doubt I would no longer be here." Raveaux addressed Fernandez directly. "I encountered the man they want to capture one time, when he hijacked a helicopter and directed it to rescue Jake and Sophie. I told them everything I knew about that situation, including that I thought he had paranormal abilities. I hope they've lost interest in me now."

"Paranormal abilities?" Sophie's eyes widened. "You never told me that." She'd seen Connor's incredible physical feats before, but nothing that could be called paranormal.

"Yes, I'm interested in hearing this, too," Fernandez said.

"I think it was my description of that which has made me of less interest." Raveaux wove his fingers together and rested them on his flat belly. "They think I was suffering some kind of post-traumatic delusion. Nonetheless, I know what I saw and heard."

Sophie narrowed her eyes in irritation. *"Son of a flatulent yak.* Quit stalling, Raveaux."

Raveaux narrowed his eyes right back at her. "I didn't understand that phrase, but I don't believe it was polite."

Fernandez harrumphed. "My time is costing Ms. Smithson a good deal, Monsieur Raveaux. Please proceed."

"Well, first of all, the man known as Connor found them by tracking a GPS chip he had embedded on Sophie, which I gather you are still wearing?" Raveaux raised his brows at her.

"Yes." Sophie flushed—*she needed to figure out what to do*

about that chip! Maybe Fernandez would have guidance for her. "Please, put us out of our agony and tell your tale."

"We located the general area where you and Jake were trapped in the cave. But then, instead of helping Connor's man Nine and me dig open the cavern's shaft to make it larger so we could get you out, Connor sat down and meditated. Closed his eyes, lotus position, all of that. I was angry with him at the time." Raveaux pushed a hand into his short dark hair, disordering it in his agitation. "Then, Connor said that he could see where you were. He perceived your energy fields underground. And then . . ." Raveaux seemed to falter. "I don't know how to explain this. He seemed to appear and disappear, when we were digging, and I had a sense that—he'd done something."

Sophie frowned. "That's vague."

"Yes, because I can't explain it. For me it was like this: I was digging, and he was there, meditating. And then he was at my side with a rope, and the hole was wide enough for a person to enter." Raveaux shrugged. "Maybe I was just so caught up in the urgency of the moment. We knew you both were unconscious because of the way he described your energy fields, and that you didn't respond to our hails."

Sophie picked up her teacup, holding it in both hands, but tea splashed anyway because she was trembling so badly. She saw those terrible moments from another angle: herself, passed out but breathing on the ledge above Jake. He'd lain below her, inhaling toxic gases.

Dying.

"Sophie." Fernandez's voice was soft, calling her back.

She set down her cup and reached for the tea towel. She dabbed the spill. "I'm sorry. It's still emotional to revisit that time. Please go on, Pierre."

Raveaux nodded. "An awful experience for all, especially Jake. But those were the two moments when I believe that Connor did something—unexplainable."

"I've seen him do extraordinary feats physically," Sophie said. "But nothing I would call paranormal."

Fernandez sharpened his gaze upon her. "Now, young lady. Since we're laying this all out here in the open, you've maintained to me that you were aware that Connor had two other identities, both legally deceased, and that he was wanted in connection with rumored activities as a cyber vigilante known as the Ghost. Do you continue to deny knowing anything about that?"

"I know Connor as a former lover, and current friend. Also, as the founder of Security Solutions. Yes, he willed the company over to me, along with his private island, when he chose to join that Thai espionage organization. But I know nothing about this "Ghost" aspect." Sophie made air quotes with her fingers.

"Good." Fernandez's response was definite. "Keep it that way."

The lawyer then turned to Raveaux. "There's not much I can do for you, sir, except to insist that law enforcement have cause to detain you if they try to do so. I would have no control over any deportation proceedings, though I can contact a friend of mine who specializes in immigration law. And as to this "Ghost" element of the investigation—do you have any knowledge of that?"

Raveaux stood up and paced. He moved like a shark through water, almost lazily graceful, but he was back in front of the desk again in seconds when he turned to face Sophie. "I do have something to share, and I must say it. But I regret, very much, Sophie, that it may cause you pain."

CHAPTER ELEVEN

Raveaux

RAVEAUX FACED SOPHIE, sitting in the sleek armchair with the ruddy-faced little lawyer across from her on the couch. He slid his hands into his pockets and played nervously with Gita's little gold Ganesh amulet, a token he'd given her long ago.

Sophie sat stiffly. "What could you possibly have to say that would hurt me?"

"I didn't tell you something that I should have. I thought you had enough to bear," Raveaux said.

Sophie seemed to have turned to golden-brown stone, but her eyes were wide and fierce. He was seared by her gaze from across the room. "You have no idea what I can take, what I have borne, and what I'll continue to deal with. It's not your place to make any decisions for me or about me. How dare you withhold information that I should have had!"

Raveaux winced under the lash of her words. He broke eye contact and paced, trying to find a place to begin his narrative.

"Now, Ms. Smithson," Fernandez moderated. "I'm sure Monsieur Raveaux was only trying to help. Grief makes every emotion more intense, and there's a good chance that this information would not have made a big difference—or he would have shared it with you by now. Correct, Monsieur?"

"I don't know what difference it would have made, but you're right. I should have disclosed this sooner." Raveaux turned and addressed Sophie. "Remember when I told you that I was visited by two agents who threatened me, and that was the start of my involvement in this investigation?"

Sophie gave a short nod. Her eyes were still hot, her lush mouth a folded line.

"That wasn't the whole truth. Remember when we met on the sidewalk outside of the hospital when you were discharged after being treated for smoke inhalation suffered during your ordeal on the Big Island? My involvement with the case began then, with your father."

Her glare was unwavering.

"The ambassador slipped a stick drive into my hand when he shook it that day."

The color drained from Sophie's face. She leaned forward and turned her teacup around and around.

"The storage device the ambassador gave me contained extensive information about the case against Connor," Raveaux went on. "Everything that the FBI has on him, secret interior documents from Security Solutions, even details about the retrieval of six bodies from the Thai jungle by the CIA."

"No," Sophie whispered. "My father doesn't know any of that. I made sure of it."

Raveaux forged on. "The documents show that you were somehow involved with the conspiracy around Connor. Your role is implicit in the contents of the file: the documentation you provided, declaring the man calling himself Sheldon Hamilton legally dead, a man the FBI believes was also known as Todd Remarkian, supposedly killed in an explosion. It's documented there that you once had a romantic relationship with Remarkian.

That man, calling himself Connor, is now residing at an armed compound in Thailand run by the clandestine organization, the Yām Khûmkạn. There's no way you couldn't have known all this." Raveaux paced. "What wasn't in the file was any clear connection between the man I met who rescued you and the vigilante known as the Ghost. They have no proof of that. They do seem to know that Connor was once known as both Sheldon Hamilton and Todd Remarkian—and they think you assisted in the coverup around his identities."

"You aren't worried about the evidence they're gathering against you?" Fernandez asked Sophie. "They could charge you with conspiracy to defraud, at least."

"The worst they can do, by proving I helped cover up for Remarkian, would be to strip the company and his possessions from me." Sophie shrugged. "But it would be a battle I think I'd win."

"It's significant," Fernandez warned.

But Sophie was upset about something else. "I can't believe Dad knows everything." She let loose a sharp stream of invectives in Thai. "I can't believe he'd lie to me. Pretend like this."

"That's not all on the subject of your father, unfortunately." Raveaux walked over and sat down on the end of the couch furthest from Sophie. He met her gaze squarely. "The ambassador asked to meet. During that meeting, he made it clear he . . . wanted Connor captured. He was providing intel to the task force, and cooperating with them voluntarily." Raveaux leaned forward, his fingers laced between his knees. "I want you to know everything. It might hurt now, but will save you pain later." Raveaux swallowed apprehensively. "Your father made it clear to me that—he didn't approve of your choices in men."

Sophie snorted. "Screw him. He's hardly in a position to pass judgment on me, after marrying Pim Wat." She stood up abruptly. She wore a swirl of red skirt like a matador's cape with a narrow top that showcased her superb upper body, and no jewelry but that flash of Jake's diamond on her hand. "I knew Dad didn't mean it when he said he supported me in this pregnancy. I knew he was hiding something!"

Raveaux froze, and absorbed this as best he could without giving away shock. Many years as an investigator helped him keep his facial expression neutral, his voice even. "You're—pregnant?"

"Yes, Pierre, I am. And it's none of your damn business." Sophie spun around, that skirt flaring.

Fernandez leaned forward and harrumphed. "Sophie, this is big news to anyone working with you. I would have wanted to know that, myself."

Sophie glared at Fernandez. "How is it any of your business, either? The fact that my uterus is now occupied has nothing to do with my legal defense. I'm sick and tired of these patriarchal responses. And don't you dare tell me I'm being overly emotional. I went to my father for protection, only to find out he's helping the enemy." Her hands gripped her hips. *She was magnificent.* "I'm going to the restroom. And when I get back, you two better have some useful suggestions for me."

The carpet was too thick for her stride to make much sound, but Raveaux felt her power as she swept out of the room. The heavy door shut soundlessly behind her.

Raveaux stared at that door. *She was pregnant, with Jake's baby.* A tiny bloom of happiness for her warmed him, somewhere beneath his sternum. That child would be such a comfort to her. "What a beautiful thing to come from sorrow," he said.

"Yes. And Sophie is right; her pregnancy is none of our concern." Fernandez retrieved a briefcase from beside his seat. He set it on the coffee table and popped the latches to remove some papers. "I'm afraid, in light of all this information, I'm going to have to refer you, Monsieur Raveaux. I have a colleague who deals with international and immigration law. She's a lovely woman to work with; I think you'll be an excellent fit, and I'll give her a call today to ensure that she makes room in her schedule to take you on." He handed Raveaux a card. "Now, what other suggestions are we going to have for Sophie when she returns?"

Raveaux accepted the card. His mind was whirring. "Thank you. The referral will be fine. And in the meantime, I do have some ideas for her."

CHAPTER TWELVE

Sophie

SOPHIE STOMPED past Paula at her desk and went on to the main women's bathroom in the hall. Once inside, she flipped the deadbolt to lock it—she wanted complete privacy. This restroom was well-appointed with a sitting area, a vanity with good lighting, a shower and dressing room, and a series of toilet stalls.

Sophie hurried into the nearest stall and dealt with her overactive bladder. She'd never understood this stage of pregnancy: the baby was hardly taking up any room, but she still needed to pee every hour or so.

She washed her hands, examining her image in the mirror. Her cheeks were flushed, her eyes still wide with anger.

When had she ever let herself go like that? Raising her voice? Swearing at a man?

Her early marriage to an abusive husband had taught her to retreat, to close down, to conceal all emotion behind a frozen mask. Maybe she was coming out of that, finally—*or maybe it was just hormones.* Not that either of them would dare accuse her of a hormonal outburst—she had made sure of it.

Remembering the expressions on their faces made her snort.

And then she laughed, and then that became hysteria, and then tears.

Definitely hormones.

But behind her anger, was hurt.

Betrayal.

Even shame.

Her father didn't approve of her choices. Frank was trying to manipulate and protect her by making some kind of deal with that infernal investigation team. Sophie needed protection—from her foolish choices in men, from Connor, and from Pim Wat and her powerful consort, the Master. That's what his rationale would be, she was sure of it.

The Secret Service must have been how they got to him. Sophie could imagine Kate Smith, with her honest blue eyes, approaching Frank with a proposal that he help his daughter get free from the taint of involvement with the Yām Khûmkạn and her deadly mother; and from Connor, a man with questionable motives.

That would not have been a hard sell. Her father's hatred for his ex-wife had been ignited afresh by finding out that Pim Wat was not only a manipulative depressive, but a spy and an assassin who had likely used him to gain information. Sophie still remembered the pain in his eyes when the truth about Pim Wat came to light.

But Dad could have trusted her. He could have shared that classified file with her instead of Raveaux, and discussed all of their options. He could have believed that she was competent to find her way out of the situation. Instead, he'd told Raveaux, and threatened and used *him.*

Thank God Raveaux had chosen to be honest with her!

Now she was sleeping in her father's apartment, and counting on the protection of his position—and of course, he was enjoying that. *He loved her best when she needed him.*

Sophie set her watch for five minutes of crying, something she had tried to wean herself off of—but today she needed the release.

"It's okay to let go," Dr. Wilson, her therapist, spoke in her mind. "Crying is good. Tears carry away cortisol, a stress hormone. Cry regularly."

Sophie cried for the memory of Jake, and memories of the terrible loss that had been stirred up by Raveaux's description.

She cried for the fact that her mother was a psychopath that, while pretending to ask her forgiveness, wasn't to be trusted.

She wept because her beloved father didn't believe she could manage her life, her work, or her relationships.

And she cried because she was going to lose her friend Connor because of his vigilantism—and because he was turning into someone she really didn't know anymore.

It was becoming clear that she needed to sever all ties with Connor, or find herself becoming collateral damage in the war between him and worldwide law enforcement.

There was no one around her that she could really trust.

She blew her nose on a paper towel.

Well, there were a few people: Dr. Wilson. Armita. Marcella. Maybe even Raveaux, but not if he kept anything from her. Bix would always tell her straight as far as work went. Paula was more than an assistant . . .

The alarm on her watch went off.

Sophie got up from the chair in the lounge area and went over to the sink. She splashed water on her face, then dabbed it dry with paper towels.

Her eyes were puffy, bloodshot slits. She retrieved a makeup bag from her locker under the counter and applied eyedrops. She touched up her pale cheeks and put on a bit of raspberry lipstick to bring some color to her face. She used a couple of handfuls of water to smooth her curls back from her face, but she liked the look of the mane of wild ringlets tumbling to her shoulders.

"*Those sons of a fetid pig* better have some advice for me," she growled at her reflection, and headed for the door.

RAVEAUX AND FERNANDEZ were as she had left them: Raveaux sat at one end of the couch, Fernandez on the loveseat across from him. Fernandez had taken out a briefcase, and Raveaux held a business card in his hands. The two men were bent towards each other as if she had interrupted them in conversation, but they sat back and gave her their full attention as she returned to her seat.

Sophie smoothed her skirt over her knees and folded her hands in her lap. "Recommendations, please." Her voice was cool and assertive, just the way she wanted it to sound.

Fernandez cleared his throat. "In light of the amount of crossover and the complexity of the case, I am referring Raveaux to a colleague. This conversation is still completely covered by attorney-client privilege, however, and I have given Monsieur Raveaux a signed affidavit to that effect. I believe he has some thoughts for you, and having heard them, I support them."

Sophie inclined her head toward Raveaux. "Proceed."

Raveaux leaned forward. His keen eyes fixed on her like a hawk. "Sever all ties with Connor. Remove the chip so that he cannot be lured to your location, since your father knows about the chip and has no doubt given that information to the team."

"I've come to the same conclusion. Anything else?"

"Don't let on to your father that you're aware of his involvement with the case. I know this will be difficult, but the reasons that you sought shelter with him originally are valid. You need the protection of his position, and for everything to appear as if you aren't aware of his involvement. By his side is the safest place for you to be, Sophie, and if it helps at all, I believe he agreed to help in order to protect you."

"That doesn't mean he shouldn't have trusted me by telling me what he knew." She gestured. "Go on."

"I believe the task force will move on from attempting to involve us in their scheme when they realize we have nothing further to offer." Raveaux sat back. "For what it's worth."

"Yes, it will be difficult to live with my father and conceal that I know of his betrayal. But I agree with you, at least for the moment. I'll remove the chip as soon as possible and cease all communication with Connor." Sophie turned back to Fernandez, raising her brows. "Anything further?"

"I agree with Monsieur Raveaux's opinions," Fernandez said. "And I further recommend that you move Connor's holdings that were deeded to you into a neutral LLC Trust, of which you are the owner. That will help keep them from being confiscated if your connection to Hamilton/Remarkian is challenged."

"Good idea," Sophie said. "Thank you, Bennie."

"I feel certain that your father was threatened that you would be taken into custody if he didn't cooperate with the team's plans. I hope you will not judge him too harshly. Sometimes we do foolish things to protect those we love," Raveaux said.

"I was fine with your thoughts until you crossed the line into what is none of your business, once again," Sophie kept her voice flat and cool. "That will be all, gentlemen."

"Good," Fernandez said. "Keep me posted of any changes or new activity." He snapped his briefcase shut and rolled his portly form up out of the couch. He extended a hand to Raveaux. "I'm sorry I wasn't able to help you more directly."

Raveaux stood, and shook the little man's hand. "It was a pleasure to meet you, sir."

Sophie walked to the door and pulled it open, holding it ajar. "I'll be in touch with either or both of you, should I need your services." She could tell by Raveaux's raised brow that he had not planned to leave with Fernandez, but he followed the little lawyer out with a nod.

Sophie shut the door behind them, flipped the lock, and sagged against it.

She needed a nap.

But first, she needed to get rid of the chip.

She walked over to her desk and removed a box cutter she used for opening packages. Grabbing a handful of tissues, she propped her elbow on the corner of her desk, placing the pad of tissues on the desk's surface beneath her arm. After locating the slight node of the tracker in the tender skin under her arm, she extended the box cutter's razor tip and sterilized it with an alcohol wipe that she had in her drawer.

She cut into the skin, set the box cutter down, and squeezed gently on either side of the tracker. The chip was actually cylindrical, half an inch long and a quarter-inch wide, filled with coiled material inside of a plastic case. It popped out easily from under her skin, along with a gush of fresh, bright blood.

Sophie hadn't expected the wave of nausea that hit her as she pressed the tissues to the wound in her arm. She gulped, hoping to forestall the inevitable—but a moment later, she vomited into her wastebasket.

"Pregnancy isn't for sissies. Ugh." She dabbed her mouth with more tissues, and removed a bottle of water from the cabinet under her desk. She drank a few sips, and then tied the plastic trash bag tightly shut.

Sophie felt too weak to get up just yet. She depressed a button on her desk phone. "Paula? Can you come tidy up in here? You'll have to bring your keys. The door is locked."

"Right away, Sophie."

She pressed the tissues against her arm. The bleeding had stopped. Paula came in just as Sophie got up and headed over to lie down on the couch, propping her head on one of the throw pillows. "Please put away the tea things from the meeting, and re-stock the bar," she told Paula. "And I wasn't feeling well. If you could pick up the trash and replace the liner . . ."

"Of course. Are you sick, Sophie? Do you want to go home?" Paula's pretty face showed concern.

"Just a touch of morning sickness. You might as well know,

along with everyone else," Sophie said. "I am due in six months. My fiancé left me a little surprise."

Paula cupped her face with her hands, her mouth an O, and came over to Sophie, dropping to her knees to hug her on the couch. "Congratulations! I'm so happy for you. Momi will have a brother or sister! What a blessing!"

Easy tears came to Sophie's eyes. *If only everyone had given her this kind of support at her news!* "Yes, children are always a blessing."

CHAPTER THIRTEEN

Pim Wat

P‌IM W‌AT, seated at her vanity, turned her face from side to side, admiring the new facial structure the bone surgeon had created. She'd taken the opportunity to have her face not only repaired, but completely made over.

She didn't recognize herself anymore, but in a good way this time.

Her cheekbones had been wide before, pointing to a narrow chin that set off her lush mouth and tilted eyes. Now her cheekbones were higher, her jawline squarer, and her eyelids, completely redone, were a rounder shape, giving her a look of mixed Thai and European lineage. Even her mouth looked different, but it was still sexy and full. The surgery scars at her hair and jawline were pink and raised; but a few more laser treatments over the next months would take care of that, and makeup could cover the rest.

She'd also put on the colored contacts she'd chosen to be a permanent part of her new look. These were dark green, masking her brown eyes. A hairdresser had dyed her white hair platinum blonde; it shimmered against her golden skin in a fashionable short style.

This face wouldn't register on any facial recognition software. Pim Wat was a new woman.

She smiled into the mirror, catching the eyes of the team of three plastic surgeons, hovering in the background. "This is acceptable."

They broke into delighted applause. "You are exquisite, Mistress," one of them said.

"Our very best work," another chimed in.

Pim Wat turned on her padded swivel stool to face them. "This has been stressful for all of you—everyone here wants to please the Master, including myself, and I believe he will be well pleased. My maid has prepared a congratulatory beverage for us." Kupa, standing in the corner holding a tray, came forward. "Let us toast."

Kupa's tray contained four glasses of traditional Thai rice beer. The doctors clustered around, chatting, as they took the beverages. Kupa, her eyes down modestly, brought the final glass, marked with a golden ribbon, to Pim Wat.

Pim Wat rose from her chair. She'd been working out with yoga and pilates, and her breasts had been tightened and filled. They rose proudly without need of a bra, her pert nipples lifting the cream-colored silk of her robe and drawing the eyes of the surgeons as they turned toward her, their faces wreathed in smiles, their relief palpable.

Men. They were all the same, the simple creatures.

"To my talented team. May you prosper as you deserve!" She raised her glass. They raised theirs. Everyone drank deep, as was traditional. "Thank you again for my exemplary care. Your fees will be posted today."

She'd promised an astronomical fee by direct deposit, and it was indeed on its way to their bank accounts for all of their families to enjoy.

She sat back down. Turned toward the mirror again. Looked at her face, turning from side to side to admire it. *Unfamiliar, but beautiful.* A fresh start to a new chapter in her life. "Kupa, come here."

The maid came to her side. Pim Wat still didn't like the lumpish, timid woman, but she'd had Kupa's breasts and face lifted and her hips liposuctioned; she was less of an eyesore. The facelift had brightened her eyes and tightened her sagging cheeks. Pim Wat enjoyed pretty things. "You look nice, too, Kupa."

"Mistress." Kupa ducked her head. Her graying hair was a fresh shiny black now, a smooth curtain lengthened with extensions. "You honor me."

"The team did a good job on both of us." Pim Wat drained her beer and set her glass on the tray Kupa still held. "They deserve what we paid them."

When the doctors died, it was sudden and silent. They collapsed, one by one, in the middle of talking, smiling, laughing, and toasting that they'd gotten away unscathed from working on the consort of the most powerful man in Thailand.

No foaming at the mouth, no ugly vomiting or seizing or soiling of their pants. The poison paralyzed them first, then stopped their hearts. Painless and merciful; tidy and civilized.

That poison was one of Pim Wat's favorite tinctures. An additional bonus was that the victim appeared to have died of natural causes.

Death was the most secure non-disclosure agreement, and her records were already erased. No one would ever be able to speak of what had been done to Pim Wat, of who she'd been, or what she looked like now.

Kupa, standing beside Pim Wat, trembled from head to toe. Pim Wat's empty, beribboned glass tottered on the tray.

"Stop that, Kupa. You're making me uncomfortable, and I dislike being uncomfortable."

"You said I was putting a vitamin in their drinks. A supplement to make them more comfortable in your presence, Mistress." Kupa was about to drop the tray, she was shaking so hard.

Pim Wat took the bamboo platter and set it on the vanity. "They felt nothing—an easy death. Look at their peaceful faces."

Kupa looked. They were very dead: their mouths slack, their eyes open. "I killed them, Mistress." She covered her face with her hands and burst into sobs.

"Useless twat!" Pim Wat lost patience. She set aside her glass, picked up the tray, and whacked Kupa with it, hard. "Stop that blubbering at once, and go fetch the cleanup crew."

Kupa fled.

Pim Wat went into the walk-in closet filled with designer clothes she'd bought to celebrate her new identity. She tried on outfits as the Master's ninjas removed the bodies and the glasses and tidied her suite.

Plastic surgery was a risky career, in Thailand.

CHAPTER FOURTEEN

Raveaux
Day 3 afternoon

RAVEAUX FOLLOWED Leede into a well-appointed office in a suite off of busy King Street. "Nice space you've got here."

"Offices send an important message to clients." Leede hung her petite jacket on a hanger and stowed it in a shiny carved armoire behind her desk. "I've been here for five years. Retired from a government agency job in the UK, and relocated here after my divorce." Leede gestured to a table in the corner fronted by two comfortable-looking chairs. "Why don't you have a seat? It might be best for you to become aware of how I do my work, then we can decide how your role fits in."

"Perfect." Raveaux sat in one of the chairs she indicated. He opened his worn messenger bag and removed a pad and pen.

Leede nodded to his satchel. "That looks familiar."

"I too, retired from a government job before relocating here for the weather," Raveaux said. "I was an inspector with the French police."

"Ah. I have great respect for my sister agency. I was with Scotland Yard."

Raveaux's brows shot up, and he examined his new colleague with renewed interest. "What division?"

"Forgeries and art theft." Leede seated herself. "You'd be surprised how much of that kind of work involved in-depth accounting reviews."

"I would not be at all surprised. Now tell me how you would go about tackling something like this current investigation. What did you present to the board member who hired you?"

"I planned to meet first with the accounting firm who does Kama'aina Schools' bookkeeping. From what I'm given to understand, each school has a bookkeeper staff member. Those monthly reports are aggregated, and each school's principal has a budget they've developed the previous year. Allocations are given during the summer break for the following year. The main pot of funds, filled monthly by the lease payments of the hotels in Waikiki that are on land owned by the Trust, are then administered and managed by a firm, Peerless Accounting. They also do an audit of schools that become financially strained and look for ways to get them back on budget."

Raveaux made notes rapidly. "Where did the concern about funds come up?"

"There appears to be a discrepancy between the amount that should be in the main budget pot from the leases, and what is distributed to the schools. Several million dollars is missing."

Raveaux's eyes widened. "That's significant."

"You'd think so." Leede gave a delicate snort. "But the budget is huge. Close to a billion a year."

Raveaux sat back in his chair with a creak. "What? For a school?"

"We'll go visit a campus here in Honolulu so you can see firsthand. These schools teach Hawaiian children with 'the best potential' at a college preparatory standard." She made air quotes with her

70

fingers. "They spare no expense in doing so. The rationale is that the college prep curriculum makes up for any disadvantage the children might have experienced growing up Hawaiian. Because it's funded by the remains of an illegally seized monarchy, it's not only a noble cause, but legal to discriminate in supporting exclusively Hawaiian children. Applications to the schools are extremely competitive. Parents do pay a sliding scale fee, but it's nowhere near the real cost of the education they are receiving."

"Fascinating," Raveaux brushed his fingertips over the small goatee he was experimenting with. If nothing else, the springy salt-and-pepper growth gave him something to play with. "I'm trying to imagine how such a thing would work in France."

"It wouldn't." Leede swiped through some apps on her tablet. "Now. My plan is to ask for a meeting with Peerless Accounting and get access to the spreadsheet files and computers used for Kama`aina Schools. I will start combing through those files. You can take any computers we get to Ms. Smithson to work on. I'd like you to help me begin interviews with the members of the Kama`aina Schools' Board, and I'll interview the Peerless staff. We can both record the interviews and compare notes."

"I thought they hired *you,* that we'd be doing everything together." Raveaux said.

"Not all of the board members were in favor of an outside audit, and they're the people who make me nervous." Leede's bright blue eyes narrowed. "I'll give you a list of names and contact numbers, and some general questions that I usually ask."

"Who concerns you the most?" Raveaux discovered that he already felt protective of the petite, sharp-eyed Brit.

"I'll let you form your own opinions, and we can discuss them once we get underway," Leede said. "Ready for a field trip to one of the schools?"

"Of course." Raveaux stood with alacrity. "Lead on, fair lady."

Leede gave that dry snort of humor, and reached for her valise. "We'll take my car."

Leede's vehicle was a huge, silver, older model Cadillac. Raveaux almost smiled when Leede climbed onto a booster seat to see over the wheel and he glimpsed pedal extenders so she could reach the controls—but soon, he was clinging in terror to his door handle. Leede drove the beast of a car as if riding an elephant at full speed through the streets of Honolulu.

They reached the outskirts of the city far too rapidly for Raveaux's taste, and turned into the foothills, eventually entering a long private road marked by tall, elegant gates and signage that marked the campus.

"The five-hundred-acre campus provides an environment conducive to learning, with more than fifty buildings, an Olympic-size swimming pool, tennis courts, and a new athletic complex with a football/soccer field, track, and seating for three thousand. This campus also offers a boarding program geared for students from the outer islands. Kama`aina Schools offers a well-rounded, culturally-based education designed to help students attain high academic performance, positive self-esteem, and personal and community responsibility. This campus serves four thousand students, kinder-garten through high school, and there are also schools of similar size on Kaua`i, on the Big Island of Hawaii, and on Maui."

"You sound like a brochure," Raveaux teased gently.

"I have a photographic memory. It's been a boon in my work," Leede replied.

Leede was full of surprises. He glanced over at her. Sitting on her booster seat, her beringed hands clutching the large steering wheel, she looked like a child. The smooth skin of her jawline and neck told him she was younger than the first impression she'd given; perhaps only a few years older than he was.

Raveaux scanned the property as they drove past the tennis courts, running track, football stadium, and large pool complex into a central courtyard area surrounding a large bronze fountain of a

Hawaiian family in a taro field, water splashing among the sculptural plantings. "I see why you wanted me to experience the campus."

"Nothing beats getting boots on the ground, as they say." Leede drove through the roundabout with its exits to other campus areas and continued up a smaller tributary road through gracious buildings done in white stucco with blue ceramic tile roofs that reflected the distant sea.

They wound to the top of the grounds, where a three-story building, tucked behind native hardwood trees, perched on the hill overlooking the rest of the school.

"I take it this is the administrative office."

"You take it right. We'll meet the president of the board and the headmaster of this school." Leede pulled the car into a stall; they bounced off the tire guard at the end with a minor whiplash. "Oops." She threw the column shifter into park. "That was unexpected."

"Speaking of unexpected." Raveaux reached out and plucked the rhinestone crusted glasses from where they perched on Leede's nose. He squinted through the glass. "Clear. I thought so." He handed the spectacles back to her. "You're much younger than you're presenting, Ms. Leede."

"People see what they expect to see." Her smile was pure charm. "And the secret to good business is to under-promise and over-deliver. By the way, Ms. Leede is so formal; please call me Heri."

"Then you may call me Pierre," Raveaux said. "I, however, am not any younger than I look."

"You look just fine to me," Heri winked. *The woman was flirting with him!* "Let's get this show on the road."

CHAPTER FIFTEEN

Sophie
Day 3 afternoon

SOPHIE LAY on her back on the crinkly paper on the padded exam table in the doctor's office. She stared at the ceiling overhead, where someone had taped a picture of a naked surfer and hand-written across it, *"It's all his fault!"*

Dr. Beth Kepler had been her obstetrics and gynecology physician for years, and they had a cordial relationship. The obstetrician had kind brown eyes, and that was all Sophie could see above her mask as she gently palpated Sophie's abdomen. "How are you feeling?"

"A little better. I'm less tired and woozy. Smells are still problematic, though."

"Guessing by feel, you seem about twelve weeks along."

"I know exactly when this baby was conceived." Sophie named the date.

"Well, that helps us. I have to ask, was this planned?"

"No, it wasn't." Sophie lifted her left hand to gaze at Jake's ring; it brought her such comfort. "This baby is all I have left of my fiancé. Jake passed away shortly after the baby was conceived. I'll be going through this pregnancy and birth without a partner."

"Jake's gone?" The doctor's eyes widened behind her mask. She squeezed Sophie's arm. "I'm so sorry. He was a rock for you with Momi."

"Yes, and at her delivery, too. We had opted for a homebirth, if you recall, and I don't know how I could've gotten through it without him." Sophie teared up. "He should be here." She dashed the tears off her cheeks. "He would love this baby so much."

Dr. Kepler cleared her throat. "The good news is that everything seems in order. I'd like to do a sonogram and check the baby's size and heartbeat." Dr. Kepler paused. "Is there anyone you'd like to call to share the experience with you, while I get set up?"

Sophie shut her eyes. She could call Marcella, but her friend's lackluster response still rankled. Only one face came to mind who would truly share her joy and wonder at this first glimpse of her and Jake's baby. "Yes, there is."

"Good. You make your call and I'll get the equipment going." Kepler patted her on the shoulder.

Sophie took her phone off the stand where she'd set it, inserted her earbuds, and made a video call to a number she hadn't reached out to in months.

"Sophie!" Jake's sister Patty's voice was filled with warmth and relief. Her pretty round face was wreathed in a smile clear to see on the phone's video. "I'm so glad to hear from you. I've thought of you so often, but I didn't want to bug you. Kelsie says hi." Kelsie, a blonde toddler, waved from her mother's hip.

"I'm happy to see you, too, Patty. I'm sorry I took so long to call. It's been—hard."

"Of course, it has." Patty hollered over her shoulder. "Matt, can you take Kelsie? I need a minute."

Patty's husband appeared, a tall young man with shaggy brown hair falling over his forehead. "Oh, hey, Sophie. Let me take this rascal and give you ladies a chance to talk." He plucked Kelsie off Patty's hip and the two disappeared.

"Kelsie's so good. Momi would have shrieked if she didn't want to go." Sophie smiled. "'No' is currently her favorite word."

"Kelsie's a pretty mellow kid, but she definitely knows that word, too," Patty said.

Sophie held up her hand to show Patty the ring. "Your package meant the world to me. Thank you for sharing Jake's ashes, too. And having his ring to see and wear—it's been so incredibly comforting to have our status as an engaged couple acknowledged. Especially now."

"Of course. Jake meant for you to have that ring. You're the only woman he ever offered it to. But what do you mean—'especially now'?" Patty's brows arched in puzzlement.

"Now that I'm pregnant. With Jake's baby."

A short silence, then Patty gave a scream of delight. "Oh my gracious!"

"Yes. I'm here at my obstetric exam, and the doctor's about to do a sonogram. She asked me if there was anyone I wanted to call. You were the only person I could think of." Tears flowed freely from Sophie's eyes to land on the paper-covered pillow.

Patty clasped her hands together. "Oh, Sophie, I'm so honored."

The doctor wheeled the sonogram machine over. "We're about ready to start. You'll be able to see the baby on this monitor," Kepler said.

Patty pulled herself together, grabbing paper towels off a roll on the counter to dab her eyes. "I need to see my little niece or nephew."

"Absolutely. I'll point the phone at the monitor," Sophie said.

Soon Dr. Kepler had the cool, round-tipped wand coated in gel gliding over Sophie's abdomen. Shapes appeared on the monitor in grainy black and white—but almost immediately the baby's heartbeat, fast as a hummingbird's wings, filled the audio.

More tears at that sound. "It's like Jake's alive again to hear that." Patty put into words what Sophie had been unable to.

Soon, with Dr. Kepler's guidance, they could make out the shape of the baby, curled up. Its hands and feet were already developed. "We will be able to discern his or her gender in another month or so," Dr. Kepler said. "Will you want to know the sex?"

"I would," Sophie said.

Patty clapped her hands. "Yes, yes, yes! Me too!"

Dr. Kepler gave Sophie and Patty an approximate due date and confirmed that the baby was looking healthy, and growth was appropriate to the conception date Sophie had shared. She printed a sonogram photo for Sophie, and sent an e-version for her to share, then turned off and put away the equipment as Sophie wrapped up her talk with Patty.

"Take your time on the phone," Dr. Kepler said. "This room is not being used any more today." She slipped out the door with a friendly wave.

"What do you want to do about my mother?" Patty asked. "She and Monica were so horrible to you at the hospital when Jake died— they don't even deserve to know." Patty's gray eyes were sad. "But it's just a twisted form of grief. My mom, especially, would be over the moon at this news. But I'll respect whatever you want to do about it."

"Let me think it over." Sophie sat up and reached for her clothing. "I'm already having to deal with a lot of reactions. I don't like the names your mother called me and I'm in no hurry to hear them again."

"I get it. She's going to therapy though, working on her anger about Jake's death. I hope she'll get through it soon, but we haven't been speaking either. Promise you'll call me shortly?" Patty clapped her hands. "I'm just so very, very happy about this."

Jake's sister's whole-hearted joy was a balm; Sophie didn't feel so alone. *Her baby had an aunt that cared.* "I'll keep in touch.

Thanks for always having my back. You're the sister I never had." They said an affectionate goodbye.

Her phone dinged with a reminder—she was supposed to meet Raveaux and Leede back at the office to receive any computer equipment or records they'd been able to collect for the Kama`aina Schools' audit.

She hurried to change and head out the door. This time, she stuffed her red top and skirt into a gym bag, and donned a Security Solutions polo shirt and easy-movement pants. Dressing for action helped her stay focused. She had one more task to do before she got back to work.

CHAPTER SIXTEEN

Sophie

BACK AT THE OFFICE, Sophie told Paula to hold all her calls. She locked the door and took out her tablet, seating herself comfortably on the couch where she could put her feet up.

Whom should she contact first?

Connor. Get that out of the way, so she could enjoy the second call without that difficult one hanging over her head.

Sophie logged into the anonymous chat room she used to send private messages to Connor. She'd thought long and hard about how and what to communicate. When she began typing, the words unspooled quickly, as if they'd been easy to say.

That was far from the truth.

Connor:

I hope you and Nam and Kupa are well. Tell them I miss them, and Phi Ni!

This will be my last communication with you until something changes with the investigation into the Ghost and, I believe, the ultimate agenda the multi-agency team has of capturing not only you, but the Master and my mother.

I have removed the GPS chip from my arm. It's important that I sever all ties with you; that I can't be used to lure you into a trap if I'm taken captive. I've done my best to protect myself; I've moved back in with my father. Unfortunately, he has been aiding the investigation, and I believe some kind of deal was made to protect me if he cooperated. So far, I haven't confronted him about it. I am waiting until I know how to proceed, and when. I believe I'm safest from being seized by staying close to his side, and publicly visible.

I am also pregnant with Jake's baby. It happened while we were trapped in the lava tube underground. I cannot afford to take any risks right now, physically or emotionally. Do not tell my mother. I know you tried to engineer our reconciliation, but I don't trust her. I never will.

Please also know that I will always love you and value you. I miss you, and so does Anubis. One day we'll all be together on Phi Ni again. Love, Sophie

Sophie paused before she sent the message, about to log off—then added a separate, final line. She'd done what she had to. Hopefully, it would help keep both of them safe.

She logged out of the chat room, and then sent a video call to Kaua`i, and Armita's phone.

Armita picked up. "This isn't the usual time," she said in Thai. "Momi's down for her afternoon nap." The nanny's angular, golden-skinned face looked well-rested. Alika's big Hawaiian family loved to take care of Momi and pass her around to play with her many aunties, uncles, and cousins. Armita actually got time off, which she didn't get on her months with Sophie. Realizing this, Sophie felt a stab of guilt.

"That's fine, Armita. It's the middle of my workday, anyway. But I had something to tell you. Or maybe, it's better to show you." She used her finger to find the sonogram picture of the baby, and sent it to Armita via text. "I was waiting to tell you . . . until it seemed more certain. More real."

Armita's phone dinged with the incoming text. Sophie watched her nanny's face as she opened the message.

Armita's severe features broke into a joyous grin, transforming her face into one of beauty. "Oh, Sophie! I suspected, when you were so nauseous and sleepy—but I didn't want to hope you'd be this lucky!"

"You're happy for me?" Sophie's eyes filled immediately. "You're happy about this for us? You are okay with caring for another baby with me?"

"Oh, my dear." Armita looked straight into Sophie's eyes. "Caring for you, and for your children—that is my mission. My life's work. Only that."

Sophie burst into tears. "I love you, Armita. So much!" She had to set down the tablet and grab a handful of tissues. She pulled herself together momentarily, patting her face and wiping her eyes. "I was terrified you'd say this was too much, and leave me. Leave us."

Armita's dark eyes gleamed with answering emotion. "Never. Nothing but death could take me from you."

"Thank you, thank you. I don't know what I've done to deserve you." Sophie blew her nose. "I'm so relieved. You have no idea. Doing this without Jake—or even Connor—to help me—it's overwhelming."

"You're not alone. We're together in all of it," Armita said. "I'll call you back when Momi is up from her nap and we'll tell her that the family—her *ohana*—is going to get bigger."

CHAPTER SEVENTEEN

Connor

CONNOR LAY on his belly on the massage table. Nam massaged his muscles with deep, firm strokes of his forearm, using the Hawaiian *lomi lomi* method. Connor had flown a teacher in that form of massage out to Phi Ni some years ago, and both Nam and Kupa had been certified in the art.

Connor had spent long hours training with the men using staffs that day; one of the trainees was showing good promise and had landed several blows to Connor's sides and back.

He was feeling them now.

"My wife tells me that now that she and Pim Wat have returned to the compound, we can expect to see more of them," Nam said. "The Master's consort is much changed in appearance but not demeanor, she says."

"I spoke to the Master about Kupa's situation, as you asked me to. He says she must endure until a replacement can be found, but I have been unsure how to proceed in procuring one," Connor said.

"We would like to return to our home." Nam's forearm was particularly forceful as it slid over Connor's lower back muscles.

Connor hissed out a breath, willing himself to relax. "I would very much like you to be able to, but the island remains seized by the United States Department of Justice. Sophie is fighting it in court, but until the property is released to her, we have no place there."

"I fear for my wife's life. She may displease Pim Wat in some way, and not survive." Nam's voice sounded ragged.

"I know. The Master is aware of the situation. He has apprised Pim Wat that Kupa is important to me. To us," Connor said. He hoped that was the truth; the Master gave Pim Wat directions, and she obeyed him. But had he ever told Pim Wat specifically that Kupa was not to be killed? Connor had assumed that, when his houseman's wife had been assigned to the deadly assassin as a maid, it was understood that Kupa was not to be mistreated, let alone murdered. "I will speak to the Master again. I will ask what is being done to find a replacement for Kupa at Pim Wat's side."

"I thank you." The tension that Nam's skillful hands had conveyed to Connor began to ease. The man worked Connor's back, glutes, and legs, then turned him over and did his front, starting with his arms and shoulders.

Connor fell asleep, deeply grateful to have both Nine and Nam, two men he trusted, so close to him.

CONNOR WOKE to find that the Healer's chamber, where he got his massages, had grown cool with evening. He swung his legs off the side of the stone table, feeling loose and relaxed, ready to resume nighttime work in the upper room. He donned his white *gi* and headed up the stairs to the Yām Khûmkạn's computer lab.

Once inside, he logged onto his rigs and surfed quickly through the correspondence he monitored for the compound. While a program was loading, he looked around the ascetic space, enjoying the sight of his violin on the wall—and noticing that his personal cell phone was flashing with an alert.

He picked up the phone, logging in quickly, and his pulse raced when he saw that he had a message from Sophie in their low-tech, secret chat room.

His spirits sank as he read her message about cutting him off, removing the chip, her pregnancy, and the actions of the task force that were forcing her to withdraw to her father's.

A line had been added separately at the bottom: *P.S. If I communicate here again, it's because I've been forced to. Do not heed it!*

Connor felt a deep throb of loss, of abandonment, of grief.

He was losing her.

He would no longer get even the glimpses that he'd had of her life, of his beloved honorary niece Momi, of his dog Anubis. Their time together on Phi Ni, each day perfect, seemed like a fading dream.

How had things come to this?

When he'd chosen to study with the Master, it had been to help Jake while dodging the FBI, and to add skills to his arsenal as the Ghost. With Jake gone, could the passion he and Sophie once had be re-ignited?

Connor shut his eyes to check in with himself. *Yes.* He still loved Sophie. He always would. He enjoyed his role as playful uncle with Momi; another baby was just more to love.

Perhaps, with time and proximity, they could find their way to each other as a couple again. But that was even more impossible now, because Connor was a liability to her and her growing family.

His eyes stung. His chest heaved.

He was trapped here. Trapped by his choices, by being anointed Number One, the Master's successor. Sophie would never consent to come live here in the fortress; nor would he want her to.

Connor stood up, needing to move around the upper room. It was a large, stone-walled space, with small, slit-like windows set high near the roof to admit airflow. The roof itself was made of unfinished wooden timbers; the interior lined with woven matting. Tables lined the walls, stacked with computer equipment. His violin, safe in its case, was the only adornment on the wall.

Connor paced, swinging his arms, burning off his angst. Then he reached for the violin case, took it down, and opened it. He removed the instrument, stroking its curves with his fingertips. The Master had obtained his beloved violin and installed it here as a surprise. That was not the gesture of someone who didn't care about Connor's happiness. If he were to tell the Master he wanted to be released from his vows, that he wanted to build a life with Sophie somewhere else—would the Master let him go?

"No, he would not," Connor whispered aloud. "The Master has allowed himself to need me. He is aging. He wants to hand the reins to someone he trusts. If he knew what I was thinking, he would make sure Sophie was eliminated as a threat to my succession."

A chill ripped down Connor's spine. He'd spoken aloud to himself, but it was as if another voice had taken his over to speak the truth to him. That insight had come straight from Spirit.

Connor placed the violin beneath his chin and set the bow on the strings. Gently, softly, he drew it, and began to play scales. Warming up the strings. Warming up his fingers, his arms. The massage Nam had given him had loosened the tightness in his shoulders enough to be able to play again.

If what the Master had told him in the garden was true, Connor was a force for *good* that must be balanced in some universal way by someone *evil*—like Pim Wat.

Connor continued to mull over what the Master told him about duality as his body went through the discipline of the scales.

He still wasn't sure he bought that duality philosophy. In his own estimation, people like Pim Wat were cancers in the body of human- ity. If she hadn't been the Master's woman, he'd have found a way to make sure she was cut out long before this, no matter that she was Sophie's mother.

And was he ready to accept a life without Sophie in it? Was he going to let her go so meekly? Or was there some way he could use the Ghost software to counteract this multi-agency task force attack? Not to mention the Master's inconvenient anointing of him as Number One.

Pim Wat had to go, first. She was a threat to Sophie and her children. Maybe he was the only one who could make sure she was eliminated. But if he betrayed the Master in this way, how long would he survive?

And if Pim Wat was turned over to the task force, how could he prevent her being rescued again? The way the Master had broken her out from Guantánamo amply demonstrated how easily he could've taken her back anytime. The man was above the law, above the laws of physics, even. There was nowhere in the world that could hold Pim Wat if the Master wanted her back alive.

Therefore, Pim Wat had to die.

Connor's gaze darted around the empty room. Sweat broke out on his forehead. Just thinking what he was thinking filled him with fear.

He would have to be very, very careful.

CHAPTER EIGHTEEN

Raveaux
Day 3, afternoon

REX GIBSON, the head of the Kama`aina Board, was a tall, skeletally thin man with a tonsure of hair garlanding his sun-spotted pate. He bent at the waist as he shook Leede's hand. "We regret the necessity of your services."

"I promise I will make the audit as painless as possible. I brought an associate to assist me." Leede gestured to Raveaux.

"Pierre Raveaux." Raveaux stepped forward to introduce himself.

"Welcome to our campus. This is Beverly Cho, CEO of Peerless Accounting, and Dr. Stuart Ka`ula, Headmaster of Kama`aina Schools."

More handshakes and polite murmurings. Raveaux assessed each of the officials: Cho was a mixed Hawaiian Asian woman dressed in the kind of burlap sack dress and chunky jewelry he associated with artist types; Ka`ula, a stocky man, wore the usual Hawaii business casual and a scowl.

"I appreciate being apprised of this audit, but my role is the day-to-day running of the schools. I'm not sure what I can add to these proceedings," Ka`ula said.

"I asked to meet because I have specific items I require from each of you." Leede spoke in her most precise British upper-crust tones. "Is there somewhere private where we can meet? I promise not to take up too much of your valuable time."

Soon they were seated in a conference room with a sizable coat-of-arms emblem on the wall and several whiteboards that faced a bank of windows. The table was gleaming native hardwood; the chairs were excellent quality. An assistant brought in a tray with water glasses and a carafe.

Raveaux seated himself beside Leede, who took a chair at the head of the table. Enthroned there, she somehow seemed much larger than her diminutive stature as her sharp gaze speared each person. "I understand that these proceedings are to be considered highly confidential, so please don't speak of this inquiry, our process, or what we are doing, to any of your staff. The reason for that should be self-explanatory."

Ka`ula poured himself some water. "I'd still like to hear it put into words, Ms. Leede." He appeared the most resentful of the probe.

"All right. To put it baldly, a case of embezzling is, at least ninety-nine percent of the time, what they call an 'inside job.' " Leede made air quotes with her fingers. "We don't know who among your staff is skimming this money, so the fewer people that know we're looking into it, the more likely we will be able to catch them before they can cover their tracks." She lifted her messenger bag onto the table and removed four pieces of paper. She handed one each to Ka`ula, Cho, and Gibson. "Detailed on this memo is what I need from you and your staff, to be delivered to my office address on the letterhead by tonight." She turned to Raveaux and handed him the fourth copy. "You will hold the master list of required documentation and accesses. Please go with Ms. Cho to her accounting firm right now, and pick up any computers used in working with Kama`aina Schools, and deliver them directly to Ms. Smithson, so she can copy their hard drives." She turned back to the group. "We'll also need each of your personal computers, both desktop and laptop. Mr. Raveaux will take them to the car."

Cho reached for her phone, but Leede smiled and held out a hand. "I will hold all of your phones right now, for just a few moments, while Mr. Raveaux goes to the offices here in the building and picks up your computers and then delivers them to my car." She nodded to Raveaux. "Go. Have the girl who brought in the refreshments show you where their computers are. Stow them in the trunk." She handed Raveaux the car's keys.

Raveaux slanted Leede a quick glance—she really did need him as muscle.

An eruption of indignant protests ensued from the administrators.

Raveaux rose and tugged down his jacket, happy to exit the room where the three bigwigs in charge of Kama`aina Schools had just had their privacy and sense of power removed. They weren't enjoying that—nor being without their computers for the time it would take for their hard drives to be copied by Sophie.

The receptionist needed to be brusquely told by the headmaster to cooperate; but soon she was helping Raveaux carry Gibson and Ka`ula's laptops, while Raveaux lugged the desktops, all the way out to the Cadillac. They stowed the units in the capacious trunk.

Raveaux returned to the conference room. "Done."

"Thank you for your cooperation," Leede told the three administrators. "Mr. Raveaux, please keep Ms. Cho's phone, and accompany her to her office. You may keep the keys and drive to the Peerless Accounting office, pick up the computers, and then deliver them to Ms. Smithson for duplication. Dr. Ka`ula is allowing me physical access to the records stored here at the Administration Building; they are being delivered to this conference room so that I can review them on site. I'll await your return."

"*Oui, Madame.*" No other response was possible. "Ms. Cho, after you."

Leede winked at him as he followed the stiff-backed accountant out of the conference room, and he almost smiled back.

CHAPTER NINETEEN

Raveaux

RAVEAUX CALLED Sophie from the car as he followed Cho's shiny black Mercedes toward the Peerless Accounting offices downtown. Sophie picked up on the third ring, sounding out of breath. "Yes, Pierre?"

"I've just witnessed our new client, Hermione Leede, perform a hostile takeover," Raveaux said. "I'm holding the phone of the CEO of Peerless Accounting in my pocket so the woman can't communicate with anyone, and we're headed to her office to pick up all the computers used in accounting for the Kama'aina Schools. I hope you have a work area prepped and are prepared to duplicate at least ten computers."

Sophie emitted a liquid stream of syllables that sounded distinctly profane. "I will be. When will you get back to the Security Solutions building?"

"Soon. Less than an hour. I'll just be dropping them off, then returning to pick up Heri, as she goes by to her friends." He slowed behind Cho's Mercedes as she took a left. The Cadillac glided over a pothole like it wasn't there. "Ms. Leede is quite a

95

surprise. She's ex-Scotland Yard, has a photographic memory, and is younger than she lets people think she is—no older than fifty, tops."

"You sound intrigued." Sophie's smile was readily apparent in her warm tone. "Maybe she's the woman for you. I'll be ready for the computers by the time you get back here to my office. Use the back entrance." She ended the call.

"*Merde.* Heri is *not* the woman for me. *You* are," Raveaux muttered, stowing his phone.

Cho entered a parking garage under an office building using a key card; Raveaux cursed again, as the arm on the gate refused to open for him. *She was ditching him!* Apparently, a forensic accounting investigation required anticipation and brutal efficiency.

Cho wanted to stonewall him? *Fine.* He'd inconvenience her in return.

Raveaux put the car in *Park* and locked it, leaving it parked squarely in front of the entry gate's retractable arm. He jogged into the garage and was just in time to see Cho exiting her vehicle near the stairs.

"Ms. Cho!" He ran toward her, noting the frustration in her expression. "I was forced to leave my vehicle outside your turnstile. If it's towed, we will bill your firm for our time and expenses."

"Humpf." Cho grunted. "We won't be long." She whirled to head up the stairs instead of using the elevator. Raveaux dogged her sensibly-sandaled heels as they thumped up an aluminum stairwell, heading for the fourth floor.

"Ms. Leede's methods are a bit unconventional." Raveaux ventured an olive branch as he beat Cho to the door to her level, opening and holding the heavy panel ajar in a gentlemanly way. "Thank you for being gracious with the process. I'm sure you want to catch this thief and clear your firm's name as much as we do."

Cho slanted an unfriendly glance over her shoulder. "Let's discuss this in my office."

Staffers in cubicles glanced at them curiously as they passed.

Raveaux mentally cringed at the number of computers Sophie might be dealing with.

Cho unlocked her office, ushered him in, then turned to close the door. She put her hands on her hips. "I know you think my firm has something to do with this." Her brown eyes were wide and angry. "And I don't appreciate it."

Raveaux raised his brows. "Madame, I assure you I have no opinion whatsoever on any of this. I am merely Ms. Leede's associate, and as you can see, she uses me mostly for muscle." He tried a wink. "I'm just here to fetch and carry."

Cho seemed to thaw. She turned away and slipped off her Birkenstocks. Her brown socks looked hand-knit from the hair of some unknown animal. "All right then. I will save my frustration for Ms. Leede. I don't personally handle the Kama`aina Schools' accounts, but we can get a computer trolley and pick up the units of those who do, right now. Also, I want my phone back." She padded over to her desk and depressed a button on the phone, summoning an assistant to bring the trolley.

She returned to face Raveaux and mustered a smile, seeming to really see him for the first time. Cho was attractive when she smiled. She patted her flyaway hair, tucking it behind her ears. "This investigation has been something of a shock. I didn't know about the audit until I was summoned to the campus this morning. Very stressful. I'm sure you understand."

"Absolutely." Raveaux turned and meandered around the office, noting the striking fiber art on the walls, the natural wood credenza, the meeting table and seating lounge. "Have you been with Peerless long?"

"Five years. I was an IRS analyst before I came to work for Peerless." She seated herself in her chair. "I'm from Seattle originally. This job has been practically a vacation, compared to my government one."

"I understand. I was with the French police for my entire career, and nothing ever came without sixteen forms to be filled out and submitted to different departments. We never caught up with the workload, either. I used to say I should wear a miner's light on the front of my hat, I was so buried in cases." He got her to smile again as the assistant came in with the computer cart. "Let's pick up the units, I'll give you your phone, and I'll be on my way." He took her device out of his pocket. "Would you unlock it, please? I'll put my number into your contacts, in case you need to reach me for any reason."

Cho accepted the phone and unlocked it. "I'd appreciate that."

"Of course, madame. Never know when you might need a little muscle." He winked, and added his number to her contacts.

Cho took the phone back, slipping it into the pocket of her baggy dress. "I'll be in touch, Monsieur Raveaux, should I need to reach you."

"Call me Pierre." He gave her some eye contact.

Cho looked down, flustered. "Follow me and we'll go get those computers."

RAVEAUX PULLED into the alley behind the Security Solutions building. He'd texted Sophie that he was on his way; he wasn't surprised to see her standing, arms crossed, with a dolly and three strapping security operatives. The four of them wore all-black outfits marked with the Security Solutions logo. *Where was that red outfit she'd worn in the morning?*

"Quite a car," Sophie commented, as Raveaux got out of the vehicle. "That belong to Ms. Leede?"

"Yes." Raveaux popped the enormous trunk and the men began loading the equipment onto the dolly. "She is compensating for her size, I believe."

"Apparently, not only men do that," Sophie smiled. "My father likes Cadillacs too, though." She picked up one of the laptops. "In case you need to know where the equipment is, I've set up a workroom for us in the basement of the building. Our case workstation will be in Storage Room 2A. I only have time to set up the duplicating software for these rigs tonight; it takes a couple of hours to copy each hard drive, so I'll be working on this through tomorrow. Once we have all of them copied, I'd like to meet Ms. Leede and discuss who's doing what. I cannot be the only one sifting through these computers."

"Of course. I'll let her know. We should meet tomorrow." The three men loaded the equipment onto the dolly and took it into the building. The door shut behind them with a clang. Raveaux cleared his throat. "How are you feeling?"

Sophie frowned. "Are you asking because I'm pregnant?"

The heat of embarrassment tingled the back of his neck. "I suppose."

"Well, stop that. Don't treat me any differently than you did before." Her voice was taut with annoyance. "I'll let you know if I'm having a problem." She turned to follow the computers into the building, and her hand landed on the handle of the steel door.

"Then let me fix dinner for you, sometime," Raveaux burst out. "You liked my cooking. Before."

Sophie stopped, her back to him. "I do like your cooking." She opened the door. "Text me when you're making something worth eating." She never looked back. The door banged shut.

But she would let him feed her.

Raveaux got back into the Cadillac, unaccountably lighter.

CHAPTER TWENTY

Connor
Day 4

CONNOR KNOCKED at the door of the Master's suite of rooms on one of the higher floors of the compound. He'd spent the morning meditating to control his thoughts and emotions; he still wasn't sure that the Master couldn't read his mind.

A long moment passed as he stood in front of the polished wooden portal. He heard nothing from inside the chamber.

Connor raised his hand to knock again, and the door opened.

The Master stood before him, dressed in a scarlet silk robe open to the waist and loosely knotted, as if he had arisen from bed to join Connor at the door—but it was mid-morning, a time when the Master was done with the morning drilling, and usually ate a late breakfast. Connor had timed his visit carefully.

"What is it, Number One?"

"May I come in? I'd like to speak with you privately." The walls had ears, and so did the hallways, in the compound of the Yām Khûmkạn.

The Master held the door ajar. Connor entered a sunken living area that he was very familiar with. No fire in the fireplace today, as the season had warmed, but the chess set awaited them.

Connor's gaze moved about the luxuriously appointed space; the bedroom door was ajar, but the Master's inner sanctum where he meditated was closed, and so was the bathing area.

The Master gestured to the European-style couch that faced the fireplace. "Have a seat. I'll have some tea brought up."

Connor sat, restraining himself from nervous gestures like smoothing his *gi,* as the Master used a wall intercom to summon tea and refreshments.

Finished with that small chore, the Master came over and sat in his usual place, a wing-backed armchair. The man looked like a king in his scarlet robe, his excellent musculature gleaming in natural light from carefully placed overhead slits. His pansy-purple eyes were unreadable. "What do you have to discuss, Number One?"

"Sophie has decided to cut off all communication with me, for two reasons."

A moment went by. The Master didn't respond; instead he gestured to the chess set. "It has been a while since we played. What color do you choose?"

He didn't really have a choice about playing, and he knew it.

Connor moved to sit on a small stool in front of the board. He had come to be attached to this chess set; each piece had been lovingly and beautifully carved from native hardwoods by a long-ago ninja trainee. One side was bleached white, and the other rubbed with some kind of dark stain. Every piece had been translated into a unique figure from the Thai Royal Court of millennia ago.

Connor chose white, as he usually did, and made a bold opening move. He had not intended to stay here for hours, and sometimes the Master beat him in just a few moves. Once in a while, he let Connor win.

The Master moved from his armchair and joined Connor at the table. His countermove was swift. "How does Sophie communicate with you?"

The Master had never asked this before. With his new resolution to kill Pim Wat, Connor felt an internal quiver of concern. *Was he fishing for some weakness?* "We have a secret chat room we have been using for years. Untraceable." Connor deployed his knight.

"What do you think prompted her communication?" The Master counter-moved.

"The investigation that caused me to have to withdraw from Phi Ni and flee back here with my servants is placing pressure on her. Sophie is worried about being taken captive, and being used to lure me into a trap. She believes that the larger agenda of the team is to capture you and Pim Wat, too. She removed the chip that allowed me to rescue her, so that she cannot be forced to leverage me to rescue her."

"Commendable. She has shown an admirable loyalty to your relationship. Do you want to reunite with her, now that Jake is dead?" The Master took Connor's knight.

Connor pretended to study his pieces, his heart thumping and mind scrabbling. *The Master likely knew that he was agitated by the question.* He couldn't answer without revealing his hopes, so he deflected with a new piece of information. "She is pregnant with Jake's baby."

A slight noise from somewhere behind them; perhaps a muffled gasp.

Connor swung around, and his eyes widened. Pim Wat stood in the doorway of the Master's bedroom.

Sophie's mother looked stunning, and completely different from the last time he'd seen her. She wore a robe identical to the Master's, barely tied at her supple waist, and her round, perfect breasts were semi-revealed by the gaping fabric. Her new face looked like that of the movie actress Halle Berry. Her hair, once a stark, dead white, had been colored a rich platinum blonde that contrasted beautifully with her golden-brown skin.

"Hello, Number One. I'm back." Pim Wat glided down the two steps into the living area, and rested a hand on the Master's shoulder.

Connor remembered how skeletal her hand had been; and the claw-like fingers stroking the silk of the Master's robe were the same—her hand was the only thing he recognized.

"Welcome home, Mistress. You look beautiful."

"It's good to see you, too, Number One. Tell me more of my daughter's news." Pim Wat smiled, and now Connor saw the faint pink of healing scars around her mouth, forehead, and jawline. In a few months, those traces would be invisible.

The cat was out of the proverbial bag, but he'd do what he could to make it clear whose side he was on. "Sophie did not want you to know the news of her pregnancy, Mistress. I hope that doesn't offend you."

Pim Wat shrugged. "No more than I expected. She would not want me to steal this baby, too." Her smile was shark-like.

Connor felt a wave of rage and opened his mouth to respond, but fortunately the tea arrived. The servant stopped in the doorway. "Oh, I'm sorry, Master. I did not know you had another guest." There were only two teacups on the tray.

Connor shot to his feet. "It's fine. I'll catch up with you two later. I only meant to stop in briefly and convey this news." Connor headed for the door and brushed past the servant as quickly as he could.

He had to warn Sophie that her mother knew about her pregnancy and had a new face. *But how?*

He'd start by replying to her message in the chat room. Hopefully, she would check it.

Once he had a secure location, Connor used his personal burner phone to log into the chat room.

Dear Sophie:

Pim Wat overheard me tell the Master about your pregnancy. I'm sorry that happened, but I felt I had to tell him that news. She's just come from extensive plastic surgery and has a new face that some-

what resembles the actress Halle Berry. I'm sure the task force would like a photo; I'll try to get one for them if I can.

I understand that you need to cut me off right now, but trust me, please. I will find a way to trade her to the authorities for my freedom from this place. I won't accept a life without you in it. Connor.

Connor hit *Send* before he could re-think his unvarnished declaration.

CHAPTER TWENTY-ONE

Pim Wat

PIM WAT STROKED her hand down the Master's shoulder, enjoying the feeling of silk over muscle, as the servant carried the loaded tea tray into the room. The Master lifted a hand to take hers, as he stood up from the chessboard's stool. They seated themselves on the couch in front of the refreshment table. The servant set down the tray and arranged everything needed for an English high tea.

Pim Wat's emotions warmed as she gazed at the spread of food. Great trouble had been taken to procure all of the special ingredients for an English tea way out here at the compound, but her beloved knew how much she enjoyed crumpets, clotted cream, fresh blackberry jam, *petits fours*, and cucumber sandwiches. "Darling, it looks delicious. I'm so hungry."

The Master squeezed her hand. "And I am hungry for *you*. Four weeks is a long time to be separated—though the results are spectacular." He leaned over and kissed her.

Pim Wat enjoyed his taste, his smell, the touch of his tongue that promised more.

The Master let go of her hand, picked up a plate, and chose all of her favorite things as he served her. "Number One is unhappy with losing your daughter from his life."

"What do I care? Connor is just another lovelorn swain, and Sophie has many. I have no idea how my daughter came to be so endowed with pheromones," Pim Wat said sourly.

The Master laughed his deep chuckle. "Really? You have no idea, my Beautiful One?" He tweaked her ear playfully. "She inherited that from you, of course."

Once more, Pim Wat felt herself melting. It was dangerous to love the Master so much, to be so deeply under his spell that it was hard to think clearly in his presence. Sometimes she knew he exerted that power intentionally, to control her. Other times, like now, she merely felt loved in a way that she craved, in a way that no one else had ever loved her.

"I want Number One to be content. I intend to turn the Yām Khûmkạn over to his management. In time, I would like for us to be able to enjoy our advancing age on our secret island," he said. Pali, the Master's personal island in the Philippines, was the very definition of paradise.

"I love that place." Pim Wat lowered her eyes modestly. She took a bite of her crumpet. The clotted cream and blackberry jam, as well as the pastry, were delicious on her tongue.

The Master picked up a *petit four* and ate it in one bite. "I think your daughter is a liability to that plan."

Pim Wat's pulse quickened. She hid her excitement by eating one of the cucumber sandwiches. She licked her fingers delicately. "Thank you once again for always attending to my needs. Yes, my daughter is a liability. I could tell when I met with her recently, that though she gave lip service to accepting my apology, she will never allow me to see my grandchildren." Pim Wat raised her eyes to meet those of the Master. "And I would like to see my grandchildren. Often."

"I understand, but the compound is no place for children, as I told you before when you brought her infant here. We need a larger, longer-term plan. I urge you to be patient. After all, Sophie still has to give birth to this baby." The Master poured their tea. He lifted his cup, and met Pim Wat's gaze. "How would you feel about eliminating her from the equation? Number One could settle into the role I have planned for him if Sophie were gone, along with his dream of another life spent with her."

Pim Wat's mouth still felt tight around the lips, scars impeding her wide smile. "I thought I would have to fight for permission to remove her. She must pay for trading me to the CIA."

"Then we are in accord." The Master narrowed his eyes slightly in calculation. "We have until she gives birth to plan her demise. It must be made to seem a tragic accident, or perhaps the blunder of one of the multi-agency team—we can strategize something that kills two birds with one stone. But Number One must never suspect, or I will lose his loyalty."

"Leave it to me," Pim Wat said, and added a little sugar to her tea. "I do love you."

"I know." He smiled. "Let's go back to bed."

CHAPTER TWENTY-TWO

Sophie
Day 5

SOPHIE HAD JUST SHUT her eyes for a few moments, resting on her yoga mat, when the heavy metal door opening into the basement workroom at Security Solutions screeched open.

She woke with a start, and sat up too quickly. She lowered herself back down to her elbows as her head spun. Her eyes were gritty, and a knot tightened the muscles between her shoulder blades.

Sophie had spent the night in the workroom she had set up at Security Solutions, in order to maintain the flow of copying each of the ten hard drives that had landed on the long table she had set up. Each computer required several hours to copy, depending on how much information was on the unit, and she had only two write blocker devices. She'd set an alarm on her phone, and slept on her yoga mat, getting up every few hours to switch one of the copying devices to another computer as it completed the previous one. At nine a.m. the next day, she'd set up a time for Raveaux and Leede to come in for a meeting.

Somehow, it was nine a.m. of the next day.

Hermione Leede stood in the doorway next to a Security Solutions operative who'd escorted her to the basement. She looked perfectly put together in a tiny fuchsia pant suit. Her keen eyes, bright behind cat eye glasses, took in the scene at a glance. "Oh my! No one expected you to stay up all night working on this!"

Sophie sat up at a more reasonable speed, and stood slowly to her feet, flapping a hand to dismiss Leede's security escort. "It was the most efficient way to get the work done."

She had another reason for spending the night in the work room; she hadn't wanted to see her father. She sent him a text that she was tied up with a case and spending the night at her office, working.

Avoidance was a good strategy when subterfuge was not one of her strengths.

Leede advanced into the work area as Sophie went to the phone on the corner of the table. She pressed the extension for Paula's desk upstairs. "Paula, can you bring us some fresh tea and sandwiches from the food cart? Also, fresh scones if you can find them. I haven't had breakfast yet, and Ms. Leede is here. She appreciates a good cup of tea and a scone."

"Right away, Sophie!" As usual, Paula's cheerful, positive response lifted Sophie's spirits.

"I didn't even need to tell you that I love a good scone," Leede said, smiling. "Preferably with homemade preserves."

"Anyone from England is likely to love those," Sophie said. "It wasn't much of a guess. I'm craving a warm pastry with butter, myself. Where is Raveaux?"

"I was in touch with him this morning. He said he was following up with something, and would be a little late."

"Good." Sophie combed her wild hair with her fingers. "I need to go to the restroom and freshen up, anyway." She indicated the table, stacked high with computers. "I've been able to copy all the hard drives. I have two computers set up for us here to use for review, and the drives are already loaded, labeled with their owners. If you'd make yourself comfortable, I'll be back in a few minutes."

"Excellent." Leede sat down and lifted her leather bag onto the table. "Take your time."

Sophie hurried out, her bladder acting up per usual. She made it to the bathroom in time, and took a quick shower in the locker room. Wrapped in a towel, she twisted her riotous curls into Marcella's favorite "FBI twist," and secured the roll of hair with bobby pins. She then changed into a fresh Security Solutions black polo shirt and yoga pants, and put on a little makeup.

Hopefully, with all of that, Raveaux wouldn't be able to tell she'd spent the night in the workroom. After this meeting, she'd go upstairs to her office and nap, for sure. She could feel exhaustion tugging at her bones like gravity.

Sophie returned to the basement, and smiled at the sight of Leede, already scanning the monitor of one of the computers. "I'm glad Raveaux's not here yet. I wanted to have a few moments to get to know you a little better. He seems quite taken with you."

"An interesting choice of words." Leede lifted a well-groomed brow. Her intelligent eyes sparkled. "I'm rather taken with him, too."

Sophie smiled. "I probably should have said he's impressed with you. He told me a little about your tactics yesterday."

"Setting a cat among the pigeons can sometimes flush out new game. While I had the three Kama`aina Schools' bigwigs' devices, I bugged them." She handed Sophie a palm-sized communication pad. "I'm giving this to you, as a separate layer of protection for myself. You can track their conversations and locations. I hope you don't mind me delegating this. You are subcontracted to me, so . . ."

"I see what you're doing. Plausible deniability." Sophie took the device.

"Yes. And I was up to my eyeballs in spreadsheets yesterday. The data is quite extensive, and I need to do more of that today. Would you monitor their phones for us when you aren't working on the computers?"

"That's a lot to keep track of for one person." But Sophie took the device anyway. She felt a jolt of adrenaline and interest quickening her veins. She walked over to one of the rigs she had set up for herself. *She could hook up the pad to a computer, run the verbal tracing through a voice-to-text program, and set her Data Analysis Victim Information Database program to monitoring for certain keywords related to their case.*

Running the bugged phones' conversations through DAVID would be much more efficient than monitoring long-winded personal talk from the owners of the various cell phones. It wasn't worth explaining all of that to Hermione Leede, who wanted only to divest herself of a responsibility.

"I'll see what I can do." Sophie found a USB cable, plugged it into the pad, then hooked that device to the computer, downloading its contents as her fingers flew.

Everything around her faded as she dove into the task at hand.

Sometime later, she heard the screech of the door, and the noise brought her back to the present moment.

"You really need to get those hinges oiled." Raveaux looked at the folded-up jacket and yoga mat in the corner, then glanced at Sophie's face. His brows knit together. "You spent the night down here?"

"I'm done copying all of the hard drives," Sophie said stiffly. "A significant and time-consuming commitment."

"Sophie did spend the night down here," Leede said. "And I have already informed her that no one required that level of sacrifice from her or anyone else on this team. I'm certainly not staying up all night to work on the case."

"I had my reasons." Sophie swiveled her chair to face them. "And some of them were personal."

She was relieved not to have to explain further as the door creaked open to admit Paula, burdened with tea and foodstuffs on a large tray. Raveaux hurried to help her, removing a paper bag balanced on the edge of the tray and clearing an area for her to set it down. "It took me a little while to go to the bakery on the corner for the scones," Paula said.

She set up the food on an empty table against the wall as Raveaux went to the one window in the corner, raised the blind, and brightened the lights. "It may be a basement but we don't have to sit in the dark."

"I happen to like the dark." Sophie pushed back from her chair, satisfied now that her DAVID program would be monitoring the phone taps. "I'm quite hungry. Thank you, Paula."

"You shouldn't have spent the night down here," Paula scolded. "You need your rest, and you have a perfectly comfortable couch upstairs."

"I know." Sophie stretched her arms and yawned. "I was just too lazy to keep going up and down."

"Tell me next time you're going to stay after hours." Paula shook a finger at Sophie in mock rebuke. "I'll make sure you have everything you need." She left.

Raveaux headed for the food. "I'll fix you a plate. You need to keep up your strength."

Leede frowned, clearly confused, and Sophie sighed and met the woman's eyes. "Everyone's fussing because I'm pregnant."

"Congratulations!" Leede arched her brows. "Well, as I said earlier. No more all-nighters on this job, please."

Raveaux brought Sophie a mug of tea, prepared with honey and a dollop of cream, and a plate piled with scones and cut sandwiches. "Eat everything."

Sophie rolled her eyes, but bit into a still warm, buttered scone. "Mmm. So good. Ms. Leede, you have to try these. I had Paula get them for you."

The Englishwoman was still doctoring her tea—she took it with honey and lemon. "Please, call me Heri."

"All right, Heri." Sophie finished her bite and set her plate aside; she took a sip of tea; it was perfect. She slanted a grateful glance at Raveaux, and was gratified to see the corner of his mouth tuck in—that almost-smile she could sometimes tease out of him. "You two see all of these computers? I can't be the only one sifting through them. Besides, I'm not entirely sure what we're looking for."

"Certainly." Leede sipped her beverage, eyeing the computers thoughtfully. "I understand. Pierre can take the original machines back to their owners today. I, however, have to focus on the paper trail, literally. Pierre, you said you had something to do this morning. What was it?"

Sophie glanced over at Raveaux, and was surprised to see him look away, and flush.

CHAPTER TWENTY-THREE

Raveaux

RAVEAUX STROKED the neat goatee on his chin. He avoided eye contact with the two women by taking a sip of his tea, enjoying the rich flavor. "I took Ms. Cho, CEO of Peerless, out to breakfast. I'm building a rapport with her."

"Excellent work, Pierre!" Leede clapped her hands together, and her rings sparkled as she did so. She reminded him of a child, with her quick enthusiasms. "That woman had a gleam in her eye from the moment she saw you. Did you get anything useful?"

"Not yet. It's early; these things take time. But I hope to gain her confidence." Raveaux raised his gaze to meet Leede's. "I'm playing the 'my boss is evil' card. You're making me do all of this unpleasantness, and I would never suspect her of anything, of course."

"Of course." Leede smiled. "And you're unhappy at home?"

"A widower. Which is the truth," Raveaux said.

Leede's face fell. "Oh, Pierre, I'm so sorry."

"It was a long time ago."

"Don't make light of it, Pierre." Sophie turned to Leede. "Heri, his wife and child were tragically killed in a car bomb as the result of one of his investigations. That's why he's here in Hawaii."

"As I said," Raveaux looked down—he'd crushed the scone he held without realizing it. Crumbs drifted from his fist onto his immaculate pants. "A long time ago. Five years."

"So that's why you left France and your job there." Leede leaned forward to pat Raveaux's arm. Her touch was warm and gentle. "I wondered."

Raveaux stood abruptly, brushing down his trousers. "Yes. A terrible thing, a difficult time—but it's behind me. I'd better get these computers back; I know the Kama'aina Schools' people want their equipment." He stepped forward and picked up three of the stacked machines, turned, and headed for the door.

"I'll have the men come help you," Sophie said. He heard a note of regret in her voice. Was she sorry for so flippantly sharing his tragedy with Leede? He hoped so.

Raveaux took the stairs, needing to work off the angst of stirred up emotions. By the time he reached the back exit for the Security Solutions building, two muscled operatives met him at the door and one of them held open the back of one of the company SUV's doors. "Let us help, Monsieur Raveaux."

The men came back down with him and in one more trip, thanks to the dolly, the back of the vehicle was loaded. "Secure these computers with some padding and strapping, will you? We wouldn't want to cause any machine failure for the people who own them," Raveaux said. "I have to go back down to the workroom for a few minutes."

"You got it." Perkins, one of the men, threw him a little salute.

Raveaux headed back down to the basement and was surprised to find only Sophie at the computer table. Her back was to the door, but she turned at its familiar screeching. "I have to oil that before it drives me mad."

"Where's Leede?"

"She went upstairs to talk to Bix, and then back to her ledgers."

Sophie swiveled fully in her chair to face him. If he hadn't already noticed the makeshift bed in the corner, the dark circles under her eyes would have told him of her sleepless night. "I'm sorry I just— told her your story like that. I thought Heri should know it was a much bigger thing than just—cancer or something. Sometimes I'm not as tactful as I should be. I apologize."

"An understatement, but apology accepted." Raveaux's jaw felt tight. "Do you think watching a spouse die of cancer would be easy?"

Sophie's cheeks reddened. "No. Losing a loved one is terrible, no matter how they die. But sometimes you get to say goodbye. You have time to get used to the news. Maybe their illness causes pain, and by the end, you want their suffering to end, and they want that too, and somehow a peace can be found." She met his eyes at last. "Other times—the one you love is just taken from you. Snatched away without even a goodbye, and it's your fault." She glared at Raveaux, her eyes shining with tears. "We have that in common."

Raveaux sank into the chair beside her. "Yes, we do." He leaned forward, his elbows on his knees, and rubbed his eyes because they burned. "I want it to be okay. I want it to be behind me. But five years later, it still isn't."

"How do you think I feel?" Sophie banged her fist on the table, a loud thump that made the monitor near her wobble and Raveaux jump. "Jake and I had just made a commitment to each other. We'd cleared up our old hurts and—we'd celebrated that, and just being alive together. We had one time to make love. Once! In two years! And then he . . ." She shut her eyes and fat tears rolled out of them. "Jake gave his life so I could live. I have to find a way to deal with that. And have this baby. And keep going somehow. Without him."

Raveaux met her bleary gaze. His own eyes were hot and sting-ing. "It's not fair, Sophie. It's not, and it never will be." He extended a hand to cover Sophie's fist where it rested on the table. "I don't know much, but I do know this: children are a gift to be celebrated. You are rich indeed, if you get to have two of them."

"You can be their godfather," Sophie burst out. She gave a wet laugh, as she swiped tears away with the back of her free hand. "If you want to, that is."

"Of course I will." Raveaux felt his chest swell with feeling; a painful, beautiful feeling. Joy? Hope? Love? Maybe a little of all three. Sophie's high-energy daughter Momi reminded him of his own strong-willed Lucie, but he'd avoided her because of that. Knowing that he could be in Momi's life in some kind of role, indefinitely, made his eyes brim. "Whatever I can do to help you."

"I am angry with God, right now, not even sure he or she exists, but I've always liked the idea of *godparents*." Sophie groped for a nearby box of tissues, pulled some out, and dabbed her face—and still her hand stayed under his. "My children will need other people in their lives. Male role models, since they only have me and Armita during the month that they're here. I am going to ask Dr. Wilson to be an honorary grandmother, because Pim Wat is unfit. And I had thought Connor could be their godfather, like an uncle—but I've cut off all communication with him, and I think that might have to be for a long time."

Raveaux sat up straighter, his attention sharpening. He kept his hand on hers. That small contact felt so vital. "What about the GPS chip?"

"I removed it." Sophie sniffed and wiped tears from her cheeks. "I have lost him, too. You don't know what he meant to me."

"You were lovers."

"Only for a short time. Mostly, we have been friends." Sophie finally removed her hand from under his and blew her nose. "This is what happens when I don't take my five minutes."

"Five minutes?"

"Five minutes to cry. Every day. I set a timer."

Raveaux felt that unfamiliar tug at his mouth—and this time he let the smile happen.

A grin born of the happiness she'd given him by offering to share her children with him, by sharing her grief with him, by just being Sophie—spread across his face.

He chuckled.

And then he laughed, a deep and wild laugh that loosened his gut and his knees and the knots of pain that pulled his heart in so many directions.

"You're cackling like a chicken." Sophie stared at him, wide-eyed. "I'm not usually very funny."

"You're not. It's just that . . . if I'd taken five minutes a day for my grief, instead of trying to numb it, maybe I wouldn't have spent two years at the bottom of a bottle." Raveaux shook his head, still smiling. "Who knew? A timer. Five minutes a day."

"Works remarkably well." Sophie blew her nose with dignity.

Raveaux felt the familiar stab of grief again—but it was softer now, its edge blunted by the shiny, full feeling she'd given him with her trust. "I bet you worry, some days, that five minutes won't be enough. I think that's why I never wanted to cry. I was sure I'd lose myself if I did."

"Yes. On those days I promise myself a second session, late in the night, if I need it. I've seldom needed it."

"You've already answered your question."

"What one was that?" She was smiling too.

"How you go on."

Sophie shook her head. "I know that old cliché. One minute at a time, one day at a time, etcetera. In my case, five minutes at a time." She turned back to the computers. "We didn't get to the part of the meeting where Leede told us what we were looking for on these rigs."

Sophie seemed to be fading into drowsiness before his eyes, her shoulders rounding, her eyes half-lidded.

"You look like you need a nap, Sophie. Why don't you go upstairs and use the couch Paula mentioned? Get a few hours rest. I'll deliver the original computers back to Kama`aina Schools' staff and to Peerless, then come back here, and poke around on the one you set up for us. You can come down when you're rested."

"Excellent idea." Sophie yawned. "What I could use are keywords related to the case. Names, dates, places, specific accounts used by the Kama`aina people. Anything I can set my program to search for." She stood up and stretched. "I think I'll take you up on your excellent suggestion and get a nap."

"You'll have to tell me about this program."

"Oh, I will." Sophie yawned again. "But it's a bit of a long story." She headed for the door, weaving on her feet with exhaustion.

Raveaux restrained himself from supporting her, following to close the workroom door behind her. She got on the nearby elevator.

"Rest well, Sophie," he said. She nodded as she leaned against the elevator's wall, her eyes closed. The doors shut, taking her from him.

Raveaux turned and took the stairs to the SUV parked in the alley outside, missing her already.

CHAPTER TWENTY-FOUR

Marcella

MARCELLA SAT in the FBI's conference room with Waxman, Gunder-sohn, and Pillman. The large monitor used for distance meetings had been raised up out of its slot in the table. The triangular table mic was on, and they could see small panels framing Kate Smith from the Secret Service, MacDonald and Karl Beckett from the CIA, and Stefan Voise, Interpol.

Everyone but the FBI group had been ordered back to their posts in order to work more productive cases, and today they were tuning in from London, Hong Kong, Thailand, and Smith from Washington, DC.

Pillman opened with his opinion. "The subjects have all gone to ground. Until we find a way to pry those three out of that compound in Thailand, this case is closed."

Marcella raised a finger. "What if we were to turn Connor to do our work for us with the Master and Pim Wat? I would like to propose that I look into seeing if Sophie Smithson will re-engage with him, and whether or not he is willing to trade one or both of them for immunity."

"Why would he possibly do that?" Beckett asked, impatience clear in his tone.

"Because Connor loves Sophie," Marcella said simply. "And Sophie is vulnerable and alone. His competition for her affections is dead. Maybe he still wants a chance with her."

"I saw the two of them together when I was trying to recruit Sophie as a CIA asset," MacDonald said. "The dude definitely has a thing for her."

"From what Frank says, Sophie still harbors a great deal of affection for Connor, too," Smith said. The Secret Service agent's dark blue eyes sharpened on Marcella. "But I thought you said your agenda was keeping Connor out of your friend's life."

Marcella felt hot, and unbuttoned her collar. "That *is* my agenda. But let's grab whoever Connor helps us get, then nail him, too. That man has no moral compass, and it's going to get Sophie hurt someday."

Waxman chimed in. "This idea has legs."

"Do we have any other ideas? Any contacts within the compound?" Stefan Voise's frown didn't sit well on his good-natured face.

MacDonald scratched his beefy, whiskered jowls, making a rasping sound. "Everyone in Thailand is afraid of the Yām Khûmkạn. I do have a source inside the compound. So far, he will provide only passive observation information, and I can't get leverage for more at this point—I've tried. He reported that there was a dissident contingent within the compound recently, and the entire faction was executed by sword. Their heads were displayed on pikes before the men for a week." Silence fell upon the group at his words. "We don't have an incentive powerful enough for anyone in that compound to betray the Master."

"That's medieval," Smith said. "It's bizarre to hear of something like that in the twenty-first century."

"The Master is a spiritual, military, and spy agency leader, all rolled into one," MacDonald said. "And Connor, as his Number One, or second in command, is being groomed to take over. I can't see him giving all that up. And were he to betray the Master, the world would not be a big enough place for him to hide from all of the trained ninja assassins who'd come after him."

"Well, let's let Marcella take her long shot and see what happens, since we don't have any better ideas," Waxman said. "Keep us informed, MacDonald, if your contact has any updates for us." They wrapped up the meeting.

Waxman shifted his chair to look at Marcella as the telemonitor slid out of sight. "How do you feel about using your friend this way?"

Marcella frowned. "Well, that's a stark way to put it, because the truth is, I don't think Sophie is going to be safe until both Pim Wat and Connor are out of her life. The Master, I'm less sure about. Frankly, I don't care what he does over there in Thailand as long as it doesn't affect my friend."

"Are you able to keep this team, and your role on it, confidential?"

Marcella met Waxman's gaze squarely. "I will do whatever is necessary to gain the objective of removing Connor and Pim Wat from Sophie's life. That may involve keeping my role here secret; or it may be wiser to take her into my confidence. I will know when we have that conversation."

MARCELLA NEEDED to work out after the tension-filled meeting, and there was no time like the present for implementing phase two of her plan. She hit Sophie's number on her favorites list. She was delighted when her friend picked up. "Sophie! How do you feel about a work-out? I'm headed over to Fight Club to deal with the office blues."

"I'm sorry, Marcella, I worked all night on the computers for our latest investigation, and I just woke up from a nap in my office. I'm afraid I have to keep going with this project."

Sophie had been so conscientious about her health during her pregnancy with Momi. "Are you sure keeping those kinds of hours are good for the baby?"

"Whatever keeps me calm and not too stressed is what's good for the baby," Sophie said. "And at the moment I'm avoiding my father."

Marcella's attention sharpened. "What did he do now?"

"I found out he was aiding and abetting the investigation into Connor, so I've been staying away from the apartment since I found out. It's impossible to be around him and not be angry. I don't know if I can hide that, and I'm not sure confronting him is the right thing to do right now. Currently, he doesn't know that I know he was involved with that investigation— and two agents tried to grab me the other night! I'm in full avoidance mode at the moment. I feel safest at the office." She yawned.

Marcella's mind raced—*if Sophie found out Marcella was on that task force, it could be the end of their friendship!* "I'm sure your dad only did that to try to protect you."

"I believe that, too. But I don't appreciate his interference. He thinks that he knows what's best for me and my relationships."

Marcella felt Sophie's words penetrate. "You see that as betrayal."

A long pause, then Sophie sighed. "I just wish that he would talk to me about his concerns, instead of manipulating things behind my back. If he did, I could assess whether or not going along with his plans was a good idea. Of course, I have concerns about what Connor is doing. I would never contribute to his capture because of our friendship, but Pim Wat or the Master? I would absolutely help bring them in if I got a chance. I'm sure that this team is actually much more interested in capturing Pim Wat than Connor."

Her comment was a golden opportunity for Marcella. "Well, how about lunch? You have to eat, and I have something important I want to talk to you about." Marcella still couldn't take the chance that the phone was tapped, and this was the kind of conversation she wanted to have in person, anyway.

"Let's get together at our favorite noodle place," Sophie said. "It's been too long since we went there."

"Yay!" Marcella clapped her hands. "As long as you didn't suggest my parents' restaurant, I'm down." Marcella's Italian parents ran a breakfast and lunch place that did a brisk business in the heart of Waikiki.

"Your parents' food is excellent, but they also love to stop by the table every five minutes."

"That's exactly the problem." They firmed up their plan of meeting for a meal before the noodle place got busy, and Marcella ended the call.

She felt a little better. She would lay it all out in front of Sophie, and let the chips fall where they may. That way, no matter what else happened from there, Sophie couldn't say that Marcella hadn't been honest with her.

CHAPTER TWENTY-FIVE

Marcella

MARCELLA HAD ARRIVED at the noodle house a little early. She scanned the long room with its row of simple, brown Naugahyde booths and a polished wooden bar that the cooks worked behind.

A wave of grief hit her unexpectedly: she'd met Jake for the first time at this very place when she was here last. Sophie'd called him to meet them for a meal, and Jake had walked in with all the energy of a thunderhead blowing across the horizon, and the charm of his grin had been the lightning.

Jake had been a man who was hard to ignore. She remembered the reluctant tingle of attraction she'd felt as he shook her hand. She was happily married to a very sexy man, and still, Jake had affected her.

Would there ever be someone like him again? There was no answer to that. Jake had been here, he had brightened up the freakin' planet, and now he was gone. No wonder Sophie was so happy about being pregnant. Maybe their child would have a little of that same dynamic energy. And if not, that was fine too. *Jake would always be remembered.*

"Sit anywhere," the cook called out, his face shiny with heat in the shade of a cocked paper chef's hat.

Marcella pulled herself together and chose a booth at the back. Highly unlikely that anyone from either of their cases would show up to listen in on this conversation, but it was better that the restaurant was empty.

Marcella was sipping a glass of iced tea when Sophie came in. Her friend's bright brown eyes found Marcella's across the room—and then her gaze dimmed, as Sophie was slammed by the same memory Marcella'd had.

Maybe this café had not been a good choice after all.

Sophie walked over and sat down across from Marcella. Her beautiful scarred face had settled into a familiar neutral mask. "It's been a long time since I had these noodles." Sophie picked up the slightly greasy laminated menu, but Marcella could tell she wasn't reading it.

Marcella reached a hand across the table to take Sophie's.

"I'm sorry that I brought you here. I forgot that the last time we ate here, Jake was with us."

Sophie nodded, but she didn't look up. Her glass had beaded with moisture and a wedge of lemon floated on top. She picked it up and took a sip. "Thank you for ordering me fresh water."

Marcella let go of Sophie's hand. "I wasn't sure if you'd be having caffeine."

"I can't do without my morning cup of tea, but I'm cutting down the rest of the day." Sophie set the menu aside as the cook came over.

"Nice to see you ladies again. Been a while. You going up against any interesting contenders, Sophie?"

Another thing Marcella had forgotten—the cook followed Sophie's amateur MMA fighting.

Sophie shook her head. "Those days are over for me. I'm having a baby."

The man's face broke into a wide grin. "Sweet! Your noodles are on the house." He switched his attention to Marcella. "Yours, however, are not."

Marcella laughed. "I'll remember that when I'm pregnant," she teased, shaking a finger at him. "You know what I like. The everything-on-it saimin bowl."

"And I'll have the Thai curry noodles," Sophie said.

"Uh-huh, the usual." He made a note on his pad, and bustled off.

Marcella took a fortifying sip of her iced tea. "How are you doing?"

"I'm glad to have a new case to keep me from obsessing too much on things that cannot be changed." Sophie shrugged. "I won't bore you with the forensic accounting details. You?"

"We've got cases rolling around the office, but then we always do. I want to talk to you about my current investigation. That's why I asked for this get-together." Marcella took another sip of her tea, and met Sophie's eyes. "I'm on the task force that is trying to bring in Connor, Pim Wat, and the Master."

Sophie froze, her eyes widening. "I presume you have a reason for that."

"I've made no secret of believing Connor is a dangerous criminal who has the capacity to derail your life. His activities have already caused you stress, and the risk of being caught up in the manhunt for him is dangerous. I'm doing this because I love you and want you to be safe."

Sophie frowned. "We agreed to disagree about my relationship with him. I thought you trusted my judgment."

"I do trust your judgment. But he's in deep with your mother, whom neither of us trust, and the Master—God only knows what *his* agenda is." Marcella drew a breath and mustered her thoughts. "Even if Connor has good intentions toward you, and I believe that, based on how he rescued you and Jake when no one else could—I just think he's in too deep with those other two, and they are dangerous as hell." Marcella took a sip of iced tea, holding up a hand to pause Sophie's response. "I'll cut to the chase, because I don't want this talk to degenerate into an argument. I would like to see if you can turn Connor to help us. Have him capture Pim Wat for the task force. The Master, too, though honestly, the team has little or no proof of wrongdoing against that man, though they suspect he's behind several government coups. They would be content with capturing Pim Wat. I have a green light to negotiate immunity for Connor, if he can bring her in." Marcella met Sophie's eyes. "Connor could be a free man. Reinstated in the United States under his real identity— whatever that is."

Sophie's gaze was intense. "You realize you're asking me to betray my mother, and the equivalent of my stepfather."

"That woman snatched your newborn infant and killed six men who were trying to rescue her!" Marcella exclaimed; her voice raised enough that other guests who had begun filling the restaurant looked in their direction. Marcella pulled herself together and leaned forward across the table. "You told me that she and the Master came to Phi Ni to ask your forgiveness and make peace. But do you really think she meant it? Do you really think that the baby you carry is safe from her?"

"No," Sophie whispered. Her tawny skin had paled as the conversation progressed. One of her hands slid down protectively over her abdomen. "No. I don't trust my mother to have my best interests at heart."

"As long as that woman breathes air on this planet, you and those you love are in danger," Marcella said. "I'm speaking hard truths today, Soph. Pim Wat is a cancer that needs to be cut out."

"I know that," Sophie said. "I wanted to believe that she meant her words on the island. But there was something . . . something not right about it. I do know one thing. She will not be taken alive. She tried to kill herself when I captured her before, by throwing herself down a flight of stairs. That's what ruined her face."

"And this is not just about you and your children. Didn't Pim Wat swear that she'd kill Armita, too?"

"Yes." Sophie's nanny had been Pim Wat's handmaid for close to twenty years. She'd taken Momi from Pim Wat and returned the baby to Sophie, an act Pim Wat considered betrayal.

The two women stared at each other. "I'm glad you trusted me enough to be honest," Sophie said.

Two large, savory bowls of noodles arrived at the perfect time, emitting delicious smells and wafts of steam. The cook patted Sophie on the shoulder. "I expect to see all of that gone."

"I can eat this portion with little difficulty." Sophie picked up her chopsticks and spoon, and dove in.

Marcella did the same. For a good five minutes there was no sound but that of them slurping, sipping, and chewing. The knot of anxiety in Marcella's chest began to loosen.

Finally, Sophie spoke. "I'll check our secret chat room and see if Connor has responded to my message about cutting him off. I will feel my way forward to see if there is an opening to share this opportunity." She raised her eyes to meet Marcella's. "You know that this is a very dangerous plan. The Master and Pim Wat are formidable enemies."

"I know." Marcella grasped Sophie's hand, heartened. "And I'm sorry. For all of it. No one should have to bear what you have had to."

"And yet, still I thrive." Sophie smiled. "I am finding happiness in the little things. Satisfaction in my work, and in the friends who remain, like you. Yes, I still grieve for Jake, but my life is full, and I'm grateful for that."

Marcella squeezed Sophie's hand. "Life isn't over until it's over, and you seem to have extra angels looking out for you."

"You are one of them." Sophie lifted Marcella's hand and gave her knuckles a quick kiss.

Sophie was usually so undemonstrative. She didn't even like hugging. "Don't get soft on me," Marcella growled. "Finish your noodles."

Sophie nodded, and resumed eating.

CHAPTER TWENTY-SIX

Sophie

REFRESHED by her nap and lunch with Marcella, Sophie returned to the basement, diving into the hard drive belonging to the main bookkeeper at Peerless Accounting.

From that rig's accounting file, she had been able to access the software connected to the main bank account of Kama'aina Schools. Running her DAVID software through that, searching for keywords that detected uneven ratios, she had been able to identify a series of small amounts of random numbers tied to the "office costs" column in the Peerless accounting software that looked like they could be the skimmed funds.

Where were those small amounts going? They were not flowing to any particular retailer. Rather, they looked computer-generated to her, a line item in random-created amounts that were not being closely tracked. DAVID concurred with a strong affirmative probability ratio, that the amounts were artificially randomized, and not associated with "real" purchases, which tended to follow established patterns.

Sophie stood up and stretched, which she did every half hour by following a phone alarm prompt. This time, her device toned an incoming call, and she checked the ID window.

She picked up for Raveaux. "I'm glad that you called. I've noticed a consistent anomaly in the Kama`aina Schools' records."

"A consistent anomaly. What an interesting turn of phrase." Sophie could hear the humor in Raveaux's voice. "Have you been there since I left this morning? It's five p.m."

"I took a break for lunch and the rest that you suggested." Sophie's stomach gave a loud rumble. "I do have to wrap it up for the day, and go get something to eat."

"That is why I called. I have a dinner I'm preparing, and you told me that you would eat my food, again, if you were invited."

Sophie paused. She didn't want to encourage Raveaux; give him the wrong idea about whether she was interested in him. *But how could he possibly be interested in her, a grieving pregnant woman?* She probably didn't need to worry about that.

She must have taken too long to answer, because Raveaux said, "Heri Leede will also be there. We can catch up on the case so far."

"That is perfect. I am so hungry. I had noodles earlier today, but they seemed to have burned off." Sophie leaned over and her fingers flew on the keyboard as she began shutting down programs. "Are you still at that same address in Waikiki?"

Sophie knocked at the door of Raveaux's apartment in the hotel district of downtown. He didn't answer right away, so she glanced around, taking in the bright ornamental plantings and the gleam of the ocean reflected in a window nearby. Even in the evening, a feeling of happy excitement filled the air of Waikiki. This area was the heart of the tourist zone on Oahu, and it beat to the rhythm of visitors and their vacation happiness.

Raveaux opened the door. He wore a short-sleeved shirt, something he rarely did because the scars on his arms showed—and a plain white canvas apron over slacks. His brown eyes crinkled with that almost-smile.

"Good to see you, Sophie." He stepped forward to kiss her cheeks quickly in the French way.

She chuckled as she returned the buss. "You're very continental tonight, Pierre."

"*Mais oui*. My cooking persona." Raveaux exaggerated his accent and made a bow, gesturing with the wooden spoon he held. "Please, come in."

Sophie brushed past him to enter the immaculately clean, simply furnished apartment.

Heri Leede was already seated on the couch, looking pretty in a floral dress. She had hidden a nice figure under her matronly garb for their first meeting. Her old lady glasses were also gone, and she looked twenty years younger than she had when Sophie last saw her. "Heri! I was happy to hear you were coming for dinner as well. I have news for you about what I've discovered on the computers."

"Please, ladies. Can we enjoy dinner and talk business afterward?" Raveaux handed Sophie a brimming glass of Perrier with lime and ice. "I prepared you my favorite drink."

Sophie took the glass. "Perfect."

"Yes, Pierre, I'm in favor of food first, business later, as well." Leede lifted a glass of red wine. "To French chefs disguised as investigators."

They sipped. "I don't know what to talk about, then," Sophie said, sitting down next to the other woman. Raveaux had gone back to stirring at the stove.

Heri smiled. "Tell me about what you do outside of work."

Sophie considered for a moment. "I am the mother of a toddler, but Momi is gone every other month. When she is here in Honolulu, I go to work at Security Solutions to focus on administration, and take care of her with my nanny's help. When she is not, I take new cases. I go running. I enjoy technological challenges. A simple existence." She sipped her Perrier. "You?"

"Oh, I stay busy. I try to make the most of having moved all this way to Hawaii," Leede said. "I'm part of a very active hula *halau*. When we aren't practicing new dances, I'm learning Hawaiian language and crafts. Right now, I'm making my own *ipu*."

"What is that again?"

"A dried gourd used for percussion. I'm drying mine at the moment, and working on the design I will carve on it when it's ready."

"That's fascinating," Sophie said. "I did not know foreigners were welcome in such cultural activities."

"It depends on the *kumu*, or teacher, and the purpose of the group. My *halau* is mostly geared toward education and preservation of the culture. Thus, they welcome people from other places," Leede said. "You should come to one of our practices. See if you'd like to be a part of it."

"I'd enjoy a visit, but given the small amount of free time I have, I don't see involvement as an option."

"Dinner is ready," Raveaux said. "We'll serve ourselves here at the counter, and take our plates out onto the lanai so we can enjoy the sunset—it's about time for that."

They filled their plates with a savory ragout, wild rice, and fresh sautéed snow peas. Leede exclaimed over everything in appreciation to the point that Sophie felt her praise would be excessive, but she ate all of her portion and went back for more. She would have eaten a third plateful if there had been any left.

Replete, she sat back in her chair, enjoying the last of the streaks of red, orange, and gold gilding the clouds on the horizon. The sound of the wind in the coconut palms overhead and the waves on the beach made gentle music, as Raveaux and Leede chatted.

Leede gave a ladylike belch, hidden behind her hand. "Oh, excuse me. That was so delicious, Pierre. What do we have to do to get you to cook for us every night?" She fluttered her eyelashes in exaggerated flirtation.

Raveaux smiled.

Sophie's eyes widened to see it. He really was a handsome man, and especially when he smiled. *Too bad it was so seldom.*

He waved his glass. "You are a flatterer, Heri. We who cook live for an appreciative audience." Raveaux gestured to Sophie. "Sophie's empty plate is an equal compliment to your flowery words."

Sophie smiled too, this time. "Dinner was superb, Pierre, as you must know. Thank you. Now can we talk about the case?"

"Is she always like this?" Leede gestured in Sophie's direction.

"Yes, she is." Raveaux said. "But I forbid you to discuss those damned computers until you ladies clear and clean up the kitchen before the dessert course. Then, and only then, will we discuss the case."

Leede and Sophie pushed back their chairs and grabbed up the plates and silverware. "I want to see what this dessert is," Leede said.

"Me too," Sophie echoed.

That elusive smile curved Raveaux's mouth. He tipped his head back and shut his eyes, the picture of relaxation. "I guarantee you'll enjoy it."

The two women made short work of the kitchen cleanup, filling Raveaux's dishwasher and stacking the pans. There were no leftovers to put away.

"I don't know about you, but I'm angling for another invitation to dinner," Leede said. "Preferably alone." She raised a brow inquiringly. "Do you mind?"

"Of course not," Sophie said. "Who Raveaux has to dinner—or in his bed, for that matter—is none of my business."

"Good," Leede said crisply. "Then you won't mind if I make a move." And with that, Leede left Sophie in the kitchen, in front of a sinkful of greasy pots and pans, walking outside to join Raveaux and closing the glass slider behind her.

Sophie filled the sink with hot soapy water and went to work on the cookware, scrubbing energetically. She rinsed and stacked the pans in the drainer, feeling unsettled. "Good luck to her," Sophie muttered. "She's going to need it."

"Need what?" Raveaux had come up behind her, and for a moment she thought she felt his breath at her neck. "I made a chocolate torte. It needs to warm up a little to be at its best."

He opened the refrigerator and took out the torte. The glossy dark round, garnished with raspberries, looked as perfect as if it had been made in a bakery. He set the dessert on the counter. "Come outside with me so we can discuss the case."

"Leede wanted a little alone time with you." Sophie dried her hands on a dish towel. "I can finish cleaning up here."

Raveaux arched a brow. "Come, Sophie. You know who I want to spend time with." Before she could respond, he'd moved in his graceful way back out to the deck.

Sophie took a moment to finish wiping down the stove and counters anyway, before refreshing her drink and following him out to the lanai.

"I've seen the dessert," she told Leede. "Chocolate torte. I expect there will also be a fresh raspberry sauce."

"My favorite!" Leede clapped her hands. "Now, Sophie, you said you found something on the computers?"

"I did." Sophie sat down and described what she'd uncovered. "Have you found any entries in the formal logs to match what I'm describing?"

"I have been going over the logs that are submitted to the Kama`aina Board each quarter. There does seem to be a large budget for 'office supplies' now that you mention it, but not enough to account for the major shortage our clients have asked us to find." Leede frowned. "I wonder if this is how the embezzling is being done: padding legitimate expenses with random, computer-generated deductions to the bank account and siphoning them elsewhere. The accounting program shows that certain retailers are given categories, and when the retailer is paid, that category is triggered. A good deal of the ordering is automated for an organization this size. All the embezzler would have to do is hack into that software and set up a skim to various 'retailers' that were fake accounts."

Sophie nodded. "I think that's exactly what is going on."

"And, just like that, Sophie solved the case." Raveaux stood up. "Time for dessert. Would either of you like tea or espresso?"

"No caffeine for me, thank you," Sophie said. She yawned. "In fact, I'm so tired all of a sudden. Can I get my dessert to go?"

Raveaux's mouth tightened with disappointment. "Of course. I will prepare a Tupperware." He disappeared, shutting the glass door behind him.

"Even the way that man says 'Tupperware' is sexy," Leede murmured, swirling her wineglass.

"How old are you?" Sophie asked. "Raveaux is thirty-nine, but his life has aged him. You?"

Leede's eyes twinkled. "Guess."

"I think you present yourself as at least in your sixties. Why?" Sophie sipped her Perrier.

"It helps with my work. Adds credibility. At a certain point, an older woman is more authoritative. Guess my age."

Sophie narrowed her eyes, assessing. The woman's skin was beautiful, though the white hair . . . "I don't know."

"I'm forty-eight. My hair turned white when I was twenty-five; a family thing. I discovered the advantage of looking older in my years in Scotland Yard. Men were less threatened by me, and the suspects underestimated me."

"I can see that worked well," Sophie said seriously. "I have played down my femininity too." She flexed her arm. "In favor of musculature."

"Sorry, Sophie, but you're quite beautiful and the muscles are not unattractive," Leede said. "If I batted for the other team . . ."

"What does that mean?" Sophie asked. "I'm not familiar with that colloquialism."

The door opened just then, and Raveaux appeared, carrying two beautifully garnished plates of torte with forks on the side. "Your Tupperware is on the counter, Sophie. We'll be in touch tomorrow."

Sophie had displeased him, and now she was dismissed.

"Thank you, Pierre. I will enjoy my dessert at home. Good night, Heri." Sophie stood up and gave a little wave, which only Leede returned. She shut the sliding door and left the two on the lanai with their desserts.

"Good luck, Heri," she whispered as she picked up her container with its dark treasure inside. "He needs someone, and you just might be woman enough."

CHAPTER TWENTY-SEVEN

Sophie
Day 6

SOPHIE WOKE LATER than she usually did, feeling the warm touch of Ginger's tongue on her hand.

"Stop it, girl." Sophie tucked her hand back in under the covers, savoring the soft bed, top-quality sheets, and silk comforter. Nothing like a night on a yoga mat in a basement to make her feel grateful to wake up in her father's luxurious apartment.

She really was lucky that Frank had not only taken her in, but cared for the dogs in her more than twenty-four-hour absence. They had greeted her last night ecstatically, but without the franticness she had come to expect, particularly from Ginger, when left for anything longer than a few hours.

Her father had been out when she returned; she was relieved to have gotten a text from him that he had a dinner meeting last night, so she hadn't had to see him.

But today was the day she was going to talk to him about being on the team to capture Connor. Living with him and keeping that a secret felt way too dishonest, like a wedge that would drive them apart even more than his actions already had.

Sophie got up and slipped her arms into her familiar dragon-embroidered silk robe, a robe she had left in the closet of this room when she moved out. As she tied the sash around her waist, already becoming a little rounded, she could smell the fresh, clean fabric.

Augie had laundered all of her clothes, and had even had ones that needed dry cleaning done. They hung neatly in the closet on plastic-shrouded hangers.

Augie was a busy man. He would not have thought of such a thing if her father hadn't directed him to do it. Was there no end to Frank's loving thoughtfulness? Why did that make his betrayal feel so much worse?

Sophie walked out into the kitchen and turned on the kettle for her tea. "Good morning, Dad."

Her father, seated in his usual spot on the couch, shook out his newspaper as he shifted to the next page. "Good morning, Sophie."

The dogs had followed her out, and Ginger hurried to the front door, whimpering, clearly eager for her morning pee. "I have to throw on some clothes and take the dogs out for a quick morning walk. But I'd like to talk afterward, if you have time."

"No problem." Frank's response was short. She wasn't imagining the tension she saw in his shoulders, around his mouth.

She was getting better at reading people! As hard as this moment was, she savored the tiny insight. She set up her tea and went back into the bedroom and changed. The dogs increased their excitement as they saw her putting on her shoes.

"This is going to be a short walk, you two," she said. Anubis immediately sat down at her tone of voice. Ginger, however, continued to hope for more, trotting back and forth and swinging her tail like a club against Sophie's legs.

Her father had poured her tea into its pot, and it was nicely steeped by the time she came out and put the dogs on their leashes. "Perfect, Dad. That was so thoughtful of you."

"I live to serve."

Yes, he was as ready for this fight as she was.

SOPHIE HAD TAKEN the dogs at a jog for three laps around the block, just to take the edge off their energy. The quick run had taken the edge off of her irritability, too.

Back at the apartment, she refilled her mug, adding a spoonful of honey, remembering it was okay for pregnant women to have honey —but not babies, as their gut biomes were too delicate to process some of the natural bacteria in the substance.

Sophie carried her mug over to sit opposite her father, where he was ensconced on the couch. "I need to talk with you, Dad."

"So you said." Frank shook the pages of the Wall Street Journal together, folded the paper crisply, and set it aside. "You have my full attention." He crossed his legs, interlacing his fingers to rest them over his knee. His handsome, dignified face was inscrutable.

Sophie had learned her own opaque mask from her father—*but she'd always attributed learning that to her ex-husband's abuse.* Another insight.

"You've been working with the multi-agency task force that's trying to bring in Connor, Pim Wat, and the Master. I want to know why."

"Who told you that?" Frank's expression didn't change.

"That doesn't matter. What matters is . . ."

"What matters is that you, and my grandchildren, are safe. Everything I've done, I've done to ensure that outcome."

"I'm not surprised by that, *P̆ā*." She used the Thai word for father, instead of English. He had always preferred that she call him "Dad," but that small act of defiance felt important, felt like reclaiming a piece of herself. "Working behind my back has undermined my trust. I wish you had come to me. Talked to me about your concerns, instead of working with the task force." Sophie took a sip

145

of her tea to calm herself. "In addition, we've been working at cross-purposes. I've wasted energy and stress trying to keep secrets that you already knew. And you have wasted energy scheming things I should have been included in planning."

Frank firmed his jaw. "I didn't believe I could discuss my concerns with you because you had already made your feelings for Connor abundantly clear, in spite of who he turned out to be. Why didn't you tell me about him, instead of hiding his identities, his role as the Ghost vigilante?"

"I didn't tell anybody. I couldn't." Sophie frowned. "Who Connor is wasn't my secret to share."

Frank threw up his hands in frustration. "Listen to yourself. 'Who he is.' Who is he, really? Does anyone know?"

"Does it matter what he calls himself? I know who he is, inside." Even as she said the words, doubt gnawed at Sophie. *Did she know who he was, anymore? Had she ever?*

"What I don't understand is, if he is so important to you, why hasn't Connor been your boyfriend the whole time? Why has he stayed at that compound in Thailand with Pim Wat and the Master? And why do you still care about him when he lied, repeatedly, and let you grieve his 'death'?" Frank made air quotes. "I, for one, will never forget the pain you suffered over that betrayal."

"I am a grown woman, and I get to sleep with whomever I want. Do whatever I want in my relationships—and none of it has to make any sense to you, because it's none of your business." Sophie trembled with anger and stress. "But since we're talking about it, Connor and I broke up over his role as the Ghost. I wanted him to stop his vigilante activities. He refused."

"Well, that speaks well of your character, if not of his," Frank said acidly.

"But it's not a simple thing. Connor deals with people that need to be dealt with, people that no one in law enforcement can touch." Sophie held her father's gaze. "He rescued my ex-husband's new child bride, and made sure she got back to her parents when I asked him to. Whatever else we get out of this conversation, know this: you don't get to dictate who I have a relationship with. Not after Assan Ang."

The specter of Sophie's early arranged marriage to a sadistic businessman had long lain between them. Frank scowled. "I was not in favor of that match. That was all your mother."

"But you didn't try hard to stop it! You let it go forward. I was *nineteen,* Dad!" Sophie's knuckles turned white as she gripped her mug. "Assan almost killed me a hundred times."

Frank ran a hand over his thick, closely-buzzed hair. "I didn't know! You never said anything! I would have moved heaven and earth to get you away from him if I'd known—" He blew out a breath. "And that's why it's hard to watch you flounder around in your relationships. I just want you to be safe and happy."

"I can understand that. I have a daughter now, too, and I'm very protective of her." Sophie made a chopping gesture with her hand. "But every one of my relationships has been important. I still love each of the men I've been with in a unique way. I shouldn't have to explain or justify that to you, any more than you need to tell me about the women in your life. Marrying my mother didn't make sense—let alone staying with her as long as you did. Were you using her, just as she was using you?" Sophie's eyes felt hard and hot as she pinned her father with her gaze. "It just now occurred to me. You were a spy, too."

Frank sputtered, speechless, and Sophie saw a flash of that thing again. *Guilt.*

"Ridiculous. I've had a perfectly aboveboard position with the State Department all of these years," Frank said.

"No wonder you knew about Connor. You're with the CIA," Sophie persisted. "How else would you have known about him?"

Frank stood up. "This discussion is over."

"I'll just ask Agent MacDonald or Kate Smith. They'll tell me," Sophie said. "You've been more than just an asset to the CIA; you're an *agent.* That's why you married Pim Wat. She's close to the Thai

Royal Family. You could report on the Yām Khûmkạn and the activities of the Thai court."

Her father stood over her, six-foot-plus of intimidating male. "How dare you!"

"How dare *you*, P̌ā?" Sophie stood up too. "You might as well admit it."

Frank turned and walked into the kitchen. "Enough."

"Oh, but you get to judge me? Take matters into your own hands like a patriarch of old?" The dogs, agitated by the raised voices, lifted their heads from their beds near the door. Sophie lowered her voice with an effort. "Dad. Let's be honest, for once, and talk this through. Maybe there's a way we can figure this out. Marcella had an idea that I'm thinking over."

Frank opened the cupboard over the stove. "Are you hungry? I could fix you pancakes. You loved banana pancakes when you were a girl."

Sophie flashed to their kitchen in the family's communal house in Thailand. Her father had imported a Western stove, and when he was at home, he used to fix the two of them breakfast. Pim Wat had never joined them; she didn't "feel well" in the mornings.

Yes, she remembered those banana pancakes.

"Please. I'm hungry. I'm always hungry these days." Sophie seated herself on a high stool at the marble island that contained the stove. She sipped her tea and watched her father as he gathered the ingredients and made the batter from scratch. The homey sounds and smells and sight of him, stirring the batter in the bowl, took her back. "It's nice that you remember about those pancakes."

"How could I forget?" Frank sliced the bananas. Her sensitive nose reacted favorably to their sweet, ripe scent. "Those breakfasts were some of our best times together in that house."

Sophie took out her phone and thumbed to an app that played jazz. Soon, mellow piano riffs accompanied the sizzle of butter in the cast iron pan. Frank didn't speak until he had three perfectly round pancakes browning.

"I was recruited to the CIA as a condition of getting the ambassadorship. I was one of the first black men to occupy the office, and I wanted that job. I would have done worse than be a spy to get it."

Ginger must have sensed the tension in her mistress, because she padded over to lean against Sophie's leg. Sophie played with her dog's ears as her father went on. "It started out small. Just faxing something confidential that came across my desk, here and there. Then, they engineered a meeting between me and Pim Wat." He looked up to meet Sophie's eyes. "Your mother was so beautiful."

"She's always been beautiful," Sophie murmured. "I bet you were swept away."

"Exactly. I didn't fall in love and marry her as a part of my job; no one required that of me. But was it an additional bonus? Yes." He flipped the pancakes, plated them, and passed the steaming stack to Sophie along with a glass jug of real maple syrup and a ramekin of fresh butter. "Your mother got pregnant with you right away. Pim Wat was devastated; she said she'd never planned to be a mother. I begged for her to keep you; we struck a bargain that I would be 'in charge' of your education and care. That's how you ended up going to Western schools."

"I always felt like there were things going on between you that I knew nothing about." Sophie doctored the pancakes to her satisfaction and took a big bite. "Mmm. Delicious."

Frank flipped his latest batch of cakes. "After you were born, Pim Wat had postpartum depression—and I believe it was genuine. She got better, then relapsed again and again. I know, now, that she used the excuse of her depression as her cover. But when I found out she was not only an agent but an assassin—that was a genuine shock. She'd played me, when I thought I was playing her."

"You're lucky she didn't kill you." Sophie forked up another bite of pancakes.

"I am, come to think of it." Her father fixed his plate and came around to sit beside Sophie. They ate companionably. "Now. What do you want to do about all of this?"

"Are you still working with that team?" Sophie set her plate aside.

"No. I bowed out after those agents tried to grab you. I told them that wasn't part of our deal. But—Marcella's on the team, now."

"Yes, she told me." Sophie met her father's gaze. "And because she did, we could talk freely about what was going on. She proposed that I try to turn Connor against the Master and Pim Wat, since there's no getting any of them out of that compound."

Frank blinked. "What could you offer him to take such dangerous action?"

"Marcella thinks he might still want to be with me, now that Jake's gone." Sophie bit her lip. "We tried to be together when Jake and I were broken up, but it didn't work. I don't know. I don't want to make him any false promises, but I told her I was willing to pass along the offer of immunity for his help in bringing in Pim Wat. That's who they really want."

"Yes. They suspect the Master of being behind the disruption of several governments, but they have nothing hard on him. Pim Wat? They have a case against her, and MacDonald was really burned when the Master yanked her out of Gitmo." Frank finished his pancakes. He set his fork on the plate, and laid a hand on Sophie's arm. "Please, honey. No matter what, be careful. I have a bad, bad feeling about this."

CHAPTER TWENTY-EIGHT

Connor
Day 6

CONNOR LOWERED the heavy wooden bar that blocked the door into the upper room computer lab. The method was crude but effective. He'd also taken the precaution of sweeping the room for bugs, but there were none—and he'd have been surprised if there were. Most of the men in the compound had little awareness or training in the use of such devices; but he couldn't be too careful with what he was about to say, and to whom he was about to say it.

He turned around to face the three people he trusted the most in the organization. Seated around the work table he used for meals were his faithful assistant Nine, his former houseman Nam, and Kupa.

Kupa looked unfamiliar. Nam's wife had gone away with Pim Wat, looking middle-aged, comfortably plump around the waist, with graying hair she wore in a braid. She had returned with a complete face and body makeover. For all of that, Kupa did not seem happy with the change, and her new, pretty face looked pinched and sad.

Nam, for his part, sat as close to his wife as he could, one arm slung protectively around her. From what Connor remembered of their partnership on his island, the couple had been private and independent, each engaging in their own hobbies and pastimes, though close and loyal.

Being brought to the compound and forced into the lifestyle here had made them cling to each other for support, and Connor felt a stab of guilt at the unhappy expression on Nam's normally serene face. *But what could he have done?* The Department of Justice would definitely have taken them hostage if they'd realized the couple's value to him.

Meanwhile, Nine, who'd been redeployed by the Master to lead morning drills, sat with his hands on his knees in an attitude of expectancy, his dark eyes inscrutable. "You called us here, Number One. How can we be of service?" His English was halting—he'd been studying in his spare time.

Connor approached the table and sat down, speaking in Thai to ease communication. "Thank you for coming when I asked. You are my most trusted companions, and I need you to swear not to say anything to anyone about what we will speak of here."

Three pairs of eyes stared at him unblinkingly. "I swear," each of them said aloud. Connor almost smiled. Sometimes he forgot how literal his companions were; but on the other hand, it couldn't hurt to have them take that vow.

"I know all of you have had your struggles recently, as have I." He got up again, needing to move, and paced in front of the table. "I find myself trapped in a role and a lifestyle that is not what I intended. I joined the Yām Khûmkạn for several reasons. To evade the FBI, with the hope that the investigation into my online activities would blow over, and to add to my skills in studying with the Master. I also was—heartbroken at losing Sophie. She was with Jake. I needed something else to absorb me, and studying under the Master took everything I had. But I never dreamed that he would choose me as his Number One, or that Jake would be killed." He paused, drew a breath to gather himself, and sat back down, leaning forward earnestly. "This international investigation is getting more intense rather than less, triggered by the Master's rescue of Pim Wat. Sophie has had to cut off contact with me, and it appears that Nam and Kupa's home on Phi Ni could be tied up in litigation for years. None of this is what I wanted when I originally joined the organization."

"We believe you," Nam said soberly. "We have seen all of this firsthand." He squeezed his wife. "We do not want to be trapped here. We want to go home."

"Yes. I want that for you, as well. I have had some time to think. I believe that Pim Wat is a danger to Sophie. The authorities consider her a threat to world leaders—and they've been humiliated by her escape. I want to eliminate Pim Wat, and trade evidence of that for amnesty with the investigators on the international team."

"I am so glad that you summoned me here, because I overheard Pim Wat and the Master conspiring to kill Sophie!" Kupa exclaimed.

"What?" All eyes turned to her.

"Yes!" Kupa worked a bit of her gown nervously in her fingers. "I overheard them through the servants' tunnel. The room has a narrow place where a servant can come and go or await the Master's pleasure. Pim Wat likes me to be available whenever she wants something, and she is often in the Master's chambers since our return, so I went there and sat quietly." She looked down at her nervous fingers. "The Master brought it up. He said that he wanted Sophie out of the way so that Number One would settle into his duties and his role, and he and Pim Wat could retire to his island in the Philippines. Pim Wat agreed and said that her daughter must pay for turning her over to the CIA. She also said that she wanted her grandchildren. They agreed they would wait until Sophie had the baby, and then kill her—but in a way that Number One would not suspect."

A flush of rage blew through Connor. He breathed carefully to manage the emotion. Now is not the time, nor these the people, to unleash it upon. He must use this hot anger to generate strength. "She must die."

"But what about the Master?" Nine's dark eyes were troubled. "If he finds out you have had a hand in Pim Wat's death, the world will not be big enough for you to hide in."

"I was used by Pim Wat to administer a poison to the doctors who did her surgical reconstruction. I know where she keeps her poison kit. She has many potions, but I know the one that will kill without a trace," Kupa said.

"I understand the Master's reason for wanting Sophie dead. He knows what she means to me. He wants to keep my loyalty and have me be his replacement, with no distractions." A part of Connor throbbed with pain at the news; but another part wasn't surprised at all. The Master was ruthless; his agenda was the only one that mattered.

"The solution is obvious," Nine said. "They both must go."

The four of them sat with the magnitude of what had just been said.

"I need that poison," Connor said to Kupa. "Can you get it without endangering yourself?"

Kupa bowed her head. "I will try. I will see if I can remove a toxic dose from the bottle and replace it with something, so the loss is not discernible."

Nam placed his hand upon her arm. "You don't have to do this, my beloved. We can find some other way."

"But how can both of them die and it not be suspicious?" Nine said. "The men will tear apart anyone who has harmed the Master."

"I need time to plan," Connor said. "Kupa, get me the poison. Only I will be responsible for what happens once I have it. I refuse to put any of you in danger, or make you responsible any further for what comes next."

※

CONNOR LOWERED the bar that locked the upper room behind his three co-conspirators as they left.

The revelations of their meeting still ricocheted around inside his head. That the Master would use him, and set him up this way, shocked him. Nine's willingness to go along with this assassination plot had surprised Connor too; and so had his own deadly resolve.

How had the Master been so careless as to let Kupa overhear his conversation with Pim Wat? That seemed uncharacteristic. Of course, the Master knew about the servants' passage. What if the Master had set Kupa up, and this whole thing was a test of Connor's loyalty?

Connor's heart thundered with fear.

Fear was the enemy. Fear must be dealt with.

Connor needed a break. He left the upper room to go to the Master's garden.

Once he reached it, he mounted the tiger's eye column with an easy leap, and settled himself into the lotus position to meditate.

Gradually, the stress of the upper room meeting fell away.

All he could hear was birdsong and the gentle sound of a warm breeze blowing through the leaves of the garden's flowering and fruit trees.

What possible scenario would benefit the Master by setting up Kupa to overhear their plot? There was no benefit to be had that Connor could see, and if it were a test of loyalty, obviously Connor would fail, and that would not surprise the Master. Connor's devotion to Sophie was why the Master wanted her gone.

Kupa's overhearing must've been an accident, an oversight. Even the Master made those, on occasion.

They would proceed with the poisoning plan and look for an opportunity to implement it. He would figure out a way to flee the compound with Nine, Nam, and Kupa after the deed was done. He would reach out to Sophie to contact the investigation team to tell them that he would provide proof of death of both the Master and Pim Wat, in return for asylum in the United States. There had to be a safe place where they could hide from the revenge of the Yām Khûmkạn; without the Master or his Number One to lead, the organization would fall into disarray, at least long enough for Connor and his people to establish themselves in new identities.

He meditated until his white-hot anger had solidified into icy resolve.

CHAPTER TWENTY-NINE

Sophie

AFTER BREAKFAST WITH HER FATHER, Sophie walked the dogs. She sped up as they made their way along the curving concrete path through Ala Moana Beach Park. She took a moment to look over the early morning beauty of the park: mynah birds hopped on the grass; the light morning breeze tossed the coconut palms. Gentle waves made white foam on the surf break outside of Waikiki Beach; children ran into the water while parents watched. A Tai Chi class moved gently and slowly in sync under one of the banyan trees.

Sophie pressed the number for Connor's burner phone on her list of favorites before she could overthink it. After her ultimatum cutting him off, she didn't expect him to answer right away. "Sophie, is this a secure line?"

"As good as I can make it," she said. "I'm using my satellite phone out at the park."

Connor's voice seemed to relax, settling into the warmth that brought his smile to her mind.

"I didn't expect to hear from you again, after your message."

"Things have changed. Marcella has a proposal. She has joined the team that's after you, so I guess the takeaway from that is we both should know that she's not in favor of you, in general. But the idea is sound, and I'm just passing it on." Sophie blew out a breath as she passed a plumeria tree and inhaled its flowers' delicate perfume. The scent calmed her. "The team is proposing that if you are able to bring in Pim Wat and the Master, that you be granted immunity in the United States."

Sophie had expected an immediate rejection, but Connor was silent.

The dogs smelled something over near one of the trees, and Ginger, always the worse-behaved of the two, dragged her in that direction. Sophie checked Ginger and got them back onto the path. "While you are thinking that over, Connor, there's something else you should know." Sophie cleared her throat. "My father was also on the team. He has concerns about your being safe for me to be with. Being who you have said you are. Whoever that is." She gave a little laugh, but waited tensely for his reply.

"I don't blame Frank for not trusting me. I have not been trustworthy. But it's interesting that you approach me with this proposal right now. I have found that I am . . ." Connor seemed to be considering how best to explain it to her. "In over my head." He spoke slowly, as if gathering his thoughts. "I joined the Yām to escape the law enforcement net that was closing around me. I joined because I wanted to study under the Master; learn his secrets, add tools and skills to my abilities as the Ghost. And I joined to help you, too. I wanted to make sure that Jake could be with you, because that's what you wanted. But he's gone now, and I find myself wondering . . ."

The distance seemed to hum with things they couldn't say.

"I thought we explored that, and it was not meant to be," Sophie said softly.

"I know. But you were still in love with Jake, and I was still—I guess you could say, *besotted* by the Master. I was under his spell.

Then, he chose me to be his successor, his Number One, which I never sought or expected. I'm not sure how to get out, now. The Master won't let me walk away. And since we are having an honest conversation, Nam's wife Kupa overheard a conversation between the Master and Pim Wat—a plot to kill you."

Sophie gasped. Her heart stuttered in her chest. She stopped and pressed a hand over it, feeling its irregular thump. "So much for my mother's love and forgiveness." Her head swam, and she hurried over to a park bench and dropped down onto it, grateful for the support. "That's my mother you're talking about," she said. "My mother."

"I know. I would give anything if it weren't true."

"No, it is important for me to know. Why?" The question was a cry from the heart.

"Because you're a distraction to me. You pull me away from the Yām Khûmkạn and its mission. That's the Master's reason. Your mother wants revenge for being handed over to the CIA." Connor sighed deeply. "I didn't want to hurt you with knowing that it was the Master's idea, and that Pim Wat plans on executing you—but not until after you have your baby. She wants her grandchildren."

"Foul daughter of the devil!" Sophie cursed. Further words failed her. How could any mother do such a thing to her own child? "She will never have my babies. Never."

"Good. You will need that resolve," Connor said briskly. "So yes, I will take the team's offer. But here's the condition: neither Pim Wat nor the Master can be dealt with separately. They must both be taken at the same time. Proof of their deaths will have to be enough to satisfy the team."

"I'm sure that's fine," Sophie said woodenly.

"And I want my immunity agreement in writing."

"Of course." Sophie's mind seemed to be buzzing with white noise. "I'll make that clear to the task force."

"I have logistical things to figure out," Connor said. "But I'm working on it. Monitor our chat box and I will let you know when it's done and provide proof."

"Be very careful," Sophie whispered.

"And you, too, Sophie. Be well." The phone went dead.

CHAPTER THIRTY

Connor

CONNOR WAS MAKING some tweaks on one of his algorithms when a
knock came at the door of the tower room. He recognized that knock:
two long, two short: the special knock Kupa employed.

"Enter."

Kupa slipped in and closed the door behind her. She kept her
eyes downcast, as was her way. Once again, Connor was startled by
the change in her appearance. It was hard not to feel for her, so
heavily made over into the image Pim Wat had wanted. He'd always
thought she was pleasant-looking in a modest way. Now she had a
tight, glossy appearance that didn't suit her.

Kupa's hand slid into the pocket of the lacy white apron Pim Wat
dressed her in when she was doing indoor chores. "I have it."

Connor didn't need to ask what she meant. He held out his hand.
Kupa walked forward quickly on the balls of her feet, furtive as a
mongoose. She slipped a brown plastic bottle into his palm.

"Will she be able to tell this is gone?"

"There was an extra empty bottle in her kit. I filled it with liquid
and substituted it."

"But she might notice that one's gone."

"You will have to return the bottle to me as soon as you can, so I can put it back." Kupa's dark brown eyes were expressionless.

"Thank you. I wish there was more I could do, or say. I will find a way, as soon as I can, to do what must be done."

"Three drops in each drink was what I gave Pim Wat's plastic surgeons." Kupa said. "More than that, and the poison might be detectable. Less than that, they could just be paralyzed, and not die."

Connor nodded. "This is going to work."

Kupa shrugged. "It will be what it will be." There was a fatalistic note in her voice; she was prepared for death.

"Stay positive," Connor said. "We're going to get through this. Together."

Kupa's plump, collagen-filled lips formed a mirthless smile. "I know you will do your best." She turned and slipped out the door.

Connor looked down at the bottle. Brown plastic, with a screw top—the type that aspirin came in before the label was applied.

He had asked the Master for a chess game tonight. Perhaps the chance to administer the poison would present itself, but in any case, he needed to find a way to remove the poison from the bottle, and carry it in to doctor their drinks or food less obviously than a palm-sized bottle half-full of clear liquid.

Connor went into the rustic bathroom, searching through the cabinet there for anything he could use to carry the poison in a more concealed way. *Nothing.* Being in the stone outhouse was like returning to the twelfth century. Perhaps Nam could find something appropriate in the kitchen. He rang for Nam; Kupa's husband might as well know that the plan was a go.

NAM ARRIVED MORE QUICKLY than Connor had anticipated, his normally calm face crinkled with worry. "She brought it to you?"

"She did. But I need to transfer it to something less obvious."

Connor frowned down at the bottle in his hand. "I wish we could test it, first, too."

"I have been catching rats near the kitchen. We could administer it to one of them."

"Good idea. Why don't you find me some sort of spice jar or other container, and bring up a rat when you return." The ghost of a smile tugged at Connor's mouth. "Though I don't know how you're going to explain that."

"We trap the rats and put them outside," Nam said with dignity. "We only kill humans in this compound."

Connor smiled at the black humor. "I will wait for our test subject," he said.

An hour or so later, Nam, Nine, and Connor were looking at a large, brownish gray rat in a wire trap. The creature wasn't frightened; it sat on its haunches and cleaned its whiskers. "It's downright fat," Connor said.

"The cooks put scraps outside the kitchen door for the animals," Nine said. "They all deserve to live; they are moving up the wheel of reincarnation."

"I wonder where on the wheel the rat is." Connor had transferred the poison to a small bottle of ear wax dissolver that Nine had found in the community medicine cabinet. He'd refilled the original bottle to the same height with water, and handed it to Nam. "Get this back to Kupa. See if she can replace it before tonight."

"I will." The man whisked the bottle into his garments.

Connor used the eyedropper to draw up the poison, and administered one droplet carefully to a lump of natural cane sugar. He put the lump into the cage through the entry hole at the top. The rat picked up the lump of sugar in its front paws, and ate it quickly.

A moment later, the animal keeled over without a sigh or a spasm. Nam, Connor, and Nine stared at it. "Seems dead."

Nam lifted the rodent by the tail and waggled it back and forth. "The poison's a paralytic," he said. "I can't tell if it's still alive."

"Check for a pulse," Connor said.

Nam felt the fur under the animal's jaw for a long moment. "Nothing."

The three men look at each other. "I will find a way to serve them tea as soon as I can," Connor said.

CHAPTER THIRTY-ONE

Pim Wat
Day 7

PIM WAT LOOKED out the window of the Yām Khûmkạn's helicopter as it circled over her sister Malee's adjoining properties on the outskirts of Bangkok, Thailand. As always, old memories rose up as she looked at the run-down family compound where Sophie had been born. Pim Wat and Frank had raised her for her first twelve years of life, living in close quarters with Malee and her family, until their divorce and Sophie's departure for boarding school.

Malee now lived in the adjoining house, separated from the original property by a tall fence with sharpened stakes at the top to prevent thieves. The contrast between the two dwellings was stark: Malee's house was verdant with gardens and flowers, and brightly painted in culturally popular colors; but the property where the sisters had lived together during the time they were raising young children had fallen into disrepair. The plants in the yard had died without watering or care, and shingles and tiles were missing from the wooden roof.

The pilot circled the chopper and found an open area to land in the town square. Pim Wat took off her helmet and handed it to him. She tightened the scarf that concealed her hair, and exited the aircraft. One of the ninjas from the Yām Khûmkạn jumped out lightly behind her. She didn't care to have an audience for what she was about to do, but the Master had insisted she always have a guard these days.

"I won't be long," she told the pilot. "Be back here in about an hour."

She ducked away from the prop wash as the helicopter powered up to take off. She headed down the quiet street with its well-watered, ornamental orchid trees shading the road. This quiet area of Bangkok's suburbs was no longer a fashionable neighborhood, but Pim Wat still liked the aesthetic of it, and the nearness of the mighty Ping River, visible beyond a dock area at the end of the street.

Pim Wat hadn't called her sister to let her know she was coming, so she wasn't surprised that it took a while for Malee to open the security gate and to admit her and her guard. "Sister! I am surprised to see you," Malee said.

Pim Wat could smell Malee's fear, and it made her smile. "I have been making the rounds of forgiveness," Pim Wat said. "It's your turn for a visit, Malee."

"We did not part on good terms," Malee said. "I'm glad to see you looking so well."

"No thanks to you, foul betrayer," Pim Wat said. Her eyes were hard on her sister's soft, pretty face.

"That's the Pim Wat I've always known. You've never been much of a one for forgiveness." Malee narrowed her eyes. "My husband is due back any moment."

"No, he isn't. I've been monitoring you." Pim Wat gestured toward the ninja lounging against the closed gate, looking around, his arms crossed on his chest. "Can we go inside? I'm thirsty."

"Of course." Malee made a visible effort to get her nerves under control.

Pim Wat's sister wore an unfamiliar garment, a lovely fitted kaftan that touched the back of her knees. Pim Wat hadn't seen her sister in over two years, and Malee had spent that time working on herself, it seemed. She had lost weight, her calves looked toned, and her bronze skin gleamed. "You're looking well, sister," Pim Wat said.

"As are you, Pim Wat, as I'm sure you know." They had entered the house, and Malee slammed the door behind Pim Wat, flicking the deadbolt. She fisted her hands on her hips. "You don't even look like yourself!" She hissed. "How dare you come here after what you tried to do to me!"

Pim Wat smiled. "I love it when a target makes my work easier."

Malee's shapely brows rose in consternation. "What do you mean?"

Looking at Malee's face was, for Pim Wat, like looking at herself in the past. The softness and lack of definition that had made Malee's face different from Pim Wat's was gone, likely through her sister's dieting. Her features were sharper and more beautiful. The girls had been mistaken for twins when they were younger. "You should have lost weight a long time ago," Pim Wat said.

"I want you to leave," Malee said. "You tried to kill me last time we saw each other. I have nothing to say to you."

"And you held me prisoner after stealing my grandchild from me," Pim Wat said. "And then you colluded with my daughter in turning me over to the CIA. Do you have any idea what those two years were like for me, in their interrogation camp?"

Malee's eyes dropped. Her hands flew to her cheeks. "I tried not to think about it, Pim Wat. I know you would rather have died. But you survived and overcame, as you always do."

"It's true. I am a phoenix," Pim Wat said. "I'm very good at surviving situations like Guantánamo. Unfortunately for you." She spun Malee and pushed her between the shoulder blades, shoving her towards the kitchen. "This won't take long."

"What are you going to do?" Malee's voice had gone high with alarm. Pim Wat spotted Malee's hand sliding into her pocket as she fumbled for her phone.

Pim Wat whipped the phone out of her sister's pocket and threw it across the room. It broke with a crash against the frame of the large bay window lined with brocade pillows where Malee liked to read in the afternoon.

She pushed Malee again, and this time her sister fell to her knees with a cry, landing on the cool tile floor. Pim Wat jumped onto her back, pinning her down with a knee between her shoulder blades.

"Please, please, Pim Wat. We're sisters," Malee cried. "Have mercy!"

Pim Wat took a knife from her small waist pack. "I am having mercy. I'm not going to kill you." She reached over and pulled a dish towel off of the nearby rack, and stuffed it in Malee's mouth. "You might want to bite down on something. This is going to hurt."

Malee screamed into the towel, her wail of agony only slightly muffled, as Pim Wat reached down and sawed through the Achilles tendon at the back of Malee's ankle. Blood flowed freely. Malee flopped back and forth like a fish.

Pim Wat stood up. She walked over to the sink and rinsed her blade, wiping it clean on a fresh white linen towel. She tossed the towel to Malee. "Don't worry. That's all I'm going to do. But you'll never walk normally again; just a little reminder that you shouldn't have betrayed me."

Malee curled up and applied the towel to her mutilated ankle, sobbing, as Pim Wat walked back to the front door.

"You'll be fine," she said. "We'll go shopping next time I visit." She shut the door and rejoined the ninja at the house's gate. "Let's go. I still have some time to browse the shops in the town square before the helicopter comes back."

CHAPTER THIRTY-TWO

Sophie

SOPHIE SET down the phone on the park bench beside her. She looked around the park, reorienting herself in time and space after the call with Connor. Anubis sat beside her, leaning gently against her leg, while Ginger nosed around the corners of the bench, making sure to mark every bit of it.

Off in the distance, a white egret picked its way across the smooth lawn, and a flock of mynah birds chattered loudly in the top of one of the nearby banyan trees. Beyond them, she could see the ocean, and a beautiful white boat sailing away somewhere.

If only she could get on a boat and sail away, if only there were some part of the world that was safe enough for her to hide in, with her children, with Armita. *With Connor.*

But refuges, anywhere in the world, were few for the likes of them. Maybe, by taking this next step, Sophie could expand that circle of safety just a little more.

She had just agreed to her own mother's death.

Sophie breathed through a wave of nausea. *Morning sickness.* That's what it was.

Sophie looked down at her phone, and scrolled to Marcella's number. She called with a press of her thumb.

"Hey girl!" Marcella's voice was upbeat. "The day's still young. What are you up to?"

Sophie shook her head, and then remembered Marcella couldn't see that gesture. "I don't have time to talk, Marcella. I just called to let you know that Connor has agreed to try to do away with Pim Wat and the Master in return for immunity."

A short, charged pause.

"That's amazing." Marcella's voice was tight with excitement. "I didn't really expect it to work."

"That doesn't mean he's going to be able to do it." Sophie's stomach knotted with dread. "He says they are too dangerous, separately, to leave either one alive. Both have to be taken out at the same time, and the only thing he can offer the team is proof of death. But he did offer to kill them for you."

Marcella was silent.

Sophie cleared her throat. "They're planning to kill me, Marcella. They each had different reasons for wanting me dead. Mother wants revenge because I turned her over to the CIA. And the Master thinks I'm a distraction to Connor and his duties at the compound. But, they want my children. Pim Wat plans to kill me after my baby is born."

Marcella cursed. Sophie could almost see her friend's vigorous Italian hand gestures to go with her colorful language. "This must be really hard, Sophie." Marcella's voice softened. "I can't imagine how painful. But you know your mother isn't right in the head. She isn't wired to love anybody in a normal way. It's not your fault."

"I know that." Yet the voice of the depression argued: *Your own mother wants you dead; you're not worth loving. You're cursed. How could one person have so much bad luck?*

"You should make an appointment with Dr. Wilson. Talk it through. Promise me you will."

"Yes. I will. But I have to go now. Tell the team what Connor said. He said he would provide the proof of their death in our chat box when it was done. He doesn't want us communicating anymore for safety reasons."

"I love you, Sophie. I'm so sorry about your mother."

"She's not dead yet." Sophie ended the call. She slid the phone back into her pocket and stood up from the bench. Marcella might have been saying, "I'm sorry," because it sucked to have a mother like Pim Wat.

That was certainly an understatement.

Sophie might not survive it.

SOPHIE HEADED INTO THE OFFICE. She had spent most of the morning dealing with her personal business, and it was past time she dug into the computers that Leede and Raveaux had left for her in their makeshift lab.

Sitting down in the dim basement in front of the next computer she needed to dig through was a relief to Sophie's frayed emotions. Once she was "wired in" to her classical music and the threads of the keywords she was searching using the DAVID program, her conscious mind seemed to turn off. She was pure logic: sorting, noting, following, manipulating—her brain pinging with messages of irregularities among numbers and traces.

No messy emotion marred her focus.

She was getting closer to finding someone who had activated an auto deduction system from the bank account of Kama'aina Schools' main budget, and found a way to hide small withdrawals under a variety of expense accounts.

Maybe she could identify all the categories that the deductions were occurring under, but it would be more efficient to pass that piece of it to Leede. Sophie punted those threads into a subcache for the other investigator.

Sophie needed to track where the money was going. Once they found that link, hopefully, they could trace it to whomever was accessing that account. Sophie hunched forward, her fingers flying as she hacked the bank's central server, her soul relieved to flee matters of the heart.

CHAPTER THIRTY-THREE

Raveaux
Day 7

THE NEXT MORNING, Raveaux sat in the consultation chair in front of Heri Leede's desk, one ankle cocked over his knee. He slid one of Gita's old bookmarks between the pages of his Jack Reacher paperback, as his new investigative partner walked into her office.

"I see you're making yourself right at home." Leede went behind her desk and sat down.

Raveaux tucked the book inside his jacket pocket. "I was five minutes early. I let myself in. I hope that's all right."

"Shows that you know your way around a pair of lockpicks, and that I need a little more security around here." Leede was annoyed, but trying not to show it.

"I apologize. You have nothing to worry about from me," Raveaux said gently. "I will wait in the hall next time."

Leede took off her ridiculous little plaid pork pie hat and tossed it, with perfect aim, onto the hook of a freestanding coatrack. "It's fine. I'll have a key made for you."

"That's not necessary."

"But maybe I want you to have a key." Leede leaned back in her chair. She spun back and forth, eyeing him. "Sophie rang me while I was on the way over. She has a couple of leads for us to follow up on. The first is the name of the bank, and the account number, where the deposits are being skimmed into. She is really very good at what she does." Leede flicked on her computer. Weary shadows that even her rhinestone-edged glasses could not conceal, showed under her bright blue eyes in the monitor's glare.

"Did my dinner not agree with you?" Raveaux asked. "Did you sleep badly?"

Leede took off the glasses and rubbed her eyes. "Just shoot me now, if I can't stay up for a few hours past my bedtime drinking wine with a handsome man. Besides, I had a whole day to recover."

"I enjoyed it," Raveaux surprised himself by saying. "You're good company."

"And your cooking was superb. I'm sure Sophie thought so too, even though she left early." Leede formed a little pyramid with the tips of her fingers and stared at him over them. "Are you interested in Sophie? Am I wasting my time flirting with you?"

Raveaux froze—he wasn't prepared for her to be so direct. "I don't know what you mean."

Leede flung her hands up with a snort. "I'm not blind. Sophie is beautiful and years younger than you, while I am nine years older. I'm not an idiot."

"Age has nothing to do with it," Raveaux said stiffly. "I have a professional respect for both of you."

"I wouldn't bother with you, or this conversation, if I didn't really like you, Pierre." Leede cocked her head in that birdlike way she had. "Have you thought this thing with Sophie through? I don't know if you have a chance with her. She has a lot of baggage, and will, very soon, have even more."

"If you're asking if I'm interested in dating *anybody,* the answer is no. It has been 'no' since my wife died," Raveaux said. "Sophie is . . . preoccupied, with a lot on her mind and grief on her heart. She is also pregnant, and that will take most of her attention in the coming year or two. She is not in a position to be interested in a relationship, nor would I presume that she would want one with me. But yes, I am attracted to her."

Leede seemed undaunted by his frosty manner. "It's been more than five years, Pierre. More than that for me, too. We're both in need of companionship. That's all I am proposing. It would be nice to spend time with someone interesting. Perhaps take in a concert, or an art show, or whatever Honolulu has to offer in the way of cultural activities." She arched a brow. "Maybe even a little fooling around, should we both be so inclined."

Raveaux felt the tickle at the side of his mouth—he was tempted to smile. Until now, Sophie was the only one who'd caused that effect, but Heri Leede was smart, surprising—and *fun.*

"Well," Leede leaned over the desk. "I can hardly compete with someone like Sophie, nor would I try to. Companionship is all I'm offering. Perhaps the Bishop Museum? On a day and time of our mutual choosing?"

"Yes, that I can do," Raveaux said. "I have yet to explore the museum. Sophie has mentioned it several times as a cultural treasure trove."

"Good. Now back to the case. Why don't you make us a pot of tea? I will call this bank in the Caymans, and see if I can get them to give us the name on the account." Leede slid her glasses on and reached for the phone.

Raveaux stood, smoothing his trousers, and headed for her beverage station on the credenza. "Good luck. They're highly unlikely to respond to anything but a court order, or perhaps a probe by the FBI."

Leede twinkled up at him. "That, too, can be arranged."

RAVEAUX FOLLOWED Leede into the student computer lab at Kama`aina Schools.

The room was large and toned in the mid-gray that was so prevalent in computer labs the world over, the air lowered to a comfortable temperature. New computers ranged the walls, and a central island was also equipped with several networked computers that clearly could be engaged in the same activity. One or two students occupied the stations. An adult monitoring the room got up and advanced toward them. "Can I help you?"

Leede held up her identification, as did Raveaux. "At the request of your headmaster, we are investigating a matter of a confidential information breach. We need to check these computers for unauthorized activity."

The woman's eyes widened. "I will have to verify that with our head of security."

"Please do," Leede said. She had changed her outfit before coming to the school campus, putting on one of those bright little suits and pinning up her white hair. The youth he associated with her had effectively vanished.

She had such a useful ability to project a different persona. Raveaux could see its utility, too, as the lab monitor scurried behind her desk to make some calls.

Raveaux advanced to the central computer station and sat down. Of the two of them, he had just enough background in forensic computer recovery to look at the recent search history log-ins, even if they had been deleted. Sophie might have been a better choice for this task, but she was hip-deep in computers already.

The unit at the central station was password protected. He and Leede waited patiently as the woman verified their identities and mission. "Our head of security has given me the go ahead to cooperate with your investigation. Here are the log-in codes to the computers." She paused, frowning. "Is this about porn?"

Leede waved a hand reassuringly. "That's probably what you

deal with most with these students, but this is a different matter. Administrative in nature."

The woman looked doubtful but returned to her desk.

Leede handed Raveaux one of the slips of paper. "You take this half of the units, and I'll take that. Let's meet at the entrance when we're done. Pull out and save anything that looks like it could have been used by, or left a trace of, our embezzler."

"*Mais oui, madame.*"

Leede smiled. "I like a man who knows how to say yes."

THEY MET at the front entrance after working their way through the different computers in the lab. As they walked back out to Leede's gigantic Cadillac, Raveaux held up a flash drive. "I was able to identify a computer the embezzler is using. My guess is that our perpetrator is working out of the student computer lab in order to add an additional layer of confusion and security to whatever VPN he or she is using."

"Good. I didn't find anything. Now we have a lead to give to the school's security team. After we get the air conditioning on in the car, I'll use my phone for a few minutes to pass this intel along to them."

Leede had parked the car in the overhanging shade of a monkeypod tree, but the day was warm. High cirrus clouds hardly cut the bright sunshine beaming down on the parking lot surrounded by decorative palms. Leede got in, settled herself, and turned the car on. She engaged the air conditioner, which gushed hot air over the scorching leather seats as Raveaux settled into the passenger side. After a few moments, the interior began to cool.

Raveaux removed his paperback, reclining his seatback, as Leede called the president of the board and gave him a quick report of progress on the case so far. She advised him to put a hidden security camera into the student lounge as soon as possible and to watch for anyone using their target computer. "That will give us a concrete way to trap the hacker."

Raveaux ignored their back-and-forth, tuning it out.

Sometimes Raveaux longed for the footloose, attachment-free life Jack Reacher lived—nothing in his pockets but his hands and a toothbrush. What freedom.

But he was almost there now, with his few belongings and his rented apartment. He could still get everything he owned into two suitcases, just as he'd done when he arrived in Hawaii. Was it time for a change? He stared at the print on the page, considering.

He didn't have to know right now. The right direction would reveal itself.

Leede ended the call and glanced at Raveaux. "The president seemed . . . troubled that we had made such rapid progress."

"Perhaps he's involved, or he was in denial that the embezzler was even a real threat," Raveaux said. "Either could be true."

"We're done early for the day. Want to take that trip to the Bishop now? The building's probably air-conditioned."

Raveaux closed his book. "Sounds like a great way to spend the afternoon."

Leede's smile made her almost beautiful. "*Mais oui, monsieur.*"

CHAPTER THIRTY-FOUR

Marcella

MARCELLA HAD JUST SETTLED into the chair on her back deck, her feet up on the footstool, evening glass of Chardonnay in hand, when her phone rang. She glanced down at it in irritation, but her eyebrows lifted as she saw the name: *Pierre Raveaux*.

"Aloha, Monsieur Raveaux! To what do I owe the surprise of this phone call?"

"I'm sorry to bother you at home, Agent Scott—or, if I may, Marcella. Sophie talks of you so often that I feel like I know you." Raveaux's voice was dark chocolate: something to be savored and enjoyed.

"That feeling is mutual. I assume that this is a business call?"

"*Mais oui.* Sophie, an investigator named Heri Leede, and I are all working a private case. An audit for a large prestigious private school." He sighed out a breath. "It appears, unfortunately, that a sizable amount of money is going missing into an offshore account. The bank, in the Cayman Islands, refuses to give us the name on the account. Is there a way you can procure that name for us? When we bring the embezzler to light, you can get credit for the capture."

Marcella smiled. "If it were that easy on my end, I'd say 'no problem,' but I do have to take this to my bureau chief, Special Agent in Charge Ben Waxman. A case must be opened."

"Ah, I see."

Marcella sipped her wine. "Sophie should abstain from coming into the FBI offices due to her current situation with an investigation. If you and Ms. Leede could meet me at the FBI offices tomorrow morning and present the particulars of the case to SAC Waxman, I feel confident we will be able to get the name for you eventually." Marcella paused for a beat, her eyes drifting over the mature plumeria tree in her backyard, dropping a few spent blossoms onto a shaggy lawn that neither she nor Marcus ever seemed to have time to mow. "Are you aware how seldom the names on these accounts actually trace back to anything? The reason the offshore banks do so well is that they ask so very little in the way of identification or even business documents when shady operators open accounts with them."

"We're aware. But if we had some idea who owned the account, we could monitor it more effectively. This will be one more thread we can hopefully use to flush out the embezzler."

"And, if you can show us the trail that ends with this account being illegal, we could freeze it with a court order and keep the funds from being siphoned off. Recover your money, in other words," Marcella said. "That's another way you could flush your prey."

"This has been very helpful. Thank you so much. I will inform Ms. Leede; we have to consult our client first, but hopefully they'll want to move forward with pressing charges."

A short silence went by. "How is Sophie doing? You work with her on a day to day basis. How is she holding up?" Marcella asked.

Raveaux's voice grew chilly. "I thought you were her best friend. Why are you asking me?"

Marcella frowned. "I'm asking you as someone who sees her from another direction. Really. How's she doing?"

"She is well. Using work as an escape, as I suspect she always has," Raveaux said. "She has also asked me to be a godfather for her children. I am honored, and agreed to the role."

Marcella sat up straighter. "That's surprising! She must trust you very much. There's no one she loves more than Momi, and of course, the new baby on the way."

"Sophie said she wanted the children to have male role models," Raveaux said haltingly—he clearly felt awkward. "I am a new friend, but she knows I care for children. I . . . miss my daughter very much."

Marcella shut her eyes on an unwelcome vision of the car bomb that had taken his wife and daughter's lives. "A generous thing for her," Marcella said. "But a win-win for both of you. Of course, Marcus and I will be around as much as we can, as well, but heavy workloads are a curse as an investigator."

"I learned from losing my family that time is the one thing that can never be recovered. Treasure what you have with your husband. Never let work get in the way." Raveaux ended the call abruptly.

Marcella lowered the phone, staring at it. He'd said that last bit with the kind of conviction that came from the heart.

She liked Pierre Raveaux very much.

MARCELLA BOPPED AROUND, headphones on, to eighties rock as she stirred the simple marinara that she'd made. Crushed farmers' market tomatoes, basil from a potted plant out back, a chopped clove of garlic, and a few homemade black olives. People always overdid the ingredients for a good marinara, when just the right fresh ingredients made all the difference.

A hand on her shoulder made her jump, spinning to defend herself, wooden spoon upraised—but it was only Marcus, his brown eyes sparkling, his big shoulders up by his ears as he laughed.

Marcella dropped the headphones down around her neck, threw the spoon in the sink, and launched herself at him.

She was a good-sized woman with a curvy figure at five foot seven, but Honolulu Police Department Detective Sergeant Marcus Kamuela was up for the task. He caught Marcella in his arms, hefted her up so her legs encircled his waist, and kissed her soundly as he walked over to the counter and set her butt on it, leaning into the space between her legs to nibble her neck.

"Yummy," he said. "You smell like basil and garlic."

"Key ingredients in a good sauce." Marcella lifted up the headphones, and put them on him. "I dare you not to dance to this song."

Marcus's eyes widened. He let go of Marcella and backed away, his face blooming into a grin. He held his thumb up like it was a mic, and began a falsetto impression of Madonna's *Like a Virgin,* gyrating his hips, spinning and stomping around the kitchen.

Marcella burst into laughter. "You still got it, baby," she said, sliding off the counter to grab his hands. "Show me some moves." With a touch of her finger, she rerouted the music to play from her phone through the living room speaker. Soon both of them were lip-syncing as Marcus twirled her around and pulled her in close.

"It's been too long since we went dancing." Marcus said, when the song was over. "Remember how we met?"

Marcella rubbed herself along his body, bending into a shape that fit his perfectly. "How could I forget? Not everyone meets dancing in masks at a sex club."

"Too bad it's not the kind of story we can tell at family gatherings," Marcus said into her ear.

His voice raised the hairs along the back of her neck. "I like it being our private story." They kissed until Marcella smelled the distinctive scent of browning tomato sauce.

She shoved him away and smacked him on the shoulder. "Go take a shower. Dinner will be ready by the time you come out. We'll eat outside on the deck tonight."

Marcus blew her a kiss as he walked out of the kitchen. Stirring the sauce, Marcella enjoyed the sight of him walking away. God had truly broken the mold when Marcus Kamuela was made, and he was all hers.

Would she have felt the sweetness of this encounter with her husband as deeply if Raveaux hadn't said what he did?

Probably not, and she was grateful.

CHAPTER THIRTY-FIVE

Raveaux
Day 8

RAVEAUX HANDED Beverly Cho her skinny vanilla latte. "For you, madame."

He seated himself across from her at the small table in the coffee shop.

"Thanks so much for meeting me. It's a pleasure to see you." Cho fluttered her lashes.

"And you as well. You are looking especially fine today." Cho *was* looking good. She'd styled her shoulder-length hair, and she wore a slim-fitting cotton dress instead of the floppy burlap number he had seen her in last time.

She smiled at him. "I could say the same for you, Monsieur."

Raveaux glanced down at the blue linen long-sleeved shirt he wore tucked into black dress slacks. "*Merci.* Now, you said you had something to discuss with me."

Cho sipped, and fiddled with her coffee cup. "I do, but . . . do you like music?"

Raveaux arched a brow. "Who doesn't like music?"

She laughed. "I have a favorite artist who plays folk music from all over the world, but only on ukulele. I thought you might enjoy it. The concert's next Tuesday, if you'd care to come with me."

Raveaux's brow stayed arched. "Are you asking me on a date?"

"I suppose I am."

"I feel I should tell you that I'm a widower. I haven't dated since my wife died. I'm not looking for a relationship," Raveaux said.

Cho nodded vigorously. The curled parts of her hair flopped up and down like wings. "Oh, of course! This is just a friendly outing to hear a good musician."

"Then I accept," Raveaux said. "Now back to the case . . ."

"Yes." Cho removed the lid and sipped her coffee. "One of the accountants who works on the Kama`aina Schools' account is behaving oddly. She . . . well, I don't know how to describe it. She turns in all her reports, and they look fine, but she won't meet my eye whenever we talk about the account. I think there's something odd about how she's acting, and it has something to do with the Schools. I just wanted to alert you to that."

Raveaux reached across the table, and briefly covered her hand with his. "I appreciate that very much. I will pass this along to my team." He finished his espresso in a quick gulp and stood up. "I'm so sorry. I must depart. I told you I had a meeting, and it's actually about the case. I was headed into the office when I got your text."

Cho smiled. "I take no offense. Thank you for the coffee, and I look forward to the concert on Tuesday."

Raveaux gave a slight bow. "And I as well, madame."

He walked out of the coffee shop, conscious of her eyes on him.

Hopefully, this "date" wouldn't turn into something difficult to disentangle himself from. Raveaux summoned a rideshare and gave the address for Sophie's downtown Security Solutions building.

※

RAVEAUX, Sophie, and Heri Leede gathered at the round table in Sophie's office. Sophie seemed well-rested, and Raveaux felt relieved, seeing her clear eyes and ready smile.

"I think I might have something new on the case," Raveaux said. "And we have an issue to bring up that we need clarity around."

Sophie glanced between the two of them. "What is that?"

Raveaux inclined his head toward Leede. She was in her youthful guise today, snowy hair loose over her shoulders, wearing an exercise top and matching yoga pants. She tapped her leather messenger bag. "Raveaux and I contacted your friend Marcella Scott yesterday. She wants us to come in and present the case to her SAC, Ben Waxman. She thinks she can get us the warrant that will get us the name on the bank account in the Caymans, but not without opening a formal FBI case. I'm not at all sure Kama`aina Schools wants to go in that direction."

Sophie frowned. "That is a dilemma. But I'm sure you've already considered that the name on the account may not be that illuminating. It's probably an alias, anyway."

"In light of that, I think we need to reach Rex Gibson, President of the Board, and ask him how they want to proceed, and whether or not they want to press formal charges when the perpetrator is found. I have arranged a video call. This could be our opportunity to update him on our progress," Leede said.

Sophie gestured to the large monitor on her desk. "What do you want to use to tune him in? Gibson may have other members of his team he wants included."

"Let's set up your monitor on the table, so we can see them, and they can see us."

A few minutes later, Sophie had done so, and they connected with the President of the Schools' Board. Rex Gibson looked as skeletally thin and monk-like as he had when Raveaux met him in person. Behind him stood the scowling visage of the Headmaster, Dr. Ka`ula. Cho had been left out of this meeting.

"We are eager for an update," Gibson said.

"And we have one for you." Leede proceeded to fill the two men in on what they had been able to discern so far. "We are waiting on any news from the security that is deployed to watch the computers in the student lounge. We speculate that the perpetrator is a staff member who is using one of the terminals there in order to obscure their IP address, although, of course, they're already using a VPN. We are also going to investigate someone within the Peerless Accounting office a little more closely. Ms. Smithson, why don't you fill them in on what you've discovered on the computers."

Sophie cleared her throat. "I have been digging through the mirror image hard drives of the accountants working on the Kama`aina Schools' bookkeeping. You will be pleased to know that so far, I've found nothing on any of the computers associated with the board members, or either of yours." Gibson nodded, relief and annoyance evident in his attitude, while Ka`ula rolled his eyes and gave a head shake.

"I was glad to get my computer back," Ka`ula said. "Can't do my job without it."

Sophie inclined her head, "I do understand the inconvenience. My plan today is to go to Peerless Accounting in the guise of a computer work tech, and visit this person Ms. Cho has expressed concern about. I'll plant spyware on her computer, and have the rig cast directly to my own so that I can track what our target is doing as it happens." Sophie took a sip of water and went on. "There are ways that people can clear their cache and make sure that their computer appears to be clean, and if she is activating any of the routing that has led to us being aware of how the money is being skimmed, I should be able to perceive it in real time."

"Excellent," Gibson said. "What else do you need from us?"

Leede leaned forward, making a pyramid with her fingertips. "We'd like to know how you want to proceed with prosecuting the embezzler. We have an offer from the FBI to get us a warrant to identify the owner of the Caymans bank account where the money is being skimmed to. From our end, this is not entirely necessary or useful in solving the case, because many times these accounts are listed under aliases or shell corporations. It also requires our going to the FBI, and presenting the case to them in order to get the warrant. That opens a whole Pandora's box: law enforcement involvement. I encourage you to discuss with the rest of the board whether you want us to move in that direction."

Gibson's eyebrows had risen at the same time as Ka'ula's lowered. The two men looked like opposite comedy masks, but both of their expressions showed distaste. "We will have to get back to you on that." Gibson said. "Do not proceed without talking to us, first."

"Certainly. We will wait to hear from you. Was there anything else you want to know from our end?" Leede cocked her head, an inquisitive sparrow.

"No," Gibson said. "Send your bill for this week to my inbox directly." He ended the call with a push of a button.

"Well, I guess I better get into my computer tech disguise," Sophie said. "I'm actually looking forward to getting into that coverall. It has a nice loose waistline."

Leede patted her hand. "You look blooming, young lady."

Sophie smiled. "You're lovely to say so." She stood up. "And if you two could work on the computers in the basement while I'm gone, I'd appreciate it."

Leede pointed to Raveaux. "He's all you get. I still have ledgers to cross-check." She stood and picked up her leather bag. "Off to the salt mines."

Raveaux stayed where he was. Sophie went behind her desk and bent to take a zippered carryall out of a cabinet. "You have a question, Pierre?"

"Did you speak to your father about his involvement with the multiagency task force?" Raveaux had been wondering how that went.

"It was unpleasant, but we worked it out." Sophie did not seem inclined to elaborate. She had unzipped the bag and was checking the equipment inside. "If you don't mind, I have work to do, and so do you."

He had been dismissed.

CHAPTER THIRTY-SIX

Sophie

SOPHIE PICKED up her zippered work tote and made sure her name tag was pinned onto her cotton work coverall. She pulled on a Security Solutions ball cap. Sophie was targeting Jana Kanekoa, the accountant whom Cho had shared concerns about, adding the hardware to the woman's computer that would cast to Sophie's for monitoring. She did not plan to lie about what she was doing; she would be introduced by Beverly Cho as a technician putting in a security upgrade.

Sophie appropriated a Security Solutions van and drove the relatively short distance through busy Honolulu traffic to the Peerless Accounting building. She punched the parking garage code that she had been given into the turnstile gate and parked in the cool downstairs garage.

Sophie hadn't been kidding that she liked the looseness of the coverall. She still wore a pair of running shorts and a spaghetti strap top underneath it, but her midsection was sensitive to any sort of binding, even at the early stage of this pregnancy. Experience had taught her it was better to go with everything her body was telling her than to fight it.

Sophie exited the van and took the stairs to the fourth floor, all of her senses alert as she pushed open the office's door. The Peerless floor was set up like many a workspace: a sound-deadening, short nap carpet in wear-concealing oatmeal covered the floors, and three-quarter height cubicles boxed the room into separate work areas.

Sophie walked confidently through the cubicles, heading for Beverly Cho's office. The woman's name was marked clearly on the door. She knocked, looking around for a receptionist, but there was none visible.

The door opened. Cho stood in the doorway wearing a flax dress that looked like it had been cut out on the floor of someone's barn, and a pair of Birkenstocks. Sophie blinked: she wasn't used to seeing that kind of outfit on an accounting executive. She extended a hand. "Sophie Smithson with Security Solutions. Pleased to meet you."

"Beverly Cho." They shook, and Cho held the door open and stepped aside. "Come in."

Sophie stepped inside, and Cho went on. "I'm glad to have you here so quickly. I think it's better if you install the software on all of the computers, so Jana isn't singled out."

"I agree. I came equipped for that." Sophie walked into a spacious work area, tastefully decorated with a theme of wood and fiber arts. "I see you are an aficionado of the natural look."

"Oh yes," Cho said. "Actually, I create this work in my spare time." She gestured to a woven wall hanging, and a low table made from a wood burl. "These are from my own workshop."

Sophie's estimation of the woman went up a notch. "I admire someone who can create things with their hands. I mostly work with computers."

Cho smiled. "I can manipulate numbers, but I'm not a programmer, and I admire that skill too. Jana Kanekoa, whose computer I'd like you to monitor, is the mother of a talented young man, a student at Kama`aina Schools. Jana says he's a computer genius."

Sophie's internal antennae went up. *Whoever had figured out how to skim the money from the Kama`aina accounts knew how to code.* Could the embezzler be a student? Or maybe it was a pair: the son working with his mother to steal from the schools.

"Why don't you start me on a different computer than the target one, and I'll work my way to her cubicle." Sophie held up her zippered bag. "I brought plastic nodes to plant. Most of them are dummies, but I will put a live one on Kanekoa's computer."

"Perfect."

Cho led Sophie to the first of six cubicles, and indicated the target with her head as they walked past a black-haired woman industriously working on a spreadsheet. Once she'd explained that Sophie was here to install security software on their computers, Cho went back to her office.

Sophie introduced herself politely, sent the accountant for a coffee break, and installed the dummy node.

She worked her way to Kanekoa's cubicle, and smiled brightly in the doorway, holding up her kit. "Good morning. I'm Sophie Smithson with Security Solutions, and I'm here to add a security upgrade to your unit."

Jana Kanekoa stood up with a smile. She wore a tropical print aloha shirt down past her ample hips, and a pair of leggings with heeled shoes. Her long black hair was braided in a thick cable that nearly reached her waist. Sophie could easily imagine her dancing hula with that pretty hair swishing.

"Is this tech job something you went to college for?" Jana asked, surprising Sophie as she approached the computer.

"Not a bachelor's degree," Sophie said. "But I did take several certifications in programming and hardware tech."

"I'm asking everyone I meet who's in the computer business how they got where they are." Kanekoa seemed talkative as she took up a position at the back of the cubicle, watching Sophie.

Sophie felt sweat prickling under her arms as she knelt in front of the computer. Did this woman know something more than usual?

Would she detect the casting device Sophie was installing? "What is your interest?"

Kanekoa shrugged. "I'm raising a brilliant kid who's great with computers. I'm trying to present different pathways to him."

An unexpected opportunity! Sophie set aside her kit and turned to face Kanekoa, still on her knees in front of the computer's plug-in area. "Oh, I'm always interested in young people who have a talent for tech. Tell me about your son."

"Conrad is a real genius." Kanekoa's eyes gleamed with pride. "He got into Kama`aina Schools on a scholarship. He is so good with computers that they let him fix up the school's lab and update all the units with the latest software!"

"You must be so proud. Has he ever gotten in trouble with hacking into something he shouldn't have?" Sophie smiled in a conspiratorial way. "I certainly did when I was a teen."

Kanekoa flapped a hand dismissively. "Oh, no. He's a good boy. I'm a single mother. He would never endanger anything for us, since we live from paycheck to paycheck." She seemed to realize she was over-sharing, and clapped a hand over her mouth. "I'm sorry. I do go on and on. I've had too much coffee this morning!"

Sophie shook her head as she opened her computer kit. "No problem at all. Sometimes my job is quite lonely, so I always enjoy talking to people when I have a chance."

"Usually it's men doing this kind of work," Kanekoa observed. "What got you into the tech business?"

Sophie took out the casting device. She plugged it into one of the ports on the side of Kanekoa's unit. She had come up with an explanation that made sense in case any of the accountants asked her for more information. "You're going to have to restart the system to activate this security device. What it does is help keep other devices from trying to breach your unit. It's an exterior firewall."

Kanekoa nodded. "That makes sense. We handle a lot of sensitive information. Beverly is always concerned about making sure we have the highest security."

Sophie sat back on her heels. "As to your earlier question, I just always had an aptitude for—how do I say it . . . figuring things out. I like to find better ways to do things. And once I got my hands on a computer, it drew me into another world. A world where I felt comfortable, where I instinctively knew the language. I don't have a better way of explaining it."

Kanekoa gave a huge smile. "That's exactly what my boy Conrad says!"

She was so likable.

Kanekoa pulled out her chair and sat down. "This job was a godsend. I was just doing minor bookkeeping for a few stores, when I saw an ad for Peerless. Working here is a real career, and I found my way into it because I was good at numbers! But I want so much more for my son, and he deserves that." A shadow seemed to pass across her visage.

Sophie honed in on that. "Why?"

"Conrad had a rough start. My husband and I adopted him when he was three, and his biological parents had exposed him to a lot of neglect. We don't think he was actively abused, but he wasn't given the kind of affection a baby needs, and it affected him. And since my husband left, he's been really withdrawn." Kanekoa clapped her hand over her mouth again. "I can't believe I'm telling you my life story! I'm so sorry. Conrad says I have diarrhea of the mouth."

Kanekoa had one of those "glass faces" that Marcella had said were so easy to read; she was definitely hiding something, and it showed in her eyes, in her demeanor.

Sophie patted the woman's knee. "I'm so glad you told me all of this. It makes my day to have been able to make a genuine connection with someone."

"Oh, me too. Thanks for listening." Kanekoa gave Sophie a hug goodbye. "Don't work too hard, now."

Clearly, something was on this woman's mind, and she had chosen to confide in Sophie in a way that left her vulnerable. Whatever happened going forward with the case, Sophie was going to do her best to protect Jana Kanekoa and her son.

CHAPTER THIRTY-SEVEN

Raveaux
Day 9

THE NEXT DAY, Raveaux came in from his early morning lap swim in Waikiki Bay to find an urgent text on his phone from Leede. *"Get down to my office, Pierre! The security detail watching the target computer has nabbed a suspect at the school!"*

Raveaux grabbed his towel off the sand, turning for a brief look at the turquoise water that had felt so refreshing. He enjoyed the waving palms, the seabirds, the arc of beach peopled by only a few early morning walkers. He'd decided to start looking for a more permanent dwelling, somewhere that he could have a pet of some kind, but he would miss being right next to the ocean and being able to swim every day. Maybe he would get lucky and find an apartment near the water that allowed animals.

Raveaux hurried to his apartment, pausing to wash the sand off his feet before taking a shower inside. Under the fall of water, soaping up, he thought of Sophie.

Smooth tawny skin. Shapely legs. The curve of her breasts. Those mysterious tattoos down her thighs, along her arms. Droplets of water falling from her lips; the way her neck arched.

The fact that she was pregnant only made her more attractive to him—was that perverse? He didn't know, but it didn't matter. No one knew what went on in his own private mind. He was deeply satisfied with the progress they had made in friendship. He was so grateful for the gift she had offered him in having a role with her children.

All of that was enough for now. And in the meantime, he was only human if he enjoyed the attention of a few other women for casual activities.

He shaved, dressed, and summoned a rideshare to Leede's office.

Leede opened the door. "You're a sight for sore eyes, Pierre."

Leede's rhinestone glasses were in place, her white hair in a bun, and she wore one of those suits that made her look eighty. "I see Inspector Hermione Leede is in residence," he said. "That orange really becomes her."

"You're onto my wicked ways." Leede extended a tiny fist. "Open up, I have something for you."

Raveaux held out his hand, palm up. Leede opened hers, and dropped a key into it. "You no longer need to knock. Let yourself into my office anytime."

Raveaux's neck flushed. He wasn't sure what to say. "Thank you," he managed.

Leede took in his expression and tipped her head back to laugh. "Haha! I have rendered Monsieur Pierre Raveaux speechless. Excellent!" She scooped her messenger bag off the desk. "We're taking my car and heading for Kama'aina Schools. They have the suspect in custody."

Raveaux followed her brisk walk as they exited the building and climbed into the boat of a Cadillac. Raveaux belted himself in as Leede hoisted herself onto her booster seat, adjusted the mirrors, pedal support, and steering wheel to her satisfaction, and roared out of the parking garage, hardly looking to the left as she turned onto the busy avenue. Raveaux cringed as he heard a screech of tires, and shut his eyes for the drive to Kama`aina Schools.

Dr. Stuart Ka`ula wore the disconcerting scowl that appeared to be an essential part of his standard uniform. "Follow me."

He'd met them at the entrance to the main office, an area neither Raveaux nor Leede had seen before. They walked down an immaculate, dignified hallway lined with cultural artifacts installed on the walls: an antique Hawaiian canoe paddle, sections of preserved *kapa* cloth, even a framed, professionally mounted royal feather cape.

Ka`ula opened a heavy teak door at the end, ominously labeled Headmaster, and led them inside his office. A large, burly Hawaiian man in a school logo shirt with "Security" emblazoned upon it, stood with his arms crossed against one wall.

Ka`ula's desk was a monolith of native koa hardwood taking up one side of the room. A chair was parked in front of it where he doubtless met with errant employees and misbehaving students. Raveaux could see only the shiny black hair and narrow shoulders of a teenage boy as he entered—but his brows drew together. *The embezzler wasn't supposed to be a student!*

Ka`ula went around his desk and seated himself. "Help yourself to chairs and join us, please. Conrad, this is investigator Pierre Raveaux and investigator Hermione Leede. They have been conducting a private audit for our school."

Raveaux went to a stack of plastic chairs against the wall, and removed two of them, one for himself and one for Leede. Raveaux sat on one side of the boy, Leede on the other.

Ka`ula dismissed the security guard, and the man exited and closed the door.

Ka`ula removed a tech pad, and thumbed to an audio and video app. "The school needs a record of this interview for legal reasons," he said, and set the device in an adjustable display holder, pointed in such a direction that it captured Conrad's crossed arms and sullen face, along with Leede and Raveaux. Ka`ula rolled his office chair forward into the range of the video camera as well.

He stated the date, time, and location, looking into the little red dot of the camera. "This is the interview of Conrad Kanekoa, aged sixteen, a junior student at Kama`aina Schools. Members present include Ms. Hermione Leede, investigator, Monsieur Pierre Raveaux, investigator, and myself, Dr. Stuart Ka`ula, Headmaster for the school. This interview is being conducted to determine if Conrad may have been tampering with our school computer system." Now that the formalities had been stated, Ka`ula sat back, weaving his fingers together and setting them over his stomach. "Conrad was using the computer accessed by our tamperer. Let's begin with that."

As he took in the teen seated beside them, Raveaux mentally composed his future case notes. Conrad Kanekoa wore the standard black polo shirt with the school's emblem, Bermuda shorts, black socks and tennis shoes. The boy had his hair cut short in a style that must be school regulation, because it didn't seem to match the leather bracelet he wore on one wrist and a shark's tooth pendant on a cord around his neck. He kept his eyes down and his arms crossed on his chest. "I don't know what I did wrong."

Ka`ula spoke from across the desk. "We don't know what you did wrong, either. Why don't you tell us what you were doing on that computer lab unit?"

"I was just doing some searches for charities."

Raveaux felt that sensation that he sometimes got on an investigation: a sense of something coming into focus. He made a note on his phone: *charities as motive?*

Ka`ula continued with his interrogation. "We had that computer under surveillance. You were doing something that involved keystrokes that were more than just a search."

The boy looked up, and his brown eyes were wide with anger. "Don't I have any rights?"

Ka`ula smiled dourly. "No, you don't. Not on our school campus, or on our school computers. You were perfectly aware of what you were doing because you used a VPN and were using incognito mode."

Conrad lowered his gaze, and tightened his arms across his stomach. "I haven't done anything wrong," he said again.

Leede held up a hand. "You must be wondering what we're doing here."

Conrad slanted her a side-eye, but didn't reply.

Leede went on. "We're with a company called Security Solutions, and we have been investigating a problem in the Kama`aina Schools' bookkeeping. I am a forensic accountant and spent my career with Scotland Yard as an investigator." Spoken in her precise British accent, she sounded quite intriguing. "I wonder if you can help us."

Ka`ula drew his brows down, opening his mouth to object to Leede's openness approach, but Raveaux caught his eye and gave a slight negative shake of his head, indicating to let Leede continue.

Leede leaned forward. "Conrad. May I call you Conrad?" The boy nodded. "Conrad, I have been a forensic investigator for many years, and seldom have I encountered such a clever and effective way of siphoning money as what was developed to skim from the Kama`aina Schools' general account. Whoever designed this system was very skilled. Our entire team has been stumped for weeks trying to figure it out."

An exaggeration, but Raveaux could appreciate where she was going. He felt that twitch at his mouth again: Heri Leede definitely made him want to smile.

"I nevah know no'ting about dat," the boy tried to maintain his surly attitude, but Raveaux heard the slight inflection of pride underneath his pidgin English bluster.

"Well, now that I've shared what we're here about, I wonder if we could enlist your help?"

Conrad gave a slight nod, and Leede went on. "What we were able to determine was that this person used the very same unit that you did in the school computer lab. We were looking for an adult, someone who was on the board perhaps, maybe a teacher who got fired, someone who might have had a bone to pick with Kama'aina Schools. That's why we had the computer monitored for anyone who might be using it. Might you have any ideas on how we could capture this computer mastermind?" Leede slid her cat eye glasses down her nose and batted her pretty blue eyes at the boy. "Do you know anything about hacking?"

Conrad darted a look at Ka'ula behind his desk. "Maybe."

Raveaux thought quickly. "Dr. Ka'ula, I find myself in need of the men's room. Would you mind showing me the facilities?"

Ka'ula opened his mouth to object, but once again, Raveaux signaled him, and the headmaster got the message. "All right. We might as well grab a cup of coffee, too. Can we get you anything, Ms. Leede?" He bustled around the side of the desk.

"I'm fine, thank you," she said.

Raveaux stood as well. "Call me on my cell if the kid gives you any trouble," he told Leede gruffly. The two men exited the room and shut the door behind them.

Raveaux patted Ka'ula's shoulder once they were in the hall. "Ms. Leede could get a clam to open and give up its pearl. Don't you worry, she'll get the boy talking,"

Ka'ula's habitual frown remained. He turned to the security guard. "No one enters or leaves that room," he said.

"Yes, sir."

Ka'ula turned back to Raveaux. "Well?"

"I really would like that cup of coffee," he said.

Ka'ula led him to the staff lounge where a Keurig machine stood ready to brew a variety of pods.

The headmaster's stiff attitude seemed to wilt as he entered the breakroom and no other staff were there. He shut the door and leaned his forehead against it. "I can't believe it's a student," he said. "This is going to look very bad to the board. To the community."

Raveaux chose a French roast pod and inserted it into the

machine, positioning his mug beneath the spout and pushing down the handle. "I believe we will find that something is going on with this kid that made him siphon the money. We already had a tip that his mother was acting odd; maybe he has some motive that we don't yet understand. Quite frankly, should word get out, a student hacking your system and embezzling from the general fund is better for the school than someone on the board or a staff member."

Ka`ula stared out the window, and Raveaux joined him. The view was lovely: rolling lawns, a tidy tennis court, and an Olympic-size swimming pool filled with students playing water polo, surrounded by mature coconut palms. "You might be right. In a way, this could be a compliment to the school." His gloomy expression began to brighten as he considered how to spin the news. "We cater to the 'best and brightest' of Hawaiian children. This young man must be both."

"The situation will need to be kept as quiet as possible—from what I understand, that is what the board wants," Raveaux said. "Once we determine if the boy is the hacker, we plug the holes he's made, and you get your money back. The school leadership can discuss what, if anything, needs to be prosecuted—and thus, potentially become public knowledge."

"The student's folder is at my receptionist's desk," Ka`ula said. "As soon as we identified him in the lab, I had my secretary make a copy of it for you. You and your team can take the file back to study. If Leede hasn't been able to get him to talk, we can pull in some more pressure on his mother, and try that angle."

"Excellent plan." Both men doctored their fresh cups of coffee, and returned to the headmaster's office.

Leede and Conrad were leaning close, talking, when Ka`ula opened the heavy door. They straightened up, but appeared to have become friends. Leede straightened her bright orange jacket and pushed her glasses up her nose. "Conrad, here, has a grave injustice that he would like to see rectified."

CHAPTER THIRTY-EIGHT

Raveaux

RAVEAUX FIXED his gaze on the boy as Conrad leaned forward with a sudden burst of anger, setting his elbows on the desk in front of the headmaster. "I do have a grave injustice I would like to see rectified —the racist admissions policy of this school!"

Ka`ula's lowered brows shot up in surprise. "We are following the dictates of the Kama`aina Trust: that the Kama`aina Schools support the children of Hawaii."

"There have been many challenges to that wording." Conrad said. "And I, for one, think it's racist." He sat back, crossing his arms over his chest. Once again, his spine curved into the shape of a sullen teen.

Leede cleared her throat delicately. "I think that what Conrad is trying to say, is that he has . . ."

"I can hear with my own two ears what he has to say," Ka`ula retorted. "I fail to see how a kid's opinion on our school's policies has anything to do with the matter at hand."

Leede cocked her head in that birdlike way. "Conrad, perhaps you need to explain a little further to Dr. Ka`ula."

"Explain what?" Ka`ula growled, when the boy remained stubbornly mute.

This was going nowhere fast.

Raveaux addressed the young man before him. "Did you have anything to do with the bookkeeping problems that Kama`aina Schools has experienced?"

A sly smile curved the boy's mouth. "I plead the fifth on that."

"This office is not a court of law in which you get to plead the fifth on anything," Ka`ula said. He seemed to rein himself in with an effort. "Kama`aina Schools serves the best and brightest of Hawaii's children. You seem to be one of those, young man. Perhaps you would like to tell me more about why you feel that the school's policy is racist."

"Because the trust specifies the 'children of Hawaii' but it doesn't say children of Polynesian blood!"

"I fail to see why you are upset about that, when you're benefitting from that policy," Ka`ula replied.

The boy clammed up again.

Ka`ula threw his hands up in the air. "Maybe we should just let the FBI get involved after all."

Conrad's eyes flew wide, and Leede made a gesture with her hand. "Perhaps it's time to call the boy's parent. She might be able to shed some light on the matter."

"You are absolutely right." Ka`ula reached for his phone, pressed a button, and briskly directed his receptionist to contact Jana Kanekoa at her workplace.

Leede patted the boy's shoulder. "I'm sure your mother will be very concerned."

Conrad hunched forward, covering his face with his hands, clearly mortified at the prospect of his mother's arrival. Ka`ula looked to both Leede and Raveaux. "I think we can take it from here. Once the parent gets here, she can help us get to the bottom of this. If not, we'll call the police."

"Respectfully, I disagree with calling the authorities just yet,"

Raveaux said. "We would like to get to the bottom of it ourselves, without law enforcement involvement at the moment."

"But you are right, Doctor Ka`ula, that we need his mother present. He is a minor, and thus, unable to make his own decisions." Leede said it gently, but the effect on Conrad was electric.

"Bullshit!" The boy sat up suddenly, throwing open his arms in an expansive gesture. "Don't you dare say I can't make my own decisions. I could steal you blind, and you wouldn't even know it. You idiots have no idea what's been going on. You're never going to have any idea what happened to that money, or why I did it."

"Tell us more about that," Leede led him like a lamb to slaughter with her admiring smile. "I'd like to understand how a student as brilliant as you, did what you did, and why."

Conrad flexed his skinny arms. "I can't explain that part to you, I'm sure it's too technical for you to follow," he said patronizingly. "But I did it because this school is racist. That money was going to places where it could make a difference for kids who weren't going to have the kind of opportunity I did, coming here."

"Thank you for your confession, Mr. Kanekoa," Ka`ula said. "This is all being recorded, which you were informed of at the beginning of our interview."

The color drained from Conrad's face as he realized he had been baited. "I'd like a lawyer now."

"Again, this is not a court or a police matter at this point," Ka`ula said. "You have no rights in this office. But we do need all the information so that we can make an informed decision about consequences for the crime that you've committed. You might as well tell us everything."

Just then, the door banged open. "Tell us what?" A tall, plump woman wearing a tropical print shirt and leggings with a pair of high heels strode into the room. Mrs. Kanekoa put her hands on her hips, and she was an intimidating sight as she glared at the headmaster. "How dare you interview my son without my presence. He's a minor!"

"You were called as soon as was appropriate, Mrs. Kanekoa." Ka'ula bit down on his lower lip, clearly needing a moment to deal with his irritation.

Leede stood up. She extended a hand toward Jana Kanekoa. "I'd like to introduce myself. My name is Hermione Leede, and I'm a private investigator. This is my associate, Pierre Raveaux, with Security Solutions." Raveaux waved from where he was seated—one more adult outnumbering her child would only provoke the woman's protective parental instincts.

Leede went on. "We have been retained by Kama'aina Schools to investigate a situation of missing funds embezzled through an ingenious computer programming scheme. Your son has admitted that he is involved in this crime."

Kanekoa swiveled to stare at the boy. "Conrad! I taught you better than that!" Conrad lowered his gaze, but his mouth was set mulishly.

The headmaster stood up. "Mrs. Kanekoa, let me get you a chair."

Raveaux stood up and gestured for the woman to take his. "Please. Have a seat, madame."

Kanekoa sat down beside her son. "Why wasn't I called immediately?"

"You were called as soon as we realized the seriousness of Conrad's involvement," Dr. Ka'ula said. "I must remind you that this is a private school and a private matter, not yet a police investigation. But it could become that, if we don't know and understand everything that Conrad has been up to. Also, we are recording this interview for our records."

Raveaux went over to the stack of chairs and quietly removed another one. He seated himself in the corner, out of the view of the video camera and the drama taking place in front of the desk. Mrs. Kanekoa shouldn't feel like she was so outnumbered that it prompted her to remove the boy. Should she attempt to do so, they would be unable to do anything but call the police, and he could tell that Leede was hoping that they could still resolve the whole thing right here, right now.

Leede opened her mouth and said just that. "We have identified the money trail, and it ends at a private account in the Cayman Islands. We have had the FBI offer to provide us information about the owner of that account. But, for that to happen, we need to open a formal FBI case. So far, Dr. Ka`ula and the Board of Kama`aina Schools would like to handle this matter privately. Conrad, if you will give us a full confession, and return the money that you stole, I'm sure that would go a long way to assuaging the concern that the school has about this security breach."

Conrad licked his lips. Slowly, deliberately, he turned to face Ka`ula behind his massive desk. "Screw you," the boy said, and flipped the headmaster the bird.

Mrs. Kanekoa reacted in rage; she grabbed Conrad's arm and yanked him up from his chair. "We'll be in touch with you when my son has come to his right mind," she said through gritted teeth. "Please hold off on calling the police or the FBI until I can talk some sense into him. You have my word that I'll get him to tell you what you need to know and give the money back."

The boy still refused to get up, so his mother grabbed him by the ear. Conrad yelped as she pulled him out of the chair, and marched him out of the room, all the way out through the door.

Ka`ula turned to the video recording the entire thing. "This concludes our interview with Conrad Kanekoa and his mother, Jana," he said, and pressed off.

The three of them stared at each other for a moment. Ka`ula dropped his face into his hands and made a moaning noise. "This is a nightmare."

Leede stood up. "I disagree. As I'm sure Monsieur Raveaux told you, it's much better from a PR standpoint, to have it be a brilliant student rip off the school than one of the adults on your staff. The boy is also doing something with the money that sends it to charities. There's a story here—we just need to understand what it is."

"Ms. Leede is correct," Raveaux said. "Let's give them a day or so."

"Yes. And before you come down too hard on him, or get the police involved, let my partner and me go out to their house and see what we can get him to tell us voluntarily. In the meantime, you can notify the board of the progress we've made. I'm sure that will go a long way to establishing a positive outcome." Leede smiled, and came around the desk to pat the man's shoulder comfortingly. "We know our way out."

CHAPTER THIRTY-NINE

Sophie

SOPHIE'S PHONE rang as she was waking up from a quick nap in her office. "We've had a break in the case," Raveaux's accented voice was tight with excitement. "Come and meet us at the Kanekoa residence." He rattled off the address.

Sophie grimaced. "I'm so sorry! I was supposed to get back to you and Heri about my impressions of the Kanekoa woman yesterday, and what I was able to gather from her. I think she's hiding something."

"Her son basically confessed to being the embezzler," Raveaux said. "What we don't know is why he did it, and exactly what he's doing with the money."

Sophie felt a surge of compassion for Jana Kanekoa. "Don't do anything with the interview until I get there. I've forged a good connection with the mother. It could help us."

"That's fine, but I'm still concerned about too many of us being in the room and intimidating them."

Leede piped up in the background, "I'm sorry, Sophie, you're on speaker and we're driving over to the Kanekoa residence right now. I think, if you had a good connection with the mother, that you should come and take the lead. You're a fresh face after the debacle in the headmaster's office. You also have the expertise to pry out of the boy how he did what he did from a tech standpoint. You are going to have to fix all of that and close off those holes for the school, anyway."

Sophie felt a prickle of annoyance. "Fixing their computer leaks was not part of our contract. But I *am* concerned for Jana Kanekoa, and I would like to be present."

"I guess that leaves me the odd man out," Raveaux said. "I'll wait in the car and listen in if you have any surveillance devices handy. If things degenerate, I can support by lending muscle to the situation."

"I'm always in favor of your lending any sort of muscle that you want to show," Leede said.

Sophie felt that flare of annoyance again. *She was tired of Leede's heavy-handed flirtation with Raveaux.* "I'm on my way," she said shortly, and ended the call.

Sophie grabbed her backpack of tech tools that doubled as a purse, and headed out. Soon she was in her pearl-colored Lexus SUV, using the GPS to navigate to a small apartment building in a seedier part of Honolulu. Sun-blasted, open stairs on the exterior of the building, a line of washing flapping in the breeze, and a barking dog tied on the scrap of lawn outside, all spoke to the financial state of the family.

Sophie took the battered aluminum stairs to the third floor and knocked on the door.

Jana Kanekoa opened the door. Her mouth fell open almost comically as she met Sophie's eyes. "It's you. The computer tech lady."

"Yes. I'm Sophie Smithson, with Security Solutions, in case you forgot my name," Sophie said gently. "I'm so sorry this has happened with Conrad. Let me help you through it, and hopefully we won't have to get law enforcement involved."

Mrs. Kanekoa held herself stiffly for just a moment, and then she seemed to sag into Sophie's arms in a surprising hug. "Conrad's a good boy," she said wetly. "I can't believe he did this."

"What you can do is help him open up to us," Sophie said. "We will work closely with you to persuade the Kama'aina School Board to handle this privately."

Sophie heard the clatter of heels on the aluminum stairs, and Heri Leede appeared, bright as a tangerine in an orange suit. "Mrs. Kanekoa. I'm so sorry that we are imposing upon you again, but the headmaster gave approval for Sophie and me to talk with you both, and see if Conrad will tell us the particulars of where the money went, at least. I'm sure it will go a long way in helping the school figure out some appropriate consequences and how they want to handle the matter."

"You can't get the money back," yelled Conrad from inside the apartment. "It's already gone."

"Hush your mouth," Mrs. Kanekoa hollered back. "Disrespectful boy!"

Sophie brushed past the woman to step inside the apartment with Leede behind her.

The shades were down, casting shadow over a living room filled with overstuffed, secondhand furniture; the room was tidy, but cramped. A kitchenette ran along one side of the living area, and two bedrooms opened off a short hallway with a bathroom at the end. The cupboards were scuffed Formica, and a sliding glass door behind the blinds showed a small balcony. A window air conditioner wheezed in the corner, dripping moisture into an old coffee can. "May we sit down, Mrs. Kanekoa?"

She made an impatient gesture toward the couch. "Conrad!" she bellowed. "Get out here."

Her son emerged from one of the bedrooms and came to sit in the puffy-looking lounger. The boy crossed his arms over his chest and his chin lowered belligerently. His eyes were a dark sparkle under lowered black brows. "Who are you?"

"Hello, Conrad. My name is Sophie Smithson, and I am a computer expert."

One corner of the boy's mouth twitched in contempt. He rolled his eyes. "Expert, huh. Really."

"I brought along my laptop." Sophie unzipped her bag. "I can log in remotely to your mother's rig at work, and any of the computers in the student lounge at the school from right here. We can screenshare, and you can show me how you pulled off that skim. I've already tracked your pathway, but I wouldn't mind having you explain it."

The boy unwound his arms and sat forward. "You're bullshitting me. You can't possibly know."

"I am not bullshitting you." Sophie opened her small laptop and activated it with a button. The machine woke up. Her fingers moved in a blur of motion over the keys as she activated her remote access to the different computers. "We'll be on in a moment."

Leede seated herself beside Sophie on the couch. "Good to see you again, Conrad. The headmaster has asked us to interview you. What you say and do with us is going to have a big effect on how the school decides to handle the situation."

"If by 'situation' you mean the boy's hacking and embezzling, I think the time has come to call it what it is," Sophie said. "Perhaps you'd like to start by telling us why you did this, Conrad. Otherwise, people will assume it was just because you wanted the money."

Jana Kanekoa seemed too restless to sit down. She headed for the kitchenette. "Can I get you ladies something to drink?"

Leede, ever socially appropriate, nodded. "Please. Monsieur Raveaux is waiting for us in the car, so we hope this won't take much of your time. But, like we said, if Conrad will talk to us and give us a way to recover the money, I feel certain we can persuade the administration not to press charges."

Mrs. Kanekoa poured four tall glasses of pale yellow liquid from a plastic pitcher and added some ice. "This is passion fruit juice. We call it *lilikoi* in Hawaii, and it's Conrad's favorite." She glared at her son. "Go on, boy. Tell these ladies what they want to know. I don't want you getting dragged off to jail. You should have a brighter future than that."

"Indeed, he should," Sophie said. "Your son is quite brilliant, Mrs. Kanekoa. I have been able to discover how he did what he did and where the money is, but not why." She gazed at Conrad's sullen face. "Only you can tell us that, Conrad."

CHAPTER FORTY

Sophie

SOPHIE ACCEPTED THE TALL, cool glass of lilikoi juice. She sipped. "Hmm, this is delicious, Mrs. Kanekoa."

"Please. Call me Jana." Jana handed Heri Leede a glass of juice, took one herself, and left one on the coffee table for her son, pushing it toward him. Her displeasure with the boy was evident in every gesture. Sophie glanced up to observe how he reacted to that.

The boy was stressed, it was clear to see. His light brown skin was ashy beneath his eyes and on his lips. Though she could tell that he was trying to look angry and defiant, his shoulders were hunched, and he stared at his glass of juice. "I don't want to talk to you in front of my mom."

Jana, who had just seated herself in the other lounge chair on the other side of the couch, sprang up again. "I won't have you disrespecting me! Not in front of these ladies, and not alone either! If you don't start talking, right now, I might have to send you to your dad's!"

The boy recoiled. "He's an asshole, Mom. You can't do that."

"Just watch me." Jana sat down and gulped her juice, setting down the glass with a bang. "I'm staying right here. It's my right as your guardian to hear whatever you have to say. I need to know it anyway to figure out what to do."

Leede leaned forward and took a sip of her drink. "This is delightful, Jana! Thanks so much for the refreshment. I understand that these things can be very difficult for families; and it's clear that you're shocked and upset by what your son has done. But I encourage you to keep an open mind. He might just have had a philanthropic motive." Leede angled her body to face the boy. "Do you mind if I record our conversation, Conrad? It might save you having to repeat all this again."

"Whatever."

Leede took an electronic pad out of her leather satchel. She swiped to a recording app and pressed it. "Audio only. We are recording now." Leede named the location, date, time, and the people present. "This is an informal interview, Conrad. An opportunity for you to share what you did, and why."

"I don't want to talk about it in front of my mom," Conrad repeated.

Jana threw up her hands in frustration. "Why? What is so terrible that you can't say it in front of me?"

Conrad stared at her and tightened his lips mutinously.

Sophie had her laptop fully engaged with the various computers she had been able to tap into. "Jana, maybe it would help if I explained to the group what your son has done, and we could just speculate why he did it. Then he could just say yes or no."

Jana rolled her eyes. "If that's what we have to resort to."

Sophie copied her fellow investigator's body language by angling herself toward the boy, inclining her upper body as the small laptop sat open on her knees. "Here's what I've been able to discern so far. You set up a series of randomly occurring deductions for the Kama'aina Schools' bank account, which you had hacked. You had access to your mother's computer, and you manipulated the numbers you were skimming to feed into the regular bookkeeping. No one noticed the amounts, as they were random, smaller computer-generated numbers, and appeared under various categories of legitimate purchases. You routed the skimmed money to a bank account in the Cayman Islands, opened under a currently unknown alias. Am I correct so far?"

The boy, looking miserable, nodded his head. "Yes."

Jana opened her mouth, but Leede put a restraining hand on her arm.

Sophie went on. "We also know that you were researching racial-equality type charities. What this tells us, Jana, is that your son was stealing from Kama`aina Schools, but planning to give away the money. A modern-day, anti-racist Robin Hood."

Jana's brows drew together and she leaned forward. "What were you doing, son?" Her voice had softened. Her eyes filled. "What did you care about so much that you would do something like this?"

Conrad cleared his throat. His eyes were suspiciously shiny as well. "I know how hard things are for you, Mom. But I feel like it's wrong that Kama`aina Schools discriminates against students on the basis of race as far as their admissions policy. I took the money and I . . . well, it's still in the Caymans account, but I was going to give it to a whole bunch of different charities for kids who wouldn't be able to benefit from a Kama`aina Schools' education."

"Like who?" Jana's eyebrows had risen.

"Black kids. Mexican kids. Even . . . poor white kids." Conrad stared down at his hands.

"You mean . . . kids the same race as you," Jana said. Her shoulders hunched suddenly and she covered her face with her hands. "Oh, dammit. This is all my fault."

"No, it isn't, Mom!" Conrad flew up out of his chair and ran over to kneel beside his mother, throwing his arm over her shoulders. "You were just trying to give me the best future you could."

Leede glanced at Sophie, her brows lifted, confusion written plain on her face, but Sophie had guessed the answer to this puzzle. "Conrad is adopted," she told Leede. "I believe his heritage is black,

Mexican, and white. He's not Hawaiian. His mother forged his papers to get him into Kama`aina Schools."

"Ah, I see," Leede said. "Oh, dear."

Jana's shoulders shook with sobs as she broke down.

Leede stood up and went to the kitchen, returning with a roll of paper towels. She peeled off a few and handed them to the distraught woman. Conrad continued to try to comfort his mother. "You lied about my heritage to give me a chance. I always knew you were only trying to do what you could for me, and make sure that I had a future. But you should have trusted that I could make my own future, Mom. You should have believed in me."

"I do believe in you!" Jana exclaimed. "It's because I believed in you that I wanted you to have a Kama`aina Schools' education. I wanted you to have a better life than your dad and I could provide!" She threw her arms around the boy. They hugged for a long moment.

Sophie looked down at her computer, uncomfortable with the deep emotion, her own eyes prickling. Leede settled herself on the couch closest to the pair. "Now I understand why you feel so strongly about the Schools' admissions policy," she said. "I hope that when the board and the headmaster understand that you were adopted and that you wanted to even the playing field for children of your ethnic heritage, they might dismiss the charges. Especially if the money can be returned."

Conrad separated from his mother and returned to the lounger. "I said the money is gone. But it isn't. I can return it." He looked up at them, suddenly fierce. "But I don't want to. That policy's wrong! I was only able to get in because I look Hawaiian!"

"That's a conversation for another day, with another group of people," Leede said in her reasonable way. "Sophie, Monsieur Raveaux, and I will be sure to emphasize that you had an altruistic motive."

"Not totally." The boy gestured around the shabby room. "I was going to keep a few hundred grand so Mom could get a better place for us."

"Thank you for being honest about that, too." Leede got her phone out. "I'll call Dr. Ka`ula and let him know the outcome of our talk. Conrad, can you move the money back into the Kama`aina Schools' account? I think that will go a long way to mitigating the consequences for you."

Sophie proffered her computer. "You can do it right here, right now."

The boy came to sit beside Sophie on the couch. "I need to log in."

She handed the laptop to him. "You'll pardon me if I sit right here and make sure you're following through."

Jana winced. "He just wanted to help me. He just wanted to help other kids in his situation," she pleaded with them. "He's a good boy."

"You've raised a very bright and compassionate young man," Sophie agreed. She turned to Conrad, giving in to an impulse. "I'd like to meet with you privately, Conrad, and mentor you in working with computers. Most genius in this area is innate, not taught. You will likely be expelled from Kama`aina Schools, and need to go to a public school. That's no tragedy if you continue your education privately. I could help you learn tech skills. We could still create a very bright future for you, indeed."

The boy held himself rigidly, his fingers flying on the keys as he logged into the Caymans account and made the transfer back to Kama`aina Schools. "I don't know you."

Jana lifted her face from the pile of wet paper towels. "Don't look a gift horse in the mouth, son!"

Sophie smiled when she heard one of the first American expressions she'd investigated and learned to use. "You don't know it yet, Conrad. But this is truly a gift horse you'll want to ride."

CHAPTER FORTY-ONE

Connor

CONNOR ARRIVED on time for his chess game with the Master. He knocked on the door, and heard a shouted summons. "Enter, Number One!"

Connor opened the door and stepped into the sunken living room area. The Master was still in the bedroom with the door shut, clearly occupied with Pim Wat, to judge by the muffled sounds coming from within.

Connor's skin crawled at the thought of them in bed; Pim Wat repulsed him on a cellular level. How could the Master be so blind about her? The answer *had* to be that he wasn't; and if so, the Master was as foul as she was, if not as directly so.

It had taken Connor way too long to come to that conclusion.

"You're judging an essential duality," the Master's voice said in his mind. "Where would the light be without the darkness?" *Didn't mean Connor would ever embrace that darkness, in himself, or in others.*

Connor scowled as he walked across the room to the sideboard near the fireplace.

A tea set was already arranged on the sideboard and the hot water pot gently steamed; the Master's new manservant had already set it up. The service was one of those fussy Victorian things embossed with roses; Connor could only suppose that Pim Wat had brought it to the Master's spare but luxurious quarters. Neither Pim Wat nor the Master ever poured out; the safest way to do away with both of them was to doctor the whole pot.

Connor poured half of the container of poison into the teapot, dropped in the full strainer ball, and filled the pot with hot water from the pot.

Connor breathed slowly and deliberately through his nose as he went to the nearby bathroom and dropped the poison bottle down the commode chute. He had meditated all afternoon to gain the degree of control he needed—*he must wipe away even a thought of his plans.* The Master was able to detect almost any change in Connor's electrical field or his mental state. He'd been outrageously lucky that the Master was otherwise occupied at the moment and he didn't have to try to conceal doctoring the tea; and in case the Master sensed something wrong, he'd thought of a reason he might be agitated.

Connor turned over the hourglass timer for the tea to steep, and set up the chessboard.

The Master came out of the bedroom, knotting an embroidered silk robe. He scratched his belly, his bronze, chiseled chest gleaming. He resembled any man who had recently arisen, satisfied, from the bed of his mistress. "I'll have tea before we have our game."

"I thought as much. I have prepared it." Connor kept his eyes lowered respectfully. "Will Pim Wat be joining us?"

The Master's gaze sharpened on Connor's face. "You don't want her to, do you?"

"Doesn't matter to me," Connor said.

"You lie, but I know why you do." The Master smirked, and seated himself on the stool in front of black. He always chose black, and not for the first time, Connor wondered why.

He had to ask now. This may be the last time he had a chance to. "Why always black?"

"The best strategy is to allow my opponent to show their initiative first. A smarter game is in reacting. In chess, and in many other things."

Connor felt a chill. He narrowed his eyes at the Master. "You didn't answer my question about whether or not Pim Wat is joining us."

"She is, but when she is good and ready." The Master stroked his chin, studying Connor. "Make your move."

Connor wrenched his attention back to the board. *He had to care about this match.*

"You're thinking about something else, already. I'll beat you that much faster if you don't focus," the Master said.

Connor raised his gaze to meet the Master's. "You are correct. I have something on my mind."

"Tell me. Perhaps then, we can have a decent game." The Master leaned back and yawned. His rich silk robe fell open to expose his ripped abs. *How old was he?* Connor still had no idea.

"I've heard from Sophie. She told me that the task force wants me to find a way to capture Pim Wat. They're offering me immunity in the United States if I do." When lying, always tell as much of the truth as possible. One of the Master's earliest lessons; one Connor hadn't needed. He'd always been good at lying with the wide-eyed gaze of honesty, lending truth to what he was saying.

The Master leaned forward, resting an elbow on the table, his jaw on his hand. "What was your answer?"

"Pim Wat is too important to you to be captured."

"She *is* too important. In that, you are correct."

"Too important to whom?" Pim Wat's husky voice came from the doorway of the bedroom. She walked down the couple of steps into the living area. Her loosely-knotted robe parted to expose her perfect upper body. She seemed completely unselfconscious of that, but Connor knew better.

He kept his gaze on the chessboard. "The multi-agency team is offering me immunity in return for returning you to them. I told the Master you are too important to him for me to take that deal."

"Interesting. They are getting desperate." Pim Wat approached the tea things. "How long has this been steeping?"

"The timer just ran out." Connor indicated the small hourglass that he had flipped over. Pim Wat removed the metal strainer, setting it in a waiting bowl; she picked up the pot, and poured three cups of tea.

In all of their afternoons or evenings interacting, Pim Wat had never waited on Connor and poured him so much as a glass of water. A good deal more than three drops of poison per person had been dissolved in the pot. Connor's heart beat with heavy thumps.

"How do you take your tea?" Pim Wat asked, with a glance at him over her shoulder.

Connor swallowed. He had to find a way not to drink the beverage—but even if he had to, would that be so bad? *If his life were forfeit, wouldn't that be just?* "Only a little honey."

The Master indicated the chessboard with an impatient gesture. "Make your move."

Connor refocused with an effort. He moved his first white pawn forward.

The Master countered quickly with a knight. Connor moved his next pawn.

He was executing a pawn wall. At least this play was something he could do somewhat automatically, once he had initiated the opening.

Pim Wat presented him with his cup of tea on a saucer, complete with a small silver spoon on the side. The tea, an aged Darjeeling, smelled wonderful. "I thought you could add your own honey."

"Thank you, Mistress." He took the cup and saucer but set it down quickly because his hands were shaking.

The Master frowned. "I see the shift in your energy field. You're considering taking their offer."

"I would never betray you that way, Master." Connor reached for the rose-embossed honey bowl.

"Yes, you would, if Pim Wat's daughter was in the offing." The Master accepted his teacup from Pim Wat. She seated herself on one of the slender gold Louis XIV chairs across from their table, her lips curved in a smile that did not bode well.

"What do you mean?" Connor folded his arms and rested his elbows on the table, studying the board and containing himself with difficulty. *They were baiting him!*

"Jake is dead, and you still want Sophie," Pim Wat said baldly.

"I won't discuss this with *you*," Connor snarled.

"Oh, your lapdog has fangs," Pim Wat told the Master, laying a hand on his sleeve. "He doesn't like me."

Connor pulled his self-control together—he was in a far deadlier game right now than chess. "I respect you. That is enough."

"That *is* enough," The Master echoed. He gestured. "Drink your tea. Make your move."

"No." Connor's heart pounded; his mind scrabbled. "I won't drink anything that woman's hand has touched."

Pim Wat's laugh was sexy, musical and all a woman's laugh should be. Worst of all, it reminded him of Sophie's laugh. "You're wise, Number One."

The Master turned to her. "I've chosen him, Pim Wat! This wasn't the plan."

Pim Wat pouted. "We cannot trust him. You need a new Number One."

Connor slowly released a breath. *She was trying to poison him, too!* Where was the poison? In the honey? In his cup?

But maybe the two of them would still drink their tea . . . he had to buy time.

Connor gripped his knees because the tremble in his hands had increased. "What have I done to displease you, Mistress?"

"You love my daughter more than you love the Master. Your loyalty is to her." Pim Wat set her teacup aside.

Connor looked at the Master, and discovered that the man's penetrating purple gaze was intent upon him. "My Beautiful One has a point. Perhaps I do need a new Number One."

"No. I am loyal to you alone, Master." The words tasted like sawdust. Neither of them was fooled. Connor reached for his cup. *He had to take a risk.* "Together, the three of us make the Yām Khûmkạn strong. Let us toast to our partnership. I will show my loyalty." He raised his teacup. "But I won't drink this tea without knowing you believe in me enough to drink, too."

CHAPTER FORTY-TWO

Connor

CONNOR HELD HIS TEACUP ALOFT, waiting, staring into the Master's deep purple eyes. He felt the man's extraordinary abilities sifting over and through him, searching for any weakness, for the secret he was desperately hiding.

"I, for one, have no problem with this bargain. To health." Pim Wat lifted her cup to her mouth and took a sip.

The Master moved so quickly that Connor scarcely registered it as he smashed the cup away from Pim Wat's lips. She cried out as the teacup hit the wall and smashed, and the hot liquid spilled over her open robe.

The Master lunged across the table for Connor. His hands gripped Connor's throat, squeezing. "You tried to kill us. You are no longer my Number One."

Black dots closed in, encircling Connor's vision.

From deep inside Connor, a wellspring of will, determined not to go down, boiled up and strengthened him. Connor slowed time, just as the Master had sped it up seconds before. His hands pushed up between the Master's arms, breaking the hold on his neck.

Connor sprang to his feet, employing all of his strength and abilities as he leaped up with a kick that tossed the chessboard into the air, and caught the Master on the side of the chin. The man flew backward and did a flip, landing on his feet in a ready position as the chess pieces bounced and crashed around them.

Pim Wat, bleeding where the cup had caught against her mouth, stumbled toward the bedroom.

Connor had never done anything but spar with the Master in the past; those bouts had been intense, and he'd always lost. But he couldn't think of that now; there was no room to concentrate on anything but coming out of this fight alive.

Connor circled the Master, chilled by the smile that curved the man's lips, by the intensity of his hungry gaze on Connor's face.

"You don't really want to kill me. You want to die," the Master said in that hypnotic voice—*he had always been able to plant a suggestion with just a word.*

Connor closed his senses to that seductive voice and speeded up time so that they circled each other in a spiral with the force of a tornado's vortex, a whirl of kicks and punches.

Still the Master was supreme. Blows came out of that corkscrew of spinning energy faster than Connor could even perceive.

He absorbed them. He would not let anything register as pain or damage. He glanced briefly around the room to orient himself, and, like the last time they'd fought, they were circling above the ground at least eighteen inches, nothing but motion and energy.

He had to mix it up; surprise the Master, or the outcome was a foregone conclusion. This wasn't a fight he could win.

Connor flipped, and as he spun through the air, reached for a throwing knife hidden in the custom-sewn leg pocket of his simple drawstring pants.

Nine had created that pocket for him and concealed the slender blade inside it. "You might need this," he'd told Connor, handing him the pants. "A hidden weapon."

"No honor in that," Connor had said, frowning.

"No honor when you're dead, either," his friend had responded.

Connor pulled the simple, deadly weapon, brought it up under-hand in his fist, and dove forward. He thrust blindly and hit some-thing in the wild spin of energy. He felt a warm liquid gush over his hand.

And the next moment, he was falling.

Connor landed heavily on top of the Master's legs as both of them hit the floor.

The knife was buried in the Master's gut. Connor still held it. He and the Master lay there for a moment, gasping for breath.

Connor put his hand up on the Master's shoulder, holding him down. The Master spread his arms in surrender.

"You don't have to die. I don't want you to die," Connor said. "We can fix this."

"Do you think there is anywhere in the world that I can't reach you if I'm still alive?" A bubble of blood formed at the corner of the Master's mouth. "Do what you set out to do."

"I don't want to!" Connor cried in anguish. He pulled the knife from the Master's abdomen as he sat back on his heels. Blood welled immediately, and Connor covered the wound with his free hand. "I will call for the Healer. You'll be all right."

A ghost of humor lurked in the Master's remarkable eyes. "I thought I'd have more time, but that's always how it is. This is your final graduation as my Number One. Finish me, as I finished the Master before me."

Connor felt his chest tighten and his eyes fill. "Please. There must be some other way."

"Duality." The Master said. "You have to take my place, or die trying." His teeth bared in a bloody grin as he went for Connor's throat.

Connor stabbed him. And stabbed him and stabbed him and stabbed him again, weeping the while. He collapsed over the Master's body, giving way to harsh, gasping cries of the deepest agony.

He couldn't look at the body he lay upon; but he could smell the fresh coppery scent of the Master's blood. That blood would be on him forever, staining him, soaking into his very soul.

The Master had won.

He was now the Master.

CHAPTER FORTY-THREE

Pim Wat

Pim Wat's lips buzzed and tingled, even though she had ingested barely a sip of the tea before the Master dashed the cup away from her mouth. She hurried up the three steps out of the sunken living area, terror making her heart pound as Connor and the Master flew at each other in a confrontation she knew could only end in death for one of them.

Had she been poisoned enough to be disabled? Black spots began spinning in her vision as she headed for the bedside table. *She had to get away in case Connor won the fight, and she was in no shape to help the Master.*

Just behind the table was a loose stone that opened a hidden exit point from the room, a tunnel so secret that, as far as she knew, she was the only one trusted to know about it. The Master had built it years ago, and had made sure that everyone who worked on it had died.

Pim Wat had just enough strength to push the loose stone. A strange numbness, a lack of responsiveness in her arms and legs had begun to take control as she threw herself across the threshold into the narrow space. The door, nothing more than a panel of three stones identical to those in the wall, slid shut silently, automatically.

Pim Wat lay flat on the cool, rough stone floor of the tunnel.

She lay there, no longer even able to close her eyelids.

Her mind scrambled frantically. *She'd barely had a sip.* Whatever Connor had put in the tea had been in the whole pot. Damn that trickster, she should have killed him as soon as the Master chose him!

And how had he gotten the poison? Had to be that ungrateful peasant, Kupa. She must have used the same one Pim Wat had administered to the plastic surgeons; it was the only poison the woman was familiar with.

Pim Wat hadn't taken enough to die, or she'd be dead already—the stuff was fast acting. She was probably going to be fine, but how long would she be paralyzed?

No way to tell, and the stone wall was too thick for her to hear the fight going on in the other room—but it would be fierce, and to the death.

The Master would know where she was, and come and get her if he won.

She could relax. She could let go. She had every faith in her lover.

With repeated effort and total focus, she was finally able to close her eyelids, and it felt like a victory.

Maybe she slept for a time; maybe she was unconscious. It didn't really matter. What did matter was that sensation was returning to Pim Wat's extremities, a tingling to her limbs as if waking from being asleep. She wiggled her toes, her fingers; took a great deep breath that pressed her rib cage into the stone, then lifted her back. Air rushed in and flushed her with fresh oxygen. She panted as deep and hard as she could, trying to expel the toxin the only way she had available—through pumping oxygen into her blood, and pushing that through to her kidneys and liver.

The Master had not come.

He had to be dead.

The realization broke over her with a crash like a wave, sucking her under.

Pim Wat had wondered if she wasn't like other women because she felt no remorse for the things she did. She had tried to learn compassion for the Master's sake. He had wanted her to, though he accepted her the way she was.

But this feeling . . . *this was grief.* Pim Wat recognized it, curling herself into a tight ball, the shape she had been in her mother's womb. If only she could return there and begin her life again. But she couldn't, and because he hadn't come for her, they would be looking for her.

She had to get out before they pinned this on her—that's what she would have done if she had been the survivor of that fight.

There was no way to tell how much time had passed; the passage was completely dark. But Pim Wat knew the way; she had used it before.

She rolled onto her knees, and used her hands, clawing up the rough wall, to pull herself to her feet. She stumbled down the pitch-dark tunnel, tightening her robe to protect her skin from the rough stone, her mind racing ahead to the next steps.

She exited at last, near the outer wall of the courtyard and the helicopter pad.

The Master had escape as his top priority when he created this exit, and it served Pim Wat well as she roused the pilot from the "always-ready" hut built in the corner of the helipad.

"I need to go see my sister," she told him. "You know the address. It's a family emergency." The man nodded, knuckling sleep from his eyes and running to the chopper. Pim Wat looked at the stars overhead, guessing the time. No more than an hour had passed since she had lain in the tunnel—*they hadn't had time to raise the alarm yet.*

"Hurry," she said, climbing into the passenger seat. "My sister is in danger."

The pilot hastened to obey, handing her a helmet. She put it on and buckled into her harness. She usually rode in back, disliking chopper flights with their noise, fumes, and bumpy air travel—but it was dark out on a windless night, and she was fleeing for her life. "Turn off the radio," she told the pilot. "I want to rest."

He flicked the switch without question.

The chopper lifted off. Energy came back into Pim Wat as they hurtled above the black jungle, arrowing toward the city. Her roiling emotions began to settle like the feathers on a bird coming to rest.

She rested her head against the Plexiglas window and planned as they flew.

Pim Wat redirected the chopper to the Bangkok airport, telling the pilot that she would take a cab from there to meet her sister at their lawyer's. Though he raised his brows in question, used to dropping her off right in her sister's neighborhood, she smiled and told him he deserved to have a night on the town on the Yām's expense account.

She left the chopper and headed for her "bug-out bag" stashed in a storage locker at the main terminal of the Bangkok Airport.

She had always hated that silly phrase, but was grateful that Bangkok was one of the cities where she kept one. New credit cards, a pile of cash, new identities, recently updated with her new face and photo. A hassle, for sure, but she had just completed the task through an intermediary when she'd returned to the compound.

In the women's room stall, sorting through her new passports, Pim Wat longed for Pali Island in the Philippines. How she wanted to walk the beaches of her beautiful island, how she longed to rest in the fabulous bed where she and the Master had spent so many happy hours while she was recovering from her ordeal in Guantánamo.

But would Number One anticipate that? *Yes. He would send men to look for her there.*

She needed to go somewhere faraway and new, where she could

set up everything she would need to make sure that both Connor and Sophie paid the ultimate price.

Today was a good day to begin the rest of her life.

And though she would always miss the Master, she was better off without the crippling effect of her love for him. Now there was nothing to restrain her vengeance.

CHAPTER FORTY-FOUR

Connor

CONNOR MUST HAVE PASSED out but he had no awareness of that until he felt someone shaking him by the shoulder. "Master! Master!"

He lay beside someone who wasn't moving. He turned his head away, his nostrils filled with that awful smell. *Something terrible awaited him when he opened his eyes, and he couldn't bear to see it.*

"I've barred the door. You must get up. We have to make this look like something else."

Connor kept his eyes stubbornly closed. He refused to know what his mind was trying to tell him. "Do what you must."

Dimly, from somewhere he had been suppressing it, pain signals pulsed at him.

He had been in a fight. And he had killed the Master.

Connor rolled to his side and retched.

Once again, he felt the hand upon his shoulder. He recognized the voice—someone who cared about him. Someone who wanted good things for him. *Someone trying to help.* "Master. I have an idea."

"Don't call me that." Connor felt wrung out, a husk, as if he had died too—but his sluggish mind suddenly activated. "Where is Pim Wat? She went into the bedroom!"

As Nine hurried to look into the bedroom, Connor realized what he had been waiting for: *Pim Wat's blade in his back.*

He had been waiting for her to finish him off. He had longed for that. But she'd drunk the poison. Hopefully, it had killed her.

How could he live with having killed the Master? And the way he had—no control, no finesse, no humanity. *Just rage.*

There was no atonement for a thing like this.

And yet he must provide proof of his deed to the Department of Justice. He took a photo of the body with his phone, and sent it to Sophie in their secret chat room.

Nine's voice came from above. "Pim Wat's gone."

"I saw her leave and go in there. I thought she would come to the Master's aid." Connor said. The blood he was covered with was beginning to stiffen on his clothing, on his hands. "Do what you must," he said.

"Pim Wat did this—*she* killed the Master. You interrupted them as she was stabbing him. You tried to save him, and got blood on yourself in the process."

Each word fell into Connor's mind like a separate, meaningless stone dropping into a pond. He could make no sense of it. "That's not what happened."

"Yes, it is. You're in shock." Nine wiped Connor's hands, his face. He straightened Connor's robe, muttering over his bruises and cut knuckles.

"No one will believe I didn't do this," Connor said.

"They will. You loved the Master. You never expected Pim Wat to turn on him like she did." Nine dabbed Connor's face gently with a wet cloth. Blood must have made it all the way up to his eyes. Connor turned away, retching again, but nothing came up.

He turned and crawled back to kneel beside the body. *So many wounds. So much blood.*

"Let me handle this. Trust me," Nine said. "Don't say anything."

Connor couldn't even nod. He wept, instead.

Nine screamed for help.

Feet ran on the stone stairs. Cries of horror and shock filled the room.

Connor was picked up under the arms by Nine and held close as Nine pretended to check him over for major injuries.

Connor kept his eyes closed, limp and unresponsive. He was hardly present in his body as they patted him down, supported him over to the low couch.

Connor wept on, oblivious to the stream of excited Thai conversation flying over his head. And then he heard Nine yell, "Pim Wat escaped out of the bedroom somehow! There must be a secret exit! Find her! She must be brought to justice!"

Nine was doing a very good job covering up what had happened, but Connor would always know.

He'd always know that he'd lost control and murdered a man he'd respected—maybe even loved.

But the Master had forced him to. Trapped him. Made him do it, and now he had to live with it. "I hate you, Master," he whispered.

He wouldn't think about it anymore. He couldn't afford to.

Connor finally opened his eyes.

Nine whispered in his ear. "They're looking for Pim Wat now. Come, let's get you cleaned up. You can't be seen by the Healer; he will notice the injuries from your fight and know what happened."

Connor didn't look at the still figure on the floor, already covered with a richly embroidered cloth. He let himself be led down the stairs, all the way into the bowels of the compound.

Nine stripped off his bloody clothes and escorted Connor into the bathing chamber with its hot pool. "Sit in the water. Heal yourself. Come out of this room with no injuries. I know you can do it, Master."

Connor wanted to correct him. *He wasn't the Master!* He never could be.

But his act had made him so, and if he didn't take that role, stepping into the place the Master had prepared for him, the ninjas would tear him apart like a pack of wolves.

Pinning the murder on Pim Wat was a stroke of genius.

The stone-walled room was silent but for a drip of condensation falling from the ceiling into the water of the pool. Connor had taken many a relaxing and restorative bath here. The water was warmed by an underground geothermal spring piped into the pool, keeping it circulating continually at a comfortably warm temperature, though there was a slight smell of sulfur about it.

Connor rinsed the blood from his body with brisk strokes of a rough cloth lying folded at the pool's edge. He scooped soft home-made soap onto the cloth and washed himself thoroughly.

The die was cast. He had done what he had done. He was the Master, now, in charge of this entire organization. Hundreds of men looked to him for leadership. He could not abandon them for something as prosaic as joining Sophie in domestic bliss, even if she would have him—*especially not when he still had to hunt down Pim Wat.*

That thought energized him.

Connor finished rinsing the soap from his upper torso. As he looked down at his body, bruises and lumps were forming under the skin beneath the wavering reflections of the water.

Nine had told him the truth—Connor had to be unmarked by that deadly confrontation with the Master for the men to believe the story that Pim Wat was the murderer.

Connor had always been able to heal himself at a fast rate. Now he needed to put all of his power into healing his body within an hour. He relaxed on the stone bench submerged in the water, closed his eyes, and went inward.

His body's interior was the rich indigo of his energy field, a complex series of systems within systems. He tracked the pathway of his blood through his veins, rivers of blue on blue, pulsing with life. He could identify the areas of damage—dark masses and blotches.

Connor speeded up time, compressing it within himself, accelerating the natural effect of his body's already powerful healing ability.

He followed the pathways of nerves, veins, bones; he traced through the universe of his tissues, repairing himself at a cellular level—and soon, it was done.

Connor opened his eyes and looked down at his swollen knuckles, his bruised legs, the torso that had been stippled with contusions.

All was well; he looked perfect. In fact, he glowed with optimal health.

This was how the Master had stayed ageless! The revelation broke over him, a secret the Master had never shared. But in the end, the Master had been mortal—killed by a blade, as any man could be —*as Connor could be.*

But if he was careful, he could live a long, long time. No telling how old the Master had been.

Connor stepped out of the pool and donned the fresh white robe Nine had left for him, reborn.

CHAPTER FORTY-FIVE

Connor

BACK IN HIS CHAMBERS, Connor allowed Nam to dress him in a ceremonial white *gi* to address the men. Both of his servants were
grateful for what he had done in killing the Master—he could feel it
in every touch of Nam's hands as the man tightened his robe, flicking
imaginary dust from the sleeves, and he sensed it in Kupa's gaze
from across the room.

Connor addressed Kupa. "You know Pim Wat best. Where do
you think she will have gone?"

"I would have said to her sister's house. But the helicopter pilot
did not take her to her sister's neighborhood, and Malee is still in the
hospital."

Connor's brows drew together. "What did she do to Malee?"

"She cut the Achilles tendon in the back of her ankle. She told
me she was paying Malee back for the help she gave Sophie in
recovering her child. I have not been able to get any more information from the hospital, though I have tried," Kupa said.

"Sophie will want to know this. I have to get a message to her. I
already provided her with proof of the Master's death." Connor

addressed Nam. "See what you can find out about Malee. The Yām has contacts in Bangkok Hospital."

Nam nodded.

Nine knocked briefly, his coded pattern, and entered Connor's chambers. He turned and closed the door behind him, lowering the security bar. "I have organized a team of six of our best assassins. I will lead the team to go after Pim Wat."

Connor turned to face his loyal lieutenant. "No. I will lead the hunt for her."

Nine drew himself up and put his hands on his hips. His stance was one of confidence and authority, a change since he'd helped Connor deal with the Master's death; his energy field pulsed with rich new color. "Master. Please reconsider. You need to stay here and lead the men. Keep them on their routine, reassure them. Show them that nothing has changed."

"But what if I want it to change?" Connor said.

Nine's small, dark eyes narrowed. "You must move forward to occupy the Master's role. It is what he wanted. And it is what the men, and the Yām Khûmkạn as a whole, need. Keep routines stable until we eliminate Pim Wat. Then, make changes when your authority is secure."

Connor pushed a hand through his hair, rubbing the soft bristles under his palm. "I want to deal with her myself."

"That is a luxury you cannot currently afford," Nine said in his measured way.

"We are here to support you." Nam and Kupa, arm in arm, approached Connor. "We know how hard this has been. Let Nine deal with Pim Wat. Take the time you need to grieve, and know that we are loyal only to you, and will care for you while you're vulnerable," Nam said.

"Yes," Nine said. "I, too, am loyal only to you—but also to the Yām Khûmkạn. Your place is here, for the good of all."

Connor felt his agitation settling. "Let's sit down. I need to be able to speak freely."

His co-conspirators joined him at the round work table. Connor spread his hands on the table's surface, showing them his unmarked hands. "At the moment of his death, the Master revealed that he had killed the Master before him. He told me that this was how the mantle of leadership passed from one Master to the next. But I never aspired to this role. I'm not sure I want it." He met each of his friends' eyes in turn. "I moved against Pim Wat and the Master because they threatened Sophie and her children. I have wanted to be free to pursue a life with the woman I love."

The three faces looking at him were inscrutable—but he could see by the changes in their energy fields that they didn't like what he was saying.

Connor forged ahead, mustering his focus. "Of course, the first thing we have to do is eliminate Pim Wat. She's a threat not only to me, but to Sophie and her family. We know from what she did to Malee that she is out for revenge against all those who injured her, and we know that she said she wants Sophie's children. But with the Master gone, I don't know what she'll do next."

"I have a plan, Master," Nine said. "We will activate all of our informants and their networks. I will split the team and send half of the team to the Philippines to check the Master's island there, as I lead the group going to Bangkok. You, as the new Master, command everything that he did—and the men need you now. They will be afraid, and fearful men are angry men."

Connor winced—Nine was telling the truth.

Nine went on. "Keep the routine. Do the things that the Master would have done. This transition can be bloodless and peaceful. In the end, I believe that's what *he* would have wanted." Nine met Connor's gaze honestly. Connor saw the grief in it, a grief he shared for the man they now just called "he." A man with purple eyes, who no longer had a name.

Would there be a time when Connor's name had been forgotten too, when no one alive even knew it? "If you think this is best."

Nine nodded briskly. "I do."

Connor turned to Kupa and Nam. "What do you think?"

"It's a wise plan, Master," Nam said.

Kupa nodded too. "I will comb through Pim Wat's things. I believe she has caches of money, identification, and the tools of her assassin trade stashed in cities throughout the world. She could be anywhere, so I'll look for any clues I can find."

"We all must be careful," Connor said. "She will figure out that you had to have been the one to obtain the poison, Kupa."

"I know. She will want me dead as soon as possible." Kupa addressed Nine. "Please find her quickly."

Connor stood up. "We all have our tasks, then. I will go and address the men. Good hunting, Nine."

CONNOR HAD the tiger's eye column that had been installed in the Master's garden moved to the center courtyard. The chore took hours, and while the team moving the column and reinstalling it worked on that, Connor drilled the men.

He walked among them, demonstrating and correcting, as he ran them through their most strenuous combinations of martial arts routines. He wore them out with the heat of the Thai sunshine falling down upon the stones; with sweat and effort, he bound them together in unity. Finally, when their restlessness, fear, and anxiety had been calmed by the vigor of physical exertion and the triumph of their perfect unison in the ranks, Connor bade them sit in rows as he had refreshments and water delivered. Once they'd eaten and drank, he told them to meditate facing the column. Then he left to bathe and change.

The six-foot-high, one-foot diameter plinth made of solid tiger's eye gleamed and sparkled in the late afternoon sunshine. Nam sat at the base of the plinth and played a series of brass singing bowls, striking them gently so that their hypnotic sound rippled across the seated, meditating trainees.

Nam signaled Connor when he felt the men were ready for his message. Connor walked out in front of them, stepping so lightly that his feet on the stones could not be heard. His inner-eye perception showed him the mass of tones of the men's energy fields; many of them were dark with discouragement, grief, and uncertainty.

Connor felt an unexpected tug of compassion; of genuine caring. *They needed him.*

Nine had been correct in telling him to stay at the compound.

Connor leaped effortlessly up onto the top of the column, drawing whispers from a couple of the men whose eyes were open. He lowered himself and sat with his legs folded upon the narrow, circular top, feeling fresh from a shower and clean in his ceremonial garb, a white *gi* embroidered with crystals and white silk stitchery so that he shimmered in the waning light.

He entered into meditation with the men, sending out a calming energy of peace from his place atop the column; that energy rippled over the trainees like silken ribbons.

Was this how the Master had exerted such influence? Food for thought and practice.

With his eyes closed, Connor could still see every individual man, and also their essence as a group.

For the first time, he felt not just the weight of his position, but the beauty of it.

Nam sounded a gong, and when its ringing echoes died, the men opened their eyes.

Gasps of surprise and admiration erupted from the crowd at Connor's feat, at his pure white, shining appearance from the top of the column.

Connor projected his voice over the gathering. "The Master has passed on, as I am sure you have already heard. He named me Number One, his successor, and in the moments before his death, he conveyed to me that I was to take his role; that his death was the ultimate graduation within the Yām Khûmkạn." Whispers settled into rapt stillness. "I will lead you in the way that he did. Nothing need concern you but what I put before you. We have sent a team to capture his murderer, Pim Wat. But for now, know that you are right where you're supposed to be." Connor extended his hands in blessing. "May our lives be in service. May we rule our bodies, minds, and emotions, as we serve the Yām Khûmkạn."

The men bowed forward, their foreheads touching the stones. And then they stood, and a cry rose from them that filled Connor with awe: "The Master is dead! Long live the Master!"

CHAPTER FORTY-SIX

Sophie

SOPHIE HAD GONE BACK to the office, while Leede and Raveaux went to the school to share what they'd learned about Conrad and his mother with the leadership there.

Sophie's phone sounded with the unique tone she had set up to notify her of a communication from Connor in their secret chat room. She picked up the device and thumbed to its hidden icon.

The picture on the screen made the color drain from her cheeks. A wave of dizziness swamped her. She reached for her desk, and lowered herself into her chair.

Sophie was glad to be seated as she took in the gory photo of the Master, lying on his back, dead of stab wounds—too many to count, as if whoever had done it had gone a little berserk.

She forced herself to look away and read the message in the green DOS text that accompanied the photo. *"I killed him. Pim Wat escaped."*

Sophie swallowed.

Whatever she had expected that Connor would do, it wasn't

anything this violent. *Who was he becoming?* More than ever, she didn't know.

Would they pin it on Pim Wat? An army of ninjas would be after her, and they wouldn't stop until she was dead. All Sophie would need to do was wait for her mother to be killed.

Sophie had to let Marcella and the team know. They could begin drafting the immunity agreement for Connor.

"No, no. No."

Connor was hunting her mother, and granted, there was good reason for that. But could she be with someone who killed like this? Connor's list of kills was already long and grim, but this looked like pure, rage-fueled murder.

But who was Sophie to judge? She'd brought down her ex-husband in a scene just as grisly as the one in the photo.

She and Connor were both wounded people, smirched with blood, touched by murder. They had never wanted to be those people, but the facts remained.

Sophie didn't know what she felt about it, but it wasn't good.

But Sophie was a mother now. She wanted to spend her days solving interesting puzzles like this latest case and caring for her children, not looking over her shoulder for her assassin mother to leap onto her back and kill her.

She got up and went to the workout area in the corner of her office. She got out the jump rope, and, in her easy movement clothes, flipped the rope.

The rhythm was like a heartbeat, but the weight jumping felt too strenuous on her uterus, so she moved over to the treadmill, set at a steep angle.

She inclined the treadmill to maximum uphill, and walked and walked with long lunging steps until her heart rate evened out, and the queasy surge of horror generated by the photo began to ebb.

Sophie adjusted the treadmill to an even level, and phoned her friend. She didn't let Marcella even greet her. "Marcella, I have news."

"Good news, I hope?"

"I don't know what kind of news it is. He killed the Master. Pim Wat escaped. That's all I know."

A short, charged silence. Then, "What can I do? What do you need?"

"I'm not sure I want Connor to have immunity anymore." Sophie rolled her lips inward and bit them. *Where had that come from?*

"I will take this back to the team," Marcella said briskly. "It's out of your hands now. Don't worry about it." She ended the call.

"Foul daughter of a cancerous buffalo!" Sophie swore. This chain of events was out of control—but what about Pim Wat on the loose? She had to warn Armita.

Sophie called her nanny on Kaua`i and briefed her. "I want you to be on high alert. Put Alika on, please."

She filled her child's father in on the series of events. "If you can get some extra security out at your house, maybe even take Armita and Momi somewhere off the grid, it might be a good idea for the next few days. I wouldn't put it past Pim Wat to try to grab our child."

"That's some grandma our baby girl has," Alika said, his voice tight with tension. "I know just the place."

Sophie was relieved as she ended the call. Hopefully, Pim Wat wouldn't get far.

CHAPTER FORTY-SEVEN

Marcella:
Day 10

MARCELLA CARRIED an extra-large cup of black coffee into the FBI's conference room early the next morning. Her SAC, Waxman, was already seated at the head of the conference table with the communication monitor up in front of him. He gave a nod. "Looking ready for action, I see, Agent Scott."

"Always, sir." Marcella seated herself at his right hand. In a few moments, agents Pillman and Gundersohn entered. A heaviness of dread and anxiety hit Marcella every time she looked at those two. Gundersohn wasn't bad, on his own, but when he got together with Pillman, the other man's deeply negative perspective seemed to rub off on him.

She opened her phone and forwarded the grisly photo of the dead Thai man known as the Master to each of their devices. "This is why I asked for a meeting."

Waxman's pale brows rose. "A messy one."

"Sophie got this from Connor last night. This victim is the man they call the Master. I sent it to each of you so that we could discuss the situation before we reach out to the international part of the team," Marcella said. "I thought you'd appreciate a heads-up first."

"The number of stab wounds seems excessive," Gundersohn said in his pedantic way.

No one had any response to that statement of the obvious.

"Who killed him?" Pillman asked.

"Connor told Sophie that he did. She got another communication that they're pinning the murder on Pim Wat. She escaped from the compound after the confrontation. Assassin teams are searching for her."

Waxman opened his hands to the group. "Well? What do we think? Does Connor deserve an immunity deal for doing wet work for us in Thailand?"

Pillman tightened his lips. "I don't want that vigilante murderer anywhere near the United States."

Gundersohn knit his heavy brow. "We should wait to offer the deal until he nails Pim Wat, as well. Of the two, we want Pim Wat more."

Waxman inclined his head "I concur that Pim Wat's an important target. Not only did she escape our custody, but we have a number of assassinations that we can trace back to her. The Master has always been a shadow behind the scenes—he's probably had a hand in things, but Pim Wat was the executioner, if you'll pardon the pun. Let's put this latest news out to the larger team, and hear what they have to say."

The meeting with their international partners was mercifully brief.

Marcella left the conference room with a tension headache building behind her eyes. The consensus of the group had been that, while they were glad the Master was dead, they still wanted to see Pim Wat's head on a platter, too. Connor wasn't going to be getting any thanks from the group until he brought in an additional trophy.

The whole thing made Marcella sick. She hadn't gotten into law enforcement to make deals involving murder and assassination.

"Some people just need killing," she muttered. "But I don't have to like it."

Having to look at the Master's mutilated body for the last twenty minutes and knowing the man who'd done it made the coffee go sour in her belly.

Sophie wasn't going to be happy with this news. "Or maybe she will be," Marcella murmured.

In any case, Marcella needed an exercise break to slough off the disgust and horror that seemed smeared onto her skin ever since she'd received that ugly image. She changed quickly into workout clothes in the women's locker room, and took the stairs all the way to the top of the roof.

The Bureau maintained a helipad and a running track around the edge of the building. She did a few laps, taking in the bold blue sky, the high white cumulus clouds soaring across the ocean, a few seabirds wheeling by. All of it helped to lighten her mood. Nature was a tonic through any kind of stress.

She slowed to a walk, thumbed to Sophie's number on her favorites, and called her friend.

Sophie's voice sounded raspy with sleep when she answered. "Hello? Marcella?"

Marcella frowned. "It's eleven a.m. Did I wake you?"

Sophie yawned. "I had a bad night. We're wrapping up our case with the Kama`aina Schools, so I thought I could take the morning to sleep in."

"You deserve it!" Marcella infused her voice with positivity. "I was just out doing a few laps in the fresh air, but I could meet you down at the Fight Club gym if you want to go do a heavier workout."

She could hear the smile in Sophie's voice. "I just told you I had a rough night and wanted to sleep in. I was thinking that my workout would be lifting a fork to my mouth and eating a hefty breakfast. Pregnancy has a few benefits, you know."

Somehow Marcella had forgotten Sophie was pregnant. "Yeah, of course it does. Are you still at your dad's place?"

"I am. And from what I can smell, he's making me pancakes again."

"How lovely." Marcella mustered her resolve. "I just got out of a meeting with Waxman and the international team. They don't want to offer the immunity deal to Connor until he brings in Pim Wat, as well."

Sophie didn't reply.

Marcella started walking again for something to do.

Sunlight struck the little bits of mica in the gritty surface of the running track. Someone had thrown their coffee cup into one of the corners of the building's parapet, and a few leaves had gathered there as well. Marcella paused and picked up the rubbish. *She could tidy this little corner of the world, at least.*

"I'm not terribly surprised to hear that," Sophie said at last. "And, to be truthful, I don't know how I feel about Connor getting an immunity deal. Did you . . . see that photo of the Master?"

Marcella swallowed. "It was pretty bad."

"The man I used to know would never have done something like that. I'm—disturbed."

"You don't know the circumstances. Maybe it was self-defense." Marcella couldn't believe she was defending that man! She went on briskly. "This is all moot until he gets Pim Wat, too."

"Pim Wat is a deadly, twisted psychopath, but she *is* still my mother. We're talking about having my ex-boyfriend hunt down my parent, and kill her. How are we even having this conversation?" Sophie's voice rose. "How is this who we are?"

"I don't know what to say." It was the absolute truth. "Maybe you should talk to Dr. Wilson."

"I'm sure Dr. Wilson would agree that the whole situation is insane," Sophie said. "And she can't wave a magic wand and change anything about it. Thanks for letting me know what they decided." Her friend ended the call abruptly.

"Aw, shit." Marcella stopped, put her hands on her hips, and leaned backward to gaze up at the deep blue sky. "She has a point."

But as horrifying as it was, none of them would rest easy until Pim Wat was dealt with—dead or alive. Preferably, dead.

CHAPTER FORTY-EIGHT

Sophie

THE DOGS HAD GONE OUT with her father already, so she was alone in her bedroom, the blackout drapes drawn, and until Marcella's call, she had been deeply asleep. Sophie turned the phone off and set it down on the table beside her bed.

She'd been having some kind of wonderful dream, and she wished she could return to it.

What was it? Oh yes. She, Momi, and Jake had been building a sandcastle on the pristine white beach at Phi Ni. Armita was coming down the stairs from the house on the bluff, carrying a picnic basket. Momi set a beautiful spiral shell she had picked up near the water on top of the castle. Jake held Sophie's hand, even though they were trying to build the castle together.

She'd been laughing at how silly that was.

Then the phone rang with that ugly news from Marcella. *"Boils covering a poxy whore's ass!"* Sophie threw an arm over her eyes, feeling them prickle.

That scene at the beach had never happened. A pure imaginary dream. She and Jake had not had a lot of time to play with Momi there. All wishful thinking.

This was Sophie's real life: alone in her bed, pregnant with her dead fiancé's baby—while her dangerous criminal mother was hunted by a squad of ninja assassins, and her ex-boyfriend became a murdering cult leader.

Time for her five-minute cryfest. Sophie reached over to her phone, set the timer for five minutes, and turned her face into the pillow. She let the sobs come.

FRANK KNOCKED GENTLY on the door sometime later. "Sophie! I made your favorite pancakes." He spoke in the teasing voice he'd used when she was five years old. "I put extra bananas in yours."

That promise still worked.

Sophie tossed the covers aside and set her feet on the floor. Getting up for pancakes had to be better than her bitter ruminations.

She had other good things to get up for, too: she was eager to find out what the school had decided about Conrad Kanekoa. She'd had a message from Leede and Raveaux that their meeting had gone well, and they'd meet at her office when she was ready to come in. The thought of seeing those two lifted her spirits. "Coming, Dad! I have to take a quick shower, all right?"

"I'll keep the pancakes warm in the oven for you."

Sophie padded into the bathroom and took a shower, spending a little extra time under cold water to reduce the puffiness of her eyes. Her need for five minutes of heavy crying each day had subsided of late, but here it was again: the aftermath of that disturbing photo. There was no un-seeing it.

Soon she was eating a stack of pancakes liberally daubed with butter and swimming in maple syrup, as her father handed her a large mug of strong tea. "I took those rambunctious dogs out for a run already."

The dogs, ever sensitive to any mention of them, raised their heads inquisitively from their beds near the front door.

Sophie glanced at her father. He hadn't shaved, but the salt and pepper whiskers on his chin couldn't detract from his handsomeness. "Thanks, Dad. I think you might be interested to know that Connor did away with the Master. The team has decided that that was not enough to give him an immunity deal. They want Pim Wat dead, as well. Connor has sent a team of assassins to find her."

Her father froze as he was scraping the frying pan into the sink. His shoulders sagged. "She won't come out of that alive."

"I hope not." Sophie cut a bite of pancake from the stack on her plate. "She's a danger to all of us."

"Are you okay with that?"

"Pim Wat gave birth to me. That is all the good she ever did in my life. I owe her something for that, and I have repaid it."

"I feel exactly the same." He set the pan in the sink, and came over to give Sophie a hug. "I'm sorry. You deserved better."

"So did you, Dad."

He kissed the top of her head. "Go get dressed and get to work. That'll perk you up."

LEEDE AND RAVEAUX came into Sophie's office a couple of hours later. Leede wore one of those outfits that she must have custom tailored for her tiny figure; today's was bright turquoise, worn with high-heeled Mary Janes. Her white hair had been trimmed to shoulder length. Sophie couldn't help but smile at the sight of her. "You look lovely, Heri."

"And you look like you didn't get a good night's sleep," Heri said. "You need to take better care of yourself, for the baby's sake."

"You sound just like my father." Sophie gave an eye roll. Raveaux, who'd entered just behind Heri, had been silent through this exchange. She glanced over at him. "Well? Are you going to give me a lecture, too?"

"You forget. I've been a parent. I know a good night's sleep is always a luxury," he said. Raveaux wore a long-sleeved, amethyst silk shirt and black linen slacks. Freshly shaved, he smelled of cinnamon as he walked past her to sit at the round table. "I brought the files on the Kama'aina case for us to go over, so we can submit our final billing."

"Our boy Conrad skimmed six million dollars! My fee is ten percent of the cash recovered, so a pretty good payday, at least for me." Leede smiled.

Sophie widened her eyes. "I will have to talk to Bix about billing extra for my computer expertise."

"That will be fine. I'm planning to give each of you a bonus as well," Leede said. "And I have a good outcome to report, as far as our young computer genius."

"What's that?" Sophie asked.

"Kama'aina Schools is expelling him, but they transferred his scholarship money to another very good private school in Honolulu. The rest of his year there is paid for. With any luck at all, they will extend his scholarship and keep him as a student until he graduates. They are not pressing charges since they were able to recover the funds."

"Wonderful." Sophie felt quick tears fill her eyes. She dabbed them with a tissue. "Sorry. This is the best news I could have heard today. I just keep thinking of Jana, and how worried she was."

"All three of us are relieved," Raveaux said. "I was able to hear your entire meeting through that surveillance device in the car. You and Heri were pitch perfect in that interview with the Kanekoas."

"I very much enjoyed working with you both," Heri said. "I'll look for your billing in the mail. But if that's all, I'll leave you to get on with the day. I need to go back to my office and count my filthy lucre." She clapped her be-jeweled hands like a child. "I think I deserve a new condo. Maybe two." On that note, Heri Leede wafted out the door.

Raveaux headed to the credenza. "You look like you could use another cup of tea."

"Yes, I could."

Raveaux fixed the tea as Sophie considered how much to tell him about Connor.

She might as well tell him the whole truth. He already knew it all, anyway, and maybe it would provide her a measure of relief to be honest and open with someone a little more objective than Marcella and her father.

"Connor sent me a photo of the Master's body yesterday. He had killed him per his agreement with the international task force. Marcella then told me that the team will not extend an immunity offer until he brings in Pim Wat, as well."

Raveaux assembled the tea service on the tray, and carried it to the table. "How did the Master die?"

"Does it matter?" Sophie looked down and sighed. "Connor stabbed him. Multiple times." She covered her face with her hands, trying to block out what she'd seen, as if she could. "It was—a messy crime scene."

Raveaux approached. He gently pulled her hands away from her face, and drew her up to stand. He took her into his arms. "Lean on me," he said into her ear. "It's going to be all right."

Sophie tentatively rested her cheek on the smooth silk of his shirt. She breathed in the warm cinnamon smell of his aftershave. The skin of his neck was close to her lips as he held her. She closed her eyes—and oh, how they ached from all the crying.

Sophie let herself relax, and feel all that she felt, though she wasn't willing to put any name or label to it. He rocked her gently.

Gentle. Supportive. *Loving.*

It was okay that his hug felt loving.

Finally, Raveaux set her back, squeezing her shoulders. "All right?" His eyes were the rich brown of espresso.

"I think I'll take some of that tea now," Sophie said.

"It should be ready."

They sat. He poured. They drank.

Finally, Sophie said, "I like her. Heri."

"I like her, too."

"You should date her," Sophie said. "She's attracted to you."

"We're spending time together," Raveaux said. "Heri's—fun."

"That's not a word anyone's ever called me," Sophie said morosely. "Jake was fun." Her eyes filled again. "I miss him so much."

Raveaux covered her hand with his. "You'll always miss him. I'll always miss Gita. But they are gone, and we are here, and somehow we must go on." He removed his hand from hers, and Sophie missed its warmth. "More tea?" He quirked a brow.

"Please," she said, and they finished the pot.

CHAPTER FORTY-NINE

Connor
Day 24

CONNOR DRESSED CAREFULLY in western clothing as Nam packed his bag for their trip.

Two weeks had passed since the Yām Khûmkạn teams had been sent out looking for Pim Wat. They had come up dry; Pim Wat seemed to have disappeared off the planet. Connor had even gone to Bangkok to visit Malee, Sophie's aunt, in hope of procuring more information.

Malee had told him the harrowing tale of Pim Wat showing up at her house in order to mutilate her, but she had nothing useful otherwise. "My sister likes shopping," she'd said. "And she has a new face. She's probably gone to one of the fashion capitals to make a nest for herself."

Of his little cohort, Kupa agreed with Malee that Pim Wat had taken one of her "bug-out bags" and adopted a new identity somewhere far away. "She is waiting for everyone to lower their guard before she reappears to kill those who hurt her," Kupa said with chilling simplicity.

They had activated their spy networks in Paris, Rome, Madrid, London, and New York.

Still nothing.

In the meantime, Connor had dialogued with the international team through Sophie, and submitted a hand-drawn sketch of Pim Wat's new face for their facial recognition software.

Connor hadn't been surprised at the news that the team wouldn't give him an immunity deal on the Master's death alone; and it didn't matter. He wasn't ready to return to the United States.

He and his three friends, plus a separate chopper carrying a squad of personal guards, were on their way to the Philippines to investigate the Master's hidden lair.

PALI ISLAND, owned by the Yām Khûmkạn, was nestled in a deep bay off of the coast of Palawan, considered the most picturesque, and also one of the Philippines' biggest islands.

Connor gazed around the rustic Palawan Airport as his team, consisting of Kupa, Nam, and Nine, came down the stairs of the jet. Behind them, carrying their various baggage and food supplies, was his security team of trained Yām ninjas. The island was so remote that they'd planned as if they wouldn't have any supplies, and packed for a week.

The tropical heat immediately wilted Connor's shirt collar and made his pants stick to his legs, as he strode toward the tin-roofed building that served as this part of Palawan's small airport outpost. Contacts from the Yām were everywhere, and they'd made the travel very smooth, as a driver met the group and took them in a large van to a nearby harbor. They climbed on board a flat-bottomed transport boat with benches around the sides, and a shade cover.

The garrulous captain began a conversation with Nam, who knew a little Ilocano. The two conversed as Connor sat in the bow and stared out at the small, verdant atolls and clear turquoise waters. His sunglasses cut the glare as he took in the sparkling water all around him, so transparent that he could see the bright colors of coral on the bottom and the darting movements of fish.

They were moving fast enough to get a little breeze going, and Connor was grateful as the wind dried the sweat from his brow and his shirt.

The boat trundled on for a couple of hours, navigating among several small islands. Though covered in jungle, their steep gray cliffs reminded Connor of the islets that had peppered the waters off the coast of his beloved Phi Ni.

These land masses were made of a different material: a rough looking basalt. Still, they were topped with pretty vegetation; rising from the crayon-bright water, they were stunning.

Finally, their captain guided the transport launch into the arms of a narrow bay rimmed with palm trees and black rocks. A sandy bottom and pristine white beach welcomed them at the far end of the bay's mouth. The captain and his helper tied the launch to a narrow dock protruding from the beach, the only indication of human presence.

Connor was relieved to see this sign of civilization. Nine had been to the island while searching for Pim Wat, and had told him the Master's dwelling was large and well-appointed—but even so, Connor wouldn't have put it past the Master to have lived for six months in a shack, a yurt, or some other rustic dwelling.

A houseman dressed in the Yām Khûmkạn's regulation black *gi* came running down from in the trees to greet them in the Thai language. "Welcome to Pali Island! I am so glad you graced us with your presence, Master. My name is Tran."

Connor still winced a little at the title. "I'm glad to be here. He never told me anything much about this place, but I know how much it meant to him."

"And I hope it will provide you the same kind of rest and relax-ation that it did for him," the houseman said.

The rest of his crew introduced themselves to Tran, and soon their troop was walking up a path lined with white coral stones. Large trees with paddle-shaped leaves shaded the area, immediately cutting the heat by at least fifty percent.

They wound up the pathway, rising higher and higher, and Connor frowned. Was he going to have to walk as far as his road had been, leading to the house on the headland of Phi Ni?

He remembered his beautiful house there with a pang of nostalgia. Hopefully, Sophie would get the property back from the Department of Justice at some point, but those wheels did not seem to be turning at all right now.

They came around another outcrop of the rough gray stone that made up the island, and Kupa gasped, giving voice to what all of them felt when they saw the house.

The Master's dwelling was built in a Mediterranean style of white limestone, and it rose majestically from the bluff it rested on as if growing from its rocky base. Terra-cotta tiles made up its roof, and the windows were deep, arched, and framed by hand-painted, brightly-colored ceramic tiles. Connor had a sense of how cool it was going to be inside by looking at the mansion, and his blood pressure lowered as he followed Tran through an arched front doorway.

Inside, the tile on the roof was repeated, but in a glazed, open floor plan with floor-to-ceiling sliding glass windows and a patio. All the walking uphill had brought them to the brow of a knoll that overlooked the same bay in which they had arrived. The flat-bottomed boat looked like a child's toy tied up at the dock down below. Gauzy curtains framed the windows and allowed the breeze to blow in. Pure white canvas-covered couches and lounge chairs invited relaxation. All of the furniture was hand-hewn of native woods, and the walls were decorated with large colorful shells mounted as if they were sculptures.

He should have known the Master's house would be this beautiful.

Connor felt a stab of grief that the Master had never shared this place with him. He still missed the man daily. "This looks very comfortable."

Tran bowed. "It is our team's pleasure to make your stay as enjoyable as we can for you, Master. Follow me upstairs, and I will show you the bedrooms. The security team has their own house outside."

Connor was shown to the biggest suite, which shared the same view as the living room but one floor up. Nine took the guest bedroom on one side, and Kupa and Nam took the other one. A fourth bedroom remained empty at the end of the hall.

Connor refreshed himself in the simple bathroom with its composting-type toilet and catchment water system shower. Overhead lights provided a soft glow, and he spotted photovoltaic cells perched at an angle off of the windowsill to catch the best sun.

This place was completely off the grid, and it was as refreshing inside as the thick, sun-retardant walls had promised.

Connor had planned to lie down on the comfortable bed for only a moment, but evening was slanting long blue shadows across the pure white coverlet when he finally woke up.

He lay there for a moment, staring up at the mosquito netting artfully draped around the wooden frame surrounding the bed.

They were safe here. He'd had the entire island scoured by the ninjas the moment they landed. Contacts at the Palawan Airport and Harbor had never spotted a woman matching Pim Wat's description here, nor anywhere near the area.

It had been a vigorous and non-stop two weeks since the Master's ashes had been scattered around the garden he'd loved so much.

Connor had worked hard during the transition to keep the men on a rigorous schedule, and to begin to train some of the more trustworthy elders to lead the martial arts drilling and other functions within the compound. Nine had been his constant right hand, and he couldn't have come this far without him. Nine had grown in his leadership skills, and easily commanded the men and made the kinds of decisions that he would need to as a leader.

And yet, they both knew Nine wasn't the next Master, nor did his friend want that role. "My purpose is to facilitate you," Nine had told him during one of their evening chess matches.

Connor could stay for a short time. The house was isolated, defensible, and a good alternative to his island of Phi Ni for relaxation.

Sophie still had a week or so before her custody month with Momi began; enough time for her to come visit Pali Island. He needed to see her—reconnect somehow.

Connor rose from the bed and changed into a pair of swim trunks and a light cotton robe he found in one of the closets. He headed downstairs to find some food, and then take a swim in the crystal sea —but he never stopped watching for danger. He couldn't afford to.

CHAPTER FIFTY

Sophie
Day 27

SOPHIE DESCENDED from the private jet when it landed at the remote airport in Palawan. The tropical heat hit her like a wave, and she was glad she had dressed for it in a lightweight, spaghetti strap dress. She had left the dogs with her father, and Bix in charge of Security Solutions. Her heart fluttered at the sight of Connor, standing in the shade of the tin roof of the airport building.

Her backpack bouncing, Sophie sped across the hot tarmac to meet him. She hugged him hard, and paused, pressing him close.

There was something different about him. He felt like a stranger in her arms.

Sophie pulled back, gazing into his sea-blue eyes. Connor stared down at her, his expression somber. "I wasn't sure you'd come."

"I had to come." It was as simple as that. So much had happened since Connor and Nine had flown in by chopper with Raveaux to rescue her and Jake from the volcano. They'd disappeared so quickly afterward that she hadn't even been able to say goodbye.

Sophie eyed Connor up and down. He wore a white cotton *gi* and loose pants, the summer uniform of the Yām Khûmkạn. His blonde hair, bleached by the sun, was long enough to curl over his ears, but he was as honed and fit as ever.

She hugged him again, trying to press away the sense of something alien that lay between them like an invisible barrier.

"You can't make it go away," he said softly. "Things have changed. I am the Master now."

Sophie stood back, frowned. "You will always be Connor to me."

His lips curved in a humorless smile. "I'm counting on that." He extended a hand. "I promise you will like this island, and this house, just as much as Phi Ni."

"Nothing could be as wonderful as Phi Ni," Sophie said, but as they headed towards a van parked beside the airport building, the door opened and Nam stepped out.

"Nam!" Sophie ran forward to embrace the houseman. They had become close during the time Sophie had spent on Phi Ni, getting in shape after the birth of her daughter, and on vacations since. Shy Kupa stepped down from the van as well. Nam's wife looked lovely but unfamiliar, and Sophie remembered Connor had told her about Pim Wat's makeover of the woman. Sophie embraced her, too. "I couldn't be happier to see the two of you."

"And we to see you, Mistress," Kupa said.

"Please don't call me that. I'm Sophie to you, and always will be. We are friends."

Kupa embraced her again. "You are so different from your mother," she said into Sophie's ear.

Sophie touched the woman's long, silky hair. "You look beautiful, Kupa."

"Pim Wat wanted me to look beautiful."

Sophie felt sick as she stepped back. "I'm so sorry. I cannot imagine what she did to you."

Kupa smiled. "Those days are over. I am filled with gratitude that we are away from that place, and that woman. Let us not speak of her again." She tugged Sophie's hand and led her into the van. They sat on the bench seat together. Connor got in the passenger seat, and Nam took the wheel. Soon they were bumping down the road, headed for a harbor where a transport boat to Pali Island awaited them.

Sophie enjoyed catching up with Nam and Kupa and updating them on the situation with Phi Ni. "I have a very good lawyer, and he's working on it. The chain of ownership of the property is well established, but, since charges against Connor are still pending, the Department of Justice is saying that the island is still a part of the case, and confiscated as such." Sophie met Connor's eyes as he looked back over the backrest of his seat. "Once you get your immunity deal, this whole thing will go away."

Connor tightened his jaw, and turned away.

Kupa patted Sophie's hand. "I hear congratulation blessings are in order."

Sophie turned to her, smiling. "Yes. I just had a sonogram, and I'm pleased to tell you that I'm expecting a boy."

Kupa clapped her hands, and Connor echoed the congratulations from the front seat.

Sophie placed her hand over her abdomen. She was still slim, but that low, hard bulge was growing. "I'm calling him Sean. Sean was Jake's middle name. This pregnancy has been a great comfort to me after losing Jake."

"Words cannot express how sorry we were to hear of his death," Nam said from the front. "We know how much you loved him."

Sophie nodded. There was nothing more to say. She gazed out the window of the van, as they drove through the heavily jungled countryside. The country road wound around bluffs and through valleys and over ridges, and she took in the gorgeous views.

They reached the harbor and the transport boat. That journey was just as enchanting as the van ride had been. As they pulled into the bay at Pali Island some hours later, Sophie couldn't help clapping her hands. "Connor, this is so beautiful."

"The Master always had good taste." Connor's eyes were sad.

"You still miss him, don't you?"

"I always will."

All the things Sophie wanted to ask him about the man's death clogged her throat, but this moment, here with their dear friends Nam and Kupa, was not the place for that conversation.

SOPHIE LAY in the spacious bed of the guest suite at the end of the hall. Nam had shown her around the mansion; she could still hardly believe that a house this elaborate had been constructed in such a remote area. Tran, the houseman in charge, proudly told her that the dwelling had been constructed more than thirty years ago by a previous Master.

Sophie got a bit of a chill thinking of each incarnation of the role Connor was now playing abiding in these rooms.

Connor was different in some profound way. It wasn't just that he was grieving, because that was plain in his hollow eyes and whip-cord-lean body. A darkness of spirit seemed to have fallen over him, along with the mantle of leadership.

They'd spent a lovely first evening at the house, eating a meal out on the patio overlooking the bay with Nam, Kupa, and Nine. They all spoke in Thai as Nine spoke only that language, although he had begun studying English in his spare time. Sophie loved the sound of her birthplace's words on her tongue. They enjoyed an easy companionship, and several pitchers of locally made Palawan Wit beer from which Sophie abstained.

Connor voiced no interest in the immunity deal, in returning to the United States, nor in crafting any way to be with her more regularly.

Sophie sat up in bed. *This was only day two.* Hopefully, she and

Connor would be able to find their way back to the easy friendship they'd once shared, at the very least. Throughout the evening she'd felt his intent gaze on her.

Was he hoping to get back together, now that Jake was gone?

It wasn't as if the thought hadn't crossed her mind.

But the photo of the Master's body had extinguished her interest once and for all. She couldn't imagine having the hands that had stabbed another human with such ferocity on her own body.

Sophie got up and slid into the bathing suit and a light robe Kupa had hung in the closet for her. She padded down the immaculate tile hall. Being inside this house was like walking through the chambers of a nautilus: each room was white, filled with reflected light from the bay, the trees outside, and the sky overhead. Furniture was minimal, rugs nonexistent. The only sculptures were rare shells mounted on the wall, each of them artfully lighted.

Sophie entered the living room area. Tran was in the kitchen running some sort of electrical device, a jarring sound in the serenity of the mansion. "I was making you fresh passion fruit and Cherimoya juice," Tran said. "it will cleanse your palate."

He slid a bamboo cup of pale yellow-green juice across the breakfast bar toward her. Sophie picked it up and took a sip. Tangy and tropical, the combination was divine. "Thank you, Tran. What else are you making?"

"Fried rice with local vegetables."

Sophie seated herself on a stool in front of the cooking island. "I can't wait. Pregnancy has made me hungrier than usual."

"And I'm just plain hungry," Connor's voice said from the doorway. He walked in, knotting a robe, and joined her on one of the stools. "Did Tran fix you his morning juice?"

"He did, and I love it."

Tran handed Connor a bamboo cup as well. "Enjoy, Master."

Sophie glanced at Connor. It was still strange to hear him called that, but he did not demur. He lifted the cup to his lips and drank.

"After breakfast, I was hoping to take a swim in that beautiful water. Care to join me?" Sophie asked.

"That's why I got up early this morning—so I could clear my schedule. I was already on the satellite hook-up, checking all the Yām Khûmkạn's business. I'm free for the rest of the day. Your pleasure is my pleasure, madame," Connor said.

"Hearing you call me that reminds me of Raveaux. He calls me *madame*," Sophie smiled.

Connor raised a brow. "That man likes you. And not as a friend."

Sophie shook her head. "We're colleagues. Friendly colleagues, it's true, but nothing more. He's even dating someone now."

Both of Connor's brows went up. "Is that so?"

"Heri Leede is rather fascinating. She's British, retired from Scotland Yard. Less than five feet tall, drives a huge Cadillac, wears bright colors," Sophie said. "She is a forensic accounting investigator."

Connor laughed, the first humorous sound she had heard from him. "Now I'd really like to meet her."

"Perhaps it can be arranged someday." Sophie sipped her juice until Tran handed her a large wooden bowl. The rice filling the bowl was redolent of spices, and filled with bits of egg and sautéed vegetables. "Eat all of that," Tran admonished. "You're eating for two."

"They even have that saying in the Philippines," Connor said.

"And it's perfectly true." Sophie picked up her fork and dug in.

AN HOUR OR SO LATER, Sophie and Connor made their way down the long path from the house to the bay. The Yām operatives accompanying them had secreted themselves around the area, keeping watch.

Connor had shown Sophie the surveillance cameras he'd had installed, inside and outside the house as well. If only these security measures brought more ease; but Pim Wat was better at hunting human prey than any of these men. True, there was only one of her and many of them, and this location was remote with difficult access, too.

But Sophie didn't feel safe. She'd already told Connor that she wouldn't bring Armita and Momi out for her custody month to stay at Pali Island until Pim Wat was captured, as tempting as the water and sand looked, and as much as she knew the toddler would enjoy it. "Until Mother is caught, I'm staying home. I'm secure in my building, and at my father's when I'm not with Momi and Armita at Pendragon Arches."

"I understand," Connor said, but the shadow in his eyes only darkened.

They still weren't even close to where they'd been as friends in the past.

The two of them came out from beneath the *kamani* trees, whose spreading branches and large leaves cast such effective shade. The sun-struck sand was hot, and Sophie ran to the water, untying her sarong and tossing it aside. She dove in, and swam underwater as far as she could, opening her eyes to see the lacy patterns of light against the white sand bottom, and the darting of fish. Her eyes stung from the salt water, but it was worth it.

When she came up, blowing water off her lips, Connor arose beside her at the same time, and she smiled to see how perfectly he'd matched her. They floated in deeper water off the shore, treading water. Sophie lay back, floating, and he did too.

Long moments went by. Sophie watched the clouds overhead. "This feels so good," she said, rolling over to face him.

"I've missed you," Connor said. His eyes were the color of the turquoise ocean. *Such beautiful eyes. Such a beautiful man.*

"I've missed you too," Sophie whispered.

Connor reached for her, hooking a hand around the back of her neck to draw her up against his body. His lips met hers in a kiss.

Sophie shut her eyes, reluctant to hurt him, but it felt wrong—not just the lack of chemistry they'd had the last time they'd tried to be intimate. Now the wrongness was something visceral, something deeper.

She pulled away and dove underwater, swimming back towards the shore.

She stood up when she was waist deep, and Connor joined her a few minutes later. "I'm sorry. I had to try."

"That part of our relationship is over, Connor. I thought about it too, but I'm not ready. It's too soon after Jake. It's also that—we had our chance, and we're different now."

His eyes were still the color of the sea around them. *He was as magnetic as the Master had been.* Sophie would never forget the effect of the Master in person; the hypnotic, commanding quality of his violet eyes. Connor had that same presence, now.

"You're becoming him." Sophie covered her mouth with her hand. "It's frightening."

"That's what I'm afraid of, too." Connor took her hand and pressed it against his chest, over his heart. "You remind me of who I was. Of my best self. Don't stay away too long."

He let go of her hand and walked onto the beach.

Sophie turned and swam out into the bay. She stayed in the water as long as she could, swimming laps back and forth. A little piece of her heart had broken off at what was happening to him, to them. But she didn't want to face him, either.

Sophie finally came in when she heard a helicopter overhead, and saw it descend toward the house. She wrapped up in the sarong and made her way up the path to the mansion, still unable to detect any of the ninjas supposedly deployed around the area. Meanwhile, the chopper took off again.

Nam, dignified in a loose-fitting smock, met her outside the front door. "The Master had to return home. An emergency at the compound. He said to stay as long as you like."

"Thank you, Nam. I can't stay long. I only have a few more days until it's my turn to care for Momi."

Nam smiled. "How is our Little Bean?" He and Kupa had become attached to Sophie's daughter through her visits to Phi Ni.

"As naughty and busy as ever, but I told Connor—the Master—that I couldn't bring her out here until Pim Wat is captured."

"I understand."

Sophie tightened the sarong around her. "Will he be back?"

"I don't think so." Nam's face was carefully expressionless.

"I am sorry to hear it," Sophie said, but all she felt was relief. Connor was a stranger now.

CHAPTER FIFTY-ONE

Sophie
Day 32

SOPHIE SMOOTHED out the Mexican blanket she had spread over the edge of the lawn just in front of the beach at Waikiki. Late afternoon had cooled the bright sunshine, and palm trees swished overhead. Armita, wearing a sleek tank suit, walked the dogs along the concrete walkway of Ala Moana park, getting them tired out so that they would settle down with Sophie and Momi.

Momi was already on her belly in the sand, making an angel shape with her arms and legs.

Sophie laughed at the sight. "Try it like this, darling." She lay down on her back in her bathing suit, resting her head on the blanket because it would be challenging to wash the sand out of her dense curls. She swung her arms and legs up and down, and then rolled to the side so that Momi could see the shape. "See? It works a little better that way."

Momi promptly flung herself onto her behind, and swung her arms and legs up and down. Wearing a little pink suit printed in yellow ducks with a ruffle around the waist, her daughter looked adorable.

Momi sat up and shook her head. Sand flew out of her bouncy ringlets.

Sophie admired her daughter's sand angel and took a photo of it for Alika.

"I'm thirsty, Mama."

Sophie reached for the zippered refrigerator bag. "I'm sure we have something in here." She unzipped the bag, moving lunch items around until she found a nice cold apple juice with a built-in straw. "Here you go." She handed it to her daughter.

"*Bonjour.*"

Sophie jerked around. Pim Wat as a threat was never far from her mind, but it was Raveaux looking down at her, crinkles around his eyes indicating a smile. He wore a pair of swim trunks and a sleeveless exercise shirt. Sun gleamed on his black hair with its silver wing.

Momi, drilled not to be friendly toward strangers, jumped up to hide behind Sophie. "Who's that?"

"That is our friend Pierre," Sophie said. She scrambled to her feet, taking Momi's hand reassuringly. "Pierre, this is Momi. I'm so glad you could join us for a picnic today."

"Hello, Momi." Raveaux dropped down to Momi's level. "Do you know how to fly a kite?"

Momi popped her finger into her mouth, a habit when she was unsure. She considered for a moment, glancing at her mother for guidance. Sophie nodded and smiled, and Momi tugged her finger out of her mouth. "No."

Raveaux had a large beach bag in his hand, and he reached inside and brought out a rolled up, brightly colored tube. "Do you know what a kite is?"

"No." Momi scowled and stuck her finger back in her mouth. She didn't like not knowing things.

"It's something that we fly on a string."

Momi squatted to look as Raveaux rested the kite on the sand in front of her. "Would you like to unroll it?" Momi removed her finger from her mouth, and grabbed one edge of the kite. She shook it vigorously, and it popped open to show the shape of a butterfly. She clapped her hands with delight. "It can fly?"

"Let me show you how, and then you can do it." Raveaux held the kite up by its midsection, unspooling a length of string wrapped in a ball around a handle. "I'm going to run, and toss the kite in the air. The wind will take it up and up, and I will hold the string like this." He held the handle up to demonstrate.

Momi clapped her hands. "Yeah!"

Raveaux took off. Sophie was reminded of the quick grace of a mongoose as he twisted back and forth, running backward until the kite lifted. A few minutes later, the butterfly was aloft. Sophie and Momi tipped their heads back as far as they could, to watch it rise higher and higher and higher.

Momi suddenly frowned. "What if it goes away?"

Raveaux was returning, holding the handle to the ball of twine. "It can't fly far. It's attached to us by the string." He held out the handle. "Would you like to hold it?"

Momi nodded, and he supported her small, chubby hands as she gripped the handle. "Hold it like this and let the string go out. When it's time for the butterfly to come back, we'll roll it up." He demonstrated.

Sophie sat down on the blanket, smiling at the sight of her daughter's rapt face. Soon, Armita returned. The nanny's narrow features were apprehensive, but Sophie smiled to reassure her. "I told you my friend Pierre Raveaux was joining our picnic."

"Yes, you did." Armita fastened the dogs' leashes to a portable pivot spike that she had driven into the ground. The nanny was of a petite and wiry build, with thick black hair she kept skimmed back in a tight braid, currently hidden under a large sun hat.

Anubis sat on his haunches, panting, and Ginger flopped herself onto the grass. Both of the dogs had their eyes fixed on Raveaux and Momi as they launched the kite again.

Armita filled the dogs' water bowl, and then joined Sophie on the blanket. They watched Momi running, running, running, holding the ball of twine as Raveaux jogged behind her, holding the kite—and suddenly, the wind caught it and it pulled up into the sky.

"Do you think he's safe?" Armita didn't look at Sophie.

"Yes. I've asked him to be my children's godfather," Sophie said. "They will need male influences, and Connor is no longer available. I don't know when I'll be seeing him again."

Armita inclined her head in silent assent, but her reservations were clear.

Sophie had decided some time ago that the best thing to do was not to talk about her relationships with Armita, and that seemed to be working. Armita had told Sophie that she had no use for relationships; she considered men to be babies that needed to be looked after, and she didn't understand why Sophie would want another one.

Momi ran back towards them, holding the ball of string aloft, the kite soaring overhead. Her face was alight with joy. "It flew up! Perro made it flew up!"

"Perro?" Sophie asked.

Raveaux joined them. "I guess my name is 'dog.'" His eyes twinkled in that almost-smile. "I hope that means she likes me."

Sophie introduced him to Armita, and soon the four of them were eating the tasty picnic lunch Armita had packed. Later, Armita took Momi down to the water, and Sophie and Raveaux packed the food back into the bag.

Sophie raised her eyes to Raveaux's. "Are you sure you want to do this? It's not too late to back out. But, if we move ahead, you can't . . . abandon them. My babies."

Raveaux definitely smiled this time, that rare gem of an expression that transformed his face. "You don't know what you've given me, inviting me to be your children's godfather. I see so much of my daughter in Momi's bright spirit. Knowing that I can be her honorary

uncle does something to me. I have no words for it, but it's in here."
He thumped his chest, his eyes bright. "Besides. How could I miss being called Perro?"

Sophie laughed. "Good. This baby," Sophie patted her stomach, "baby Sean, as I've been calling him—will not have a father at all, and I want to make sure he has male role models. But I don't want my children to become attached to someone I'm dating. It's too volatile."

Raveaux, zipping shut the refrigerator bag, stilled. "Does that mean that you would never date me?"

Sophie kept her gaze on Armita and Momi, down near the water. "I didn't say that. I just said that your role has to be something separate. A commitment. That way, you can always be there for my children, no matter what our relationship is like."

"Well, no need to worry, because I don't date," Raveaux said. "And I appreciate your making my role clear. I want only the best for all of you."

"We would never have come this far if that wasn't something I already knew," Sophie said. "Want to go cool off?"

Raveaux stood up, and reached down to tug Sophie to her feet. "I thought you'd never ask."

Turn the page for a sneak peek of, *Wired Revenge*, Paradise Crime Thrillers book 13.

SNEAK PEEK

WIRED REVENGE, PARADISE CRIME THRILLERS BOOK 13

Six months after Wired Strong

FASHION WEEK in Paris could be deadly.

Pim Wat retrieved her name card from the brocade seat, and sat carefully on the tiny gold imitation Louis XIV chair facing the runway of the show. "Pleased to see they gave me a front row seat," she told her companion in French, tweaking the folds of her flowing white silk pant suit so that it draped beautifully over her legs.

"Of course, they did, *ma petite*," Pietro said, settling in his place beside her. "They wouldn't dare do otherwise."

Pim Wat didn't contradict him. The reason for her favored status was quite different than it had been in the past, but getting a front row seat for the Dior show was always a big deal.

The long black runway, currently unlit, was surrounded by draped, ruched tulle in luxe purple. Pim Wat's heart beat with excitement that echoed the thumping bass of the heavy techno music. *How she loved her new identity!*

She'd come up with it ten years before, but had not actually used it until her complete facial overhaul and departure from Thailand six months before. Fortunately, she'd had all the photos in her identification documents updated before she'd had to go on the run.

No time to dwell on that unfortunate series of events. She'd landed on her feet, as she always did. "More lives than a cat, my Beautiful One," the Master's voice whispered in her mind.

Thank the gods, Pietro had responded to her contact when she'd arrived in Paris. He'd helped her build that identity out into the fully-fleshed woman who sat beside him now. Pietro's loyalty was a weathervane that swung to the highest bidder, but she'd been able to secure that from her hidden source of funds. Besides, he knew her history—and was aware that saying no to her would likely have deadly consequences.

Pim Wat adjusted the square-framed, tortoise shell glasses perched on her nose, scanning for threats. The glasses, embedded with a facial recognition program, circled each face briefly and flashed identities and employers in the upper left corner of the clear lenses. She'd learned, through many hours of practice, to be able to monitor as she looked about in a normal way. "A good crowd so far."

"And an even more exciting collection." Pietro scrolled through his social media feed on a diamond-encrusted phone. Dressed in a lavender silk suit and taupe fedora, he played the part of gay man about town flawlessly, hiding a shark-like constitution that Pim Wat found comforting—she always knew where she stood with her old friend Pietro.

The lights dimmed. The runway lit up with lines of embedded lighting and strobes encircled the ceiling. Spontaneous applause broke out as the first model strode out in that ground-eating way they affected. Pim Wat checked the rapt faces turned up to watch the progression of the model down the runway, the spin-turn, spin-turn at the end, a hand on a protruding hipbone, the outfit shimmering under the lights.

No one she needed to worry about was watching the show, at least so far. She'd do another scan before it ended. Pim Wat stowed the glasses in their case in her golden clutch purse. She sat back to enjoy the spectacle; phone ready to photograph the outfits she might want to try.

☀

Sophie Smithson, CEO of Honolulu-based Security Solutions, gestured to the small round conference table in the corner of her office. "Welcome to Security Solutions, Dr. Ka'ula. Please have a seat."

The headmaster of prestigious Kama'aina Schools pulled out a chair and sat. Sophie's colleague and friend, Pierre Raveaux, seated himself as well. Raveaux, an elegant blade of a man, spoke in his accented voice. "I'm pleased Stuart thought to bring his problem to us, Sophie, after the way things went on our last case."

Dr. Ka'ula wore a frown that seemed stitched onto his forehead in deep furrows. "Actually, it was Security Solutions' good work finding that embezzler at the Schools, that brought me back with our current situation."

Sophie hefted herself out of her office chair to join them, carrying her tech tablet. At almost nine months pregnant, just maneuvering from one side of the room to another was a bit of a project. She wore a simple black A-line shift that minimized her girth, but still, Dr. Ka'ula's eyes widened as she approached. "I didn't realize you were expecting."

"And yet, my brain remains unimpaired." Sophie forced a smile. Reactions to her pregnancy, especially at a male-dominated security firm, continued to irritate her. "Let's get down to business. What can Security Solutions do to help?"

☀

***Wired Revenge*, Paradise Crime Thrillers #13, will continue in spring of 2021 : tobyneal.net/WRwb**

ACKNOWLEDGMENTS

Aloha dear Readers!

I don't know about you, but I always reach the end of one of these stories with my hair blown back and sweat on my brow, and this one was no different! Whew!

In case you wondered what my "master plan" for the Paradise Crime Thrillers with Sophie is…I haven't a clue. That's the honest truth.

I **do** try to plot these books. Mystery/thrillers are puzzles, and thus, must be planned—but I never plot past the two-thirds mark, because that's when the characters take over, and that's when the real fun and surprises begin.

The men and women of these stories have taken on a life of their own on the page, and feel as real to me as they do to you. Steven King says "stories already exist, like fossils, and it's the writer's job to exhume them" (paraphrased.) I think it's more like we writers open a window into a very nearby alternate universe. Readers can then peek in and watch lives, loves, agonies, obsessions, griefs and ultimately, triumphs.

These characters have something to teach us, and while they do, we're flies on the wall of their world, and grateful for the chance to escape our own.

I wanted to tie everything in this series up with a tidy bow by the end of this book, and once again, Sophie and her friends and family refused to let me do that. Pim Wat is crafty, and refused to die. Connor has made difficult choices whose repercussions are still reverberating. Frank has his daughter close once again, and is loving it. And Sophie? She's compelled to protect that which is closest and most precious.

As always, thanks to my wonderful support team: Jamie, Don and Bonnie, and Angie, the keeper of the characters! You, and my fabulous ARC team, keep errors to a minimum in these thrill-filled books. Thanks so much!

I hope you will hang in there for more of Sophie's journey, coming soon in Wired Revenge. Until then, I'll be writing!

Much aloha, Toby Neal

FREE BOOKS

Join my mystery and romance lists and receive free, full-length, award-winning ebooks of *Torch Ginger & Somewhere on St. Thomas* as welcome gifts: tobyneal.net/TNNews

TOBY'S BOOKSHELF

PARADISE CRIME SERIES

Paradise Crime Mysteries
Blood Orchids

Torch Ginger

Black Jasmine

Broken Ferns

Twisted Vine

Shattered Palms

Dark Lava

Fire Beach

Rip Tides

Bone Hook

Red Rain

Bitter Feast

Razor Rocks

Wrong Turn

Shark Cove
Coming 2021

Paradise Crime Mysteries Novella
Clipped Wings

Paradise Crime Mystery
Special Agent Marcella Scott
Stolen in Paradise

Paradise Crime Suspense Mysteries
Unsound

Paradise Crime Thrillers
Wired In
Wired Rogue
Wired Hard
Wired Dark
Wired Dawn
Wired Justice
Wired Secret
Wired Fear
Wired Courage
Wired Truth
Wired Ghost
Wired Strong
Wired Revenge
Coming 2021

ROMANCES
Toby Jane

The Somewhere Series
Somewhere on St. Thomas
Somewhere in the City
Somewhere in California

The Somewhere Series
Secret Billionaire Romance
Somewhere in Wine Country
Somewhere in Montana
Date TBA
Somewhere in San Francisco
Date TBA

A Second Chance Hawaii Romance
Somewhere on Maui

Co-Authored Romance Thrillers
The Scorch Series
Scorch Road
Cinder Road
Smoke Road
Burnt Road
Flame Road
Smolder Road

YOUNG ADULT

Standalone
Island Fire

NONFICTION
TW Neal

Memoir
Freckled
Open Road

ABOUT THE AUTHOR

Kirkus Reviews calls Neal's writing, *"persistently riveting. Masterly."*

Award-winning, USA Today bestselling social worker turned author Toby Neal grew up on the island of Kaua`i in Hawaii. Neal is a mental health therapist, a career that has informed the depth and complexity of the characters in her stories. Neal's mysteries and thrillers explore the crimes and issues of Hawaii from the bottom of the ocean to the top of volcanoes. Fans call her stories, *"Immersive, addicting, and the next best thing to being there."*

Neal also pens romance and romantic thrillers as Toby Jane and writes memoir/nonfiction under TW Neal.

Visit tobyneal.net for more ways to stay in touch!
or
Join my Facebook readers group, *Friends Who Like Toby Neal Books,* for special giveaways and perks.